A Case of
Syrah, Syrah

Also available by Nancy J. Parra

The Perfect Proposals Mysteries

Newlywed Dead

Bodice of Evidence

Engaged in Murder

The Baker's Treat Mysteries

Flourless to Stop Him

Murder Gone A-Rye

Gluten for Punishment

A Case of Syrah, Syrah

A WINE COUNTRY MYSTERY

Nancy J. Parra

CROOKED LANE

NEW YORK

Copyright © 2017 by Nancy J. Parra

Published in the United States by Crooked Lane Books, an imprint of The Quick Brown Fox & Company LLC.

Crooked Lane Books and its logo are trademarks of The Quick Brown Fox & Company LLC.

Library of Congress Catalog-in-Publication data available upon request.

ISBN (hardcover): 978-1-68331-433-2
ISBN (ePub): 978-1-68331-434-9
ISBN (ePDF): 978-1-68331-435-6

Cover illustration by Jesse Reisch
Book design by Jennifer Canzone

Printed in the United States.

www.crookedlanebooks.com

Crooked Lane Books
34 West 27th St., 10th Floor
New York, NY 10001

First Edition: December 2017

10 9 8 7 6 5 4 3 2 1

For my mom

Chapter 1

"Taylor, your cat is on my car again." Aunt Jemma's tone told me that she was in a mood.

"She's a cat," I explained as I got up from the kitchen table where I was working on my laptop. "She loves to sun on the roof of your convertible. Besides, you love her."

"I also love the new finish on my car," Aunt Jemma scolded. "I don't want cat paws on it."

I pushed out the screen door and snagged my orange-and-white-striped cat, Clementine, from the warm roof. "Aunt Jemma's on a tear," I said as I kissed and cuddled my kitty. "She must have broken up with her latest boyfriend."

Clemmie settled into my arms for a quick hug, then leaped down as I entered the kitchen again. She slinked away to find a nice box in the hall closet. Since she was a fan of hiding in small spaces, I kept a few empty boxes for her around the house. Some she used; others she ignored until I started to fill them with other things. Then she pushed those things out and climbed in. It was a game she liked to play with me. For example, she knew she shouldn't be on Aunt Jemma's convertible but loved to sneak up there anyway. She was a cat. She did what she wanted. I admired her for it.

"Your car is rescued," I said as I made a cup of tea. Aunt Jemma and I lived in Sonoma, California. She owned a small winery with a midcentury modern home settled on the top of a hill. Grapevines—zinfandel, to be exact—surrounded the house. I stayed in the pool house in the back. Beyond the pool house was a small building where the winery offered wine tastings, a place to picnic, a bocce ball field, and a gazebo for small weddings and parties.

Aunt Jemma had made a killing in the dot-com boom of the nineties and bought the little winery because she loved the drama and prestige of being a proprietor. What little she'd known about wine making hadn't mattered because she'd hired Juan Martinez to make the wine. Juan's family had been making wine in Sonoma County for a hundred years.

"What are your plans for the day?" I asked and sat down at the table. This house had been remodeled to an open concept with vaulted ceilings. There was a huge fireplace in the middle of the house. Spanish-tile floors appeared in the kitchen, while wood ran throughout the rest of the sprawling four bedrooms. My favorite part was the atrium patio adjacent to the living room. Floor-to-ceiling windows acted as the living room walls, and there were redwoods sheltering the patio from the sun. When you sat on the patio, you looked out over the vineyard toward the rolling hills.

Right now though, I didn't have time to sit on the patio dreaming. I was busy planning out my first Wine Country Tour.

"I have lunch with the ladies at the club," Aunt Jemma said airily. She was a tall, thin woman who loved to play up her hippy roots with flowing bohemian clothing. She kept her long gray hair pulled back in a loose braid. "I thought you were going to yoga with your friend Holly."

I glanced at the time. "Darn, I'm going to be late." I closed my laptop and grabbed my yoga bag near the door. Luckily I'd dressed for yoga an hour before. Today I wore black capris-cut yoga pants and a flowery T-shirt. I slipped my feet into all-purpose fitness shoes.

"Don't forget there's a wine-tasting group coming by at two. It's supposed to be two busloads of seniors, and Cristal is going to need help."

"I'll be back by two," I said and left the house. Cristal Bennet was a young sommelier who worked days at the winery and evenings at one of the pricier restaurants in town. Wineries in the area were mostly sprawling farms, and the two-lane road to town was narrow and winding. I recently had traded my Mini Cooper for a 1970s VW van. The van had been painted green and reminded me of the Mystery Machine. But the engine was solid, and the inside could comfortably carry seven passengers plus the driver, which made it the perfect vehicle to haul my little tour groups.

I'd grown up in Sonoma but moved out after high school. For most of my twenties, I'd been working in San Francisco as a high-powered advertising executive. Then Aunt Jemma had had a heart attack. My mom had died early of heart disease, and Aunt Jemma was my only living relative, so I'd given up my job to move back to Sonoma with her and ensure that she remained healthy and active. Which, apparently, she was. At sixty-five, she got around more than I did. I often wondered if her heart attack hadn't been a health scare at all but a way to get me to move closer. I wouldn't have put it past her.

I'd been living out on the vineyard for six months now, and I was restless. Aunt Jemma didn't really need me, but every time

I mentioned going back to advertising, her chest would hurt. I loved the winery, but it wasn't my passion. I might have liked to be a sommelier, but I didn't have the nose needed for being a wine expert. I could fake it, but I was a straightforward kind of person who loved people—I wasn't much into faking things. So instead of advertising, I had dreamed up my own small business. Taylor O'Brian Presents "Off the Beaten Path" Wine Country Tours. My premise was that I would take guests to some of the hidden gems in Sonoma County. There were a lot of them, like the Henry farmhouse, full of Californian art; the Witches Brew Winery, which catered to pagans; and Sonny's Open-Air Winery, which featured the work of plein air artists and other paintings.

As far as I was concerned, there was a real need for niche-market wine tours. There was more to Sonoma County than the endless ornate, Tuscan-looking wine-tasting houses that dotted the main roads, attracting tourists.

Why, even Aunt Jemma's winery was niche. It was called Sookie's Vineyard because it was supposed to be haunted by a spirit named Sookie. Aunt Jemma held séances out in the yard once a month and hosted psychics and psychic fairs. "It adds to the charm," she declared.

Also she said that it had been her favorite psychic, Sara Goodwyn, who'd told her that a heart attack loomed on her horizon and that I needed to come out to stay with her. The story always made me roll my eyes in secret.

Truth was, I had not been having a great time in San Francisco. It was too big for me, too impersonal. I'd also broken up with my longtime boyfriend, Mark. We'd been dating since high school. He'd texted me that we should start seeing other people, and within a week he was engaged.

I pretended that it was no big deal, but my heart was broken. He'd gotten married a few months ago while I hid at my aunt's house, licking my wounds.

My new business venture had finally pulled me out of my gloominess. I loved to make a plan, set goals, and see them through. Putting together my first tour had taken work, but I was nearly ready. Tomorrow was the big day.

I arrived late at the studio, Divine Yoga. I grabbed my stuff, then entered the building. I quickly put my shoes and purse into a cubby and entered the largest classroom.

"We're starting with our feet up against the wall," the teacher said. She gave me a look that told me she wasn't happy that I was late. "You'll need a bolster, two blankets, and a sandbag."

Holly was in the corner with her feet up against the wall, a sandbag across the soles of her feet. "I saved you a space," she whispered.

"Thanks!" I unrolled my mat and wiggled into place. "How're things?"

"No talking!" The instructor came over to stand by us as she continued her lesson. Yoga started slow, but before long we were stretching and twisting in crazy poses that limbered my body and helped drive out the blues that dogged me.

Holly Petree, my best friend since elementary school, looked amazing. Her thick brown hair was pulled back in a high pony-tail. She had a lean dancer's body, and the cropped pants and bra top showed off the lines of her muscles.

I was more normal. At five-foot-six, I had the stocky bones of my pioneer ancestors. My hair was a wild mix of every color—I had some fine blonde streaks framing my face, while the rest of my color was a mix of dark brown, thick black, and a few strands of curly, coppery red. All in all, it made a mass of brindle-colored waves. Those waves were currently tamed with a headband and ponytail, although a few bits had pulled free from their moorings. Especially after doing my seventh downward-facing dog.

We finished the class with a few moments of relaxation poses. Some of the older ladies began to snore while I worked at getting my breathing under control. The instructor, Laura Scott, rang a bell and called the class to a close.

"People, let's all try to get here a few minutes prior to class," Laura chided. I knew she was talking about me since I had been the last person to arrive. "It's better for your practice if you come in focused and unrushed."

"Where were you?" Holly asked as she sat cross-legged on her mat.

"I forgot the time," I said.

"You do that a lot."

"I was double-checking all the plans for tomorrow's tour. My first tour group—I want to get it right."

"Taylor," Laura called. She seemed all calm and nice during the classes but was actually high-strung and easily irked outside of class. Right now she was none too pleased with me. "If you're late again, I will have to ban you from class."

"What?" I sat up straight. "I pay for this class."

"So do my other students, and they don't need your negative energy. If you're late again, you will not be allowed in." Her tone was sharp.

"I promise I won't be late again."

"You said that last time."

"But I paid in advance."

"Any advanced payments will be refunded," Laura said, her tone rising an octave. "Since you were late yet again, I can't trust you to keep your word. I thought I could, but you are proving me wrong."

"That's a little harsh, don't you think?"

"Not considering we're doing business together. I certainly hope your tardiness is not indicative of the way you run your tour business. I expect everything to go smoothly for my team tomorrow. I've put a lot of money into you and your start-up. At this point, it's too late to pull out of our excursion, so I'm going to do my best to trust you to arrive on time and do what I paid you for. Trust me, you don't want to let me down. I have connections in this community." She sent me a superior look. "Namaste," she said shortly and walked away with her back as straight as a poker.

"Wow, almost kicked out of yoga class," Holly said with a semistraight face. "You are such an outlaw."

"She's a jerk," I said. "I'm not the only one who has been late before. Besides, she doesn't own the studio. She's just here to teach this class. Let's take a class with one of the other instructors."

"I agree. It seems Laura doesn't like you much," Holly said as we rolled up our mats and slid them in our bags.

"Do you know that Laura runs a yoga teacher mentoring business out of her home? Apparently she makes a living teaching other yoga teachers how to expand their businesses. You would think that a yoga teacher—a mentor—would be more chill."

"It's weird how uptight she really is. I've heard some of the other yoga instructors talking. The way she talked to you right now is better than how she deals with her staff. I hear they call her a petty dictator behind her back."

"How does she stay in business?"

"Apparently people like her authority and can't wait to take her mastermind class."

"I don't get it. If she's such a mastermind, why does she teach this little local class?"

"To keep her skills up, I imagine," Holly said as we took our shoes out of the cubbies and headed toward the door.

"Well, she needs to work on her personal skills," I said right before I noticed Laura was behind the desk as we walked by. I sent her an insincere smile. "Have a nice day!"

Holly and I had a good laugh when we left the building. "Oh, boy, did she give you the look."

"I guess I do have to find a new yoga class now."

Holly put her arm through mine. "Come on, I'll buy you a smoothie, and you can tell me all about your first tour."

I glanced at my watch. "As long as I'm back at the winery by two. There are two buses full of seniors scheduled to come in for an afternoon of wine tasting and bocce ball."

"I bet Cristal will love that."

"She loves waiting on seniors. They're like little kids—you never know what will come out of their mouths after the second glass of wine."

"Tasting is done in flights of five, right?"

"Yes, we generally offer ten wines and let them choose five."

"Five white and five red?" Holly said.

"That's pretty standard," I agreed. "Aunt Jemma and Juan have two originals from the petite sirah and zinfandel grown on the farm and then three blends."

"And the white?"

"All tastes of Pettigrew's next door. Mary Pettigrew is ninety-seven years old and has shut down her wine tasting. I still see her on her daily walks through the vineyard."

"Is she still making wine?"

"She loves the vines. They've been in her family for over one hundred years. But she doesn't do anything with them anymore. She lets Juan harvest the grapes. I think he is set to purchase the place once she dies."

"That means he may not be working for your aunt for very long," Holly pointed out as we walked into the coffee shop three doors down.

"Aunt Jemma has it in her mind that I'll take up wine making," I said. We both ordered green tea smoothies, picked up our drinks, and went outside to sit on the patio.

"You, make wine?"

"Is that so crazy?" I asked. "You know Aunt Jemma's been grooming me ever since the psychic predicted I would take over the winery."

"But you don't want to be a wine maker, do you?" Holly asked between sips. The tea had matcha in it to give it a powerful antioxidant.

"No, I want to do tours, but I figure the more I know about wineries, the better my tours will be."

"You always did love to plan a good party. Are you starting with a Meetup group?"

I'd thought about doing that. In fact, many people did run guided tours as Meetup groups where people met in one area, and the tour guide took them from place to place. Technically it was illegal to charge a tour fee. A Meetup was for people to find other groups of people and do things they liked to do together. But around wine country, there were a lot of people who charged the groups they led and used it as a small business.

"No, I'm not doing a Meetup," I said and sipped the green stuff, feeling healthier by the minute. "I'm doing an actual tour group. I've got the VW wagon, and I'm applying the logo and decals today."

"Logo?"

"Taylor O'Brian Presents 'Off the Beaten Path' Wine Country Tours." I splayed my hand out as if writing a headline in the air.

"That's a mouthful," Holly said.

"It tested well with audiences," I said, hearkening back to my advertising days.

"You tested the name?"

"Of course," I said and drew my eyebrows together. "Things don't go well if you don't use a name that tests well. People liked 'Off the Beaten Path' Wine Tours. I added my name to make it more personal. I think over time it'll be shortened to Taylor's. But for now it tells everyone who and what I am."

"That's why you have the van," Holly said with a nod. "A name that big takes a big vehicle side to put it on. I'm surprised you don't have an actual bus."

"I thought about an old school bus," I said, "but I want to keep the groups small so I don't forget and leave anyone behind."

"You need a mascot," Holly said. "Everyone loves an adorable mascot."

"Clemmie would be a good mascot," I said.

"Your cat hates everyone," Holly said. "You need a puppy."

"Clemmie does not hate everyone. She's particular."

"She's bitten every boyfriend you ever had."

"She likes women better," I said. "She hasn't bitten Aunt Jemma . . . yet. They have sort of a truce worked out."

"You'll need extra insurance if you take Clemmie with your tours as mascot."

"I guess I'd better leave the cat home then," I said and finished drinking my smoothie. "I have to go. Cristal will kill me if I'm late."

"Fine," Holly said. "But a mascot is still a good idea."

"My first tour is tomorrow with Laura's group. I doubt there's time to adopt a mascot," I said as I hitched my yoga bag over my shoulder.

"You are braver than I am," Holly said and walked me to my car.

"What do you mean?"

"I mean, it takes guts to do anything for Laura. It's pretty clear she doesn't like you much, plus I hear she's a crazy control freak."

"I'm learning how to work with the control thing," I said and opened my car door. "It's good practice. I'm sure Laura won't be the last cranky client. So far it's okay. She's already approved of all the stops and verified that I've only charged her for the tastings that have her stamp of approval. It seems she believes in organic, full-bodied red wines only."

"So are you going to take her to Aunt Jemma's place? You guys are organic, right?"

"No, I'm keeping my business and Aunt Jemma's winery separate," I said. "At least for now."

"Why?"

"So Aunt Jemma won't get sued if anything bad happens."

"What could possibly go wrong with a wine-tasting tour group?"

"Nothing," I said and gave her a quick hug good-bye. Still, with any event, you had to be prepared. It was why I carried liability insurance. I didn't want to tempt fate.

Chapter 2

The wine-tasting room was hopping.

"The zinfandel is the most well-known of the California grapes," I said as I poured an ounce of zin in each glass for the five people in front of me. "Old zin vines, such as Aunt Jemma's, are known for their big bold fruits. A portion of her vines are over one hundred years old and survived Prohibition."

The gray-haired woman in front of me sipped the wine. "I understand Prohibition closed many of the vineyards. How did they manage not to get torn out?"

"Well, these vines are up on a hill and carefully cultivated inside a circle of brush and scrub trees. The rest of the land was changed to fruit trees and hay fields. That's why you taste dark cherry in the red and hints of peach in the whites."

"Interesting," said the gentleman wearing a fedora and a bow tie. "I taste coffee in this selection."

"It has a darker aroma of coffee, and the next one has a chocolate hint," I said. "People like complex tastes. Some of the uniqueness comes from the old vines, and the rest comes from the earth the vines are growing in."

"Do you still have fruit trees?" asked a woman with champagne-blonde hair and an "I Love My Grandchildren" sweat shirt.

"There's a small orchard left on site," I said, "but most of the acres have been converted back to grapes."

"How are you doing with the drought?" asked the first lady.

"Grapes like harsh conditions. We're also lucky to have a natural spring running under the property, so we use drip irrigation for the vines when needed."

"The grapes use less water than the fruit trees, so it's smart to go back to vines," the gentleman explained.

The tasting room was filled with the scent of freshly poured wines, cheese and crackers, and hard sausages. Inside, there were five small café tables with red-and-white checkered tablecloths. I practically had to shout to be heard above the din of people talking and drinking. Outside were picnic tables and benches. Every seat in both areas was filled with people from the two buses that had come in. After the tasting, many people would buy a bottle or two, and we would uncork them and offer glasses so they could picnic under the trees. The bocce ball field was full of players—the seniors knew how to have a good time on a sunny afternoon.

"What is the origin of the California zin?" a second man with a bald head and intelligent green eyes asked.

"Some thought the grape was native to California," I said. "Then it was thought to have come from Italian stock. But with DNA testing, they discovered the California zinfandel were original to Croatia. It turns out there were several vines sent over in the early 1800s from Austria. These vines made their way across the United States with the gold miners during the

Gold Rush era. The vines flourished in this part of California, and an industry was born."

"Hey, I'm Croatian too," said the bald man. He lifted his glass. "Here's to the wine of my ancestors."

"Hear, hear," the group said and toasted each other.

I made my way to another group that was ready for white wines. Juan, Cristal, and I worked as a team, talking and laughing with customers, filling and refilling their glasses, ringing up purchases of wine and food, and holding IDs in exchange for wineglasses. We let them buy bottles of wine and asked that they give us their IDs in exchange for wineglasses to use outside at the picnic tables. When they were finished, they returned the glasses, and we returned the IDs. The group stayed for two hours and climbed back on the buses happy and pleasantly tired.

We waved good-bye and studied the carnage left behind.

"That went well," Cristal said. "I signed up twenty new wine-club members." The true goal of wine tasting was to entice new subscribers, who signed up for a year and received quarterly wine selections. Some were shipped, but most were opportunities to return to the winery and pick up their selections and perhaps buy more. Wine-club memberships were the bread and butter of the winery business.

"I signed up two but sold thirty bottles," I said.

"That was a good group," Juan said with a nod. "I sold eighteen memberships. Jemma should be very happy."

"The white wines went as well as the reds," I said. "Juan, you and Mary must be happy."

"I'm happy when any of my wines sell," Juan said with pride showing on his round, weathered face.

"It's four thirty," Cristal said. "Let's clean up. I have a date."

"A date," I teased her. "What the heck is that?"

"A good time with a handsome fellow. You should try it sometime," she teased back.

I shook my head. "Too busy," I said.

"Too picky," she shot back.

Juan chuckled. "I've got my Esmerelda. She and the kids keep me sane." He nudged me with his shoulder. "A good man would be a nice addition to your life."

"That's what I've heard," I said, "but I'm fine the way I am, thank you very much."

He shrugged. "That's what everyone says before they fall in love. Once you taste love . . ." He left the rest of the sentence up to me as he walked away. Juan was a small man—I'd say about five foot four, since he was three or four inches shorter than I was. But his thin, wiry frame was strong from years in the fields. He usually wore denim jeans, a T-shirt, and a dusty old jean jacket with long sleeves to protect him from the sun. My favorite part of his ensemble was his hat with long flaps of thin cotton that shielded his neck and face. But all his protection didn't make much difference; his skin was still dark and leathery from a life spent outside.

Cristal, on the other hand, was so fair it was nearly blinding. She had long white-blonde hair that was thin and currently pulled back into a low ponytail. Her skin was pale enough that you could see the blue veins underneath. Her eyebrows and lashes were also white blonde and could only be seen with makeup darkening them. It gave her an elfin look. I half expected her ears to be pointy. She had three stars tattooed on her right cheek bone. The blue ink mirrored the cornflower-blue of her eyes.

She was thin and long but not tall. She played up her fairylike looks with flowy bohemian blouses and skirts. She liked to wear moccasins because we did a lot of standing and walking whenever a tasting group came in. We were both twenty-eight—close enough to thirty to start worrying that our lives would never get themselves together.

Aunt Jemma would laugh at me whenever I mentioned how old I was. She said that your twenties were meant to be spent discovering who you were and what you wanted. I was afraid that I'd be fifty before I really had my answers. As for now, I was glad to try my hand at my own small business.

We spent another hour cleaning up after the groups. The bocce balls had to be picked up and stowed away until the next group came in. Dishes were washed, and trash was taken to the dumpster. Aunt Jemma was a fiend about recycling, so we composted any leftover foods and recycled glass bottles. It was a few extra steps, but recycle bins on the property encouraged people to help out and not simply stuff everything in the trash containers.

I was sweeping the floors when Juan came in with a tan cocker spaniel under his arm. "Who's this?" I asked.

"I don't know," Juan said and held the puppy out to me. "I found her under the old vines."

"Not again," Cristal said sadly.

I took the puppy, and she cuddled in my arms and licked my face. "What do you mean, 'not again'?"

"This is the third dog in as many years that has been abandoned in the old vines."

"Who would do such a thing?"

"Some people seem to think they can leave puppies in the country and the dog will fend for itself."

"That's horrible," I said and looked into the puppy's brown eyes. "Who could give you up?"

"There's no tag or collar," Juan pointed out.

"Maybe she's microchipped," I said.

"We should take her to the vet," Cristal said. "They'll be able to scan for a chip."

"I like her," I said and held the puppy tight. She licked my face. "Holly said I needed a mascot. I could make her my tour mascot."

"We need to take her to the vet to see if she is healthy," Cristal pointed out.

"I bet she's starving," I said. "Come on, baby. Let's see what we have for you to eat." I walked her up to the big house. Clemmie met me at the door. One look at the puppy, and she jumped up on the countertop. Her tail twitched angrily. "Aw, Clemmie, don't be like that. She's only a baby." I pulled out two bowls and put water in one and some canned stew in another, then set them down in front of the puppy. She wagged her tail and wolfed down the food. Clemmie jumped down to drink from the water bowl and check out the stew. The stew bowl was empty, and the cat batted the puppy's nose and then walked away.

The puppy yipped, more startled than hurt since Clemmie hadn't extended her claws. I picked up the pup and hugged her tight. She squeaked at the attention. "It's okay, baby," I said. "Clemmie's ornery." I looked the pup in the eyes. "I think I'll call you Millie. Do you like that name?" The pup licked my cheek and wagged her tail. "Millie it is."

"What do you have there?" Aunt Jemma asked as she walked into the kitchen.

"It's a puppy Juan found in the old vine growth. Cristal thinks someone abandoned her. I fed her." I cuddled the dog. "I'm going to name her Millie."

"Oh, dear," Aunt Jemma said and looked at me through her reading glasses, which were perched at the end of her nose.

"It's okay," I said. "Millie is going to be my tour mascot."

"As long as she stays with you in the pool house," Aunt Jemma said. "I don't have time to housebreak a dog. Your cat is nuisance enough."

"I'll see to her needs, I promise."

"How did the wine tasting go?"

"It went well. We sold several club memberships and a case or two of wine."

"That's senior citizens for you." Aunt Jemma chuckled. "They're in their second childhood with permission to drink, God love them."

Suddenly the puppy decided to start peeing. I raced her outside and put her in the grass, but not before my pant leg got wet.

"Have fun with that," Aunt Jemma called to me.

I stuck out my tongue at her. The puppy wandered away from me for a bit but then headed back the moment I called her name. I sent Aunt Jemma a smug smile and took Millie back to the pool house. There was a lot of planning to do before my first tour. But before that, I changed into a new pair of pants and called the local veterinarian to make an appointment to see if Millie was chipped and then to get her started on her well-doggie care with shots and such. I was lucky—they'd had a cancelation and could see me today.

"Come on, Millie," I said as I sat down at my desk and opened my laptop. "We have a few minutes before the appointment. Let' see what all is left to do for our first tour."

An hour later, Millie didn't seem at all upset to be at the vet and, in fact, picked up the leash I'd bought her and walked herself right up on the scales. She was eighteen pounds of fluff and love.

"Dog's healthy," the veterinarian, Kathi Summers, said. "I would guess she is about three months old."

"Does she have a microchip?" I almost hoped that she didn't.

"Most dogs do these days. If so, we can contact the chip company and see if they can find her owner. She's in very good health. My guess is she ran away. There's no way anyone would abandon such a beautiful puppy." The vet ran a scanner over Millie's body. There was a small beep.

"So she has a chip in her?"

"Yes." The vet showed me the information that popped up on the screen of the scanner. "Looks like the previous owner didn't fill out the paper work to verify the dog's address. I'll contact the company, and they will get me the name, address, and phone number of the dog's breeder. They can tell me who the owner was."

I hugged the dog. "I'll take her home until her parents come for her," I said. "I like her and would rather house her with me than leave her with you, if that's okay? Besides, she's used to my place."

"Okay," Dr. Summers said. "But I wouldn't get too attached if I were you. Fostering a puppy is a lot of work, and then you must give the dog to its forever home."

"I'm not going to get attached," I lied and picked up the pup along with a heartworm pill and some expensive dog food. "Come on, Millie. Let's make you comfortable in your new place."

"Don't get attached," the vet called after me. I waved my acknowledgement.

"Too late," I whispered into Millie's ear. The pup licked me on the cheek. We went straight to the pet store, where I bought a sparkling pink halter, a warm fluffy princess bed, a tote full of toys, a dog kennel, and a book on how to house-train a dog.

"Aunt Jemma is going to learn to love you," I said. "You watch. She might still complain about Clemmie, but she sneaks her treats. I know because Clementine told me so."

"How does a cat talk to you?" Holly asked. She was standing next to my car as I came out of the pet store.

"She has her ways," I said. "What are you doing here?"

"I was going to ask you the same thing." Holly peered at the puppy. "I was walking by when I saw your car, but it looks like you took my advice on getting a mascot."

"It wasn't planned," I said. "Juan found this beautiful puppy in the old vineyard. I named her Millie. Millie, meet Holly. Holly's my best friend and therefore is your best friend as well."

The pup looked at me with big brown eyes, then wiggled to get closer to Holly. My best friend's heart melted as she picked Millie out of my arms.

"Oh, my goodness, aren't you the sweetest thing?" Holly said as she took Millie and held her against her chest. "What did you buy her?"

I spent the next ten minutes showing her everything I'd bought the puppy, including a small pink T-shirt that said "Mascot" on the side. "She's going to be the perfect little guide to keep my tour lively."

"Speaking of tours, how's the planning going? You never did tell me where you were going."

"I plan on taking them through the Quarryhill Botanical Gardens and then down the road to one of the hidden wineries."

"What's in Quarryhill?" Holly asked. "Do I know it?"

"It's a botanical garden with the most live native Asian plants in the United States. It's got a creek running through it and these great bridges. Really good scenery."

"But I thought you were doing wine-tasting tours."

"I'll have snacks and wine in the back of the van. We'll do the hike through the gardens, stop for wine and snacks at the picnic area, then visit the wineries in the area. It's my premise. 'Off the Beaten Path' means we'll visit some of Sonoma's hidden gems while we tour wineries."

"Sounds like fun."

"That's what I thought when we started planning this tour. I like that it's different than just a wine tasting. As a health-conscious person, Laura liked the idea of a hike."

"Be sure it's okay to take the puppy before Laura shows up," Holly said and kissed Millie, who was eating up all the attention.

"I thought you wanted me to have a mascot," I said. "Besides, who doesn't love a puppy?"

Holly sent me a look.

"Fine, I'll check with Laura first," I muttered. "Say, why don't you come home with me? I'm sure Aunt Jemma would love to see you."

"No thanks," Holly said. "I'm actually meeting my date at the restaurant on the corner."

"Oh, right, you have a date. Awkward questions. Strange silences where you search for something to say. I'm glad it's you and not me. Have fun," I said.

"It's not always like that," Holly teased me. "You never know when you might click with someone."

"Well, let me know how you click," I said and gave her a hug.

"Oh, I will. I'm hoping this is the best yet."

I laughed. "You are always so positive."

She waggled her eyebrows at me. "You never know. This could be the one."

"I hope so for your sake," I said. As for me, I was still nursing a broken heart, and dating was the last thing on my mind.

Chapter 3

The next day, there was still no news on Millie's owners, so with Laura's permission, I packed a harnessed and leashed Millie into the back of the van and took her with me on my first tour.

"Ladies and gentleman." I stood inside the front of the van and addressed my seated tour members. We'd arrived at Quarry-hill. There were picnic tables shaded by large bay trees to the left of us and the gift shop down a short path to the right. "Quarry-hill is our first stop of the day. These botanical gardens boast of one of North America's largest and most important collections of temperate-climate Asian plants. We will hike amid waterfalls, ponds, and photo-worthy views of Sonoma Valley, so have your cameras and phones handy. Today we will see many rare and endangered varieties of flowering Asian trees and shrubs.

"Why stop at a botanical garden on a wine country tour? Well, this land was originally purchased for vineyards," I said and gave them a moment to look around. "As we walk, you'll see we are surrounded by vineyards. But due to the lovely old rock quarries that filled with water during the winter, creating a stream with ponds and waterfalls, the property owner, Jane Davenport Jansen, decided to turn twenty-five acres into these spectacular gardens. When we reach the highest summit, there's a prayer tree and views that will astound you.

"Your tour includes admission, so pack up your hats, sunscreen, and water bottles for a few hours of gentle hiking." I could feel my excitement for the tour building. "When we come back down, I'll have snacks and wine available. Then we'll head to Sunset Winery, where we will taste Sunset wines and dine on their expansive lawns. Are there any questions before we go?"

"Yes," Laura called out. She had a frown on her face and looked at Millie. "I know I said she could come, but are you sure dogs are allowed in the gardens? Won't she dig up important plants?"

"I have special permission to bring Millie," I said. "She's a puppy, and I have promised that she won't harm any plants or leave anything behind." I looked at all seven expectant faces of my charges. "I've also promised that you would leave nothing behind, so please keep track of your things. Also, please don't pick any 'souvenirs.' We'll have time to visit the gift shop before we leave. You can get things there. Now are we ready?"

"Yes," the group sang out.

"Let's go." I opened the van door. I had to pat myself on the back. The botanical gardens were a great idea for my concept.

Laura was the first to step out. A bit of a control freak, she'd even told everyone where to sit in the van, ensuring that she was across from the driver's seat. Next out was Laura's husband, Dan. Dan was an older man, a new-age marketer by trade and the type of guy who would throw himself in front of a bus for Laura. I could never figure out why mean people had nice spouses. Then there was Amy Hampton, the general assistant;

Sally Miles, the freelance human resources manager and yoga teacher; and finally Emma Summerton, Rashida Davis, and Juliet Emmerson, the three master yoga instructors who studied under Laura and, from what I understood, helped her teach her mastermind classes.

Everyone was appropriately dressed in yoga pants, good hiking shoes, and T-shirts except Dan, who'd worn jean shorts and a T-shirt. I was kind of glad that he'd skipped the yoga pants.

"Let's get going," Laura said. "Everyone take three deep breaths in through your nose and out through your mouth, making a 'shhhh' sound." I watched in amazement as everyone complied, closing their eyes and taking the required deep breaths—even Dan, who seemed smitten by Laura. "Good. Now remember to walk mindfully through the gardens."

"Don't forget to take plenty of pictures," I said. "You can share them on your website and social media."

We started up the trail and settled into small groups, with Laura and Dan leading the way. I walked beside Sally, who appeared to be in her early sixties. "Is she always this intense?" I asked. "I mean, I take her class, and she is not what I imagine a yoga instructor to be."

"You mean all soft and light?" Sally laughed. "No, that's not Laura. She knows she needs to work on her interactions with people. But you should see her teaching in her mastermind classes. There's a reason she does so well. She loves her craft, and it shows when she's instructing other yoga instructors."

"It's strange. I always thought that yoga would make a person more . . . peaceful."

"Oh, it has," Sally said. "You see, I knew Laura when she was a neonatal nurse. Her intensity was a hundred times what the Laura you see today is like."

"Wow."

"I know. She couldn't sustain a life that way. Eventually illness led her to yoga. Once she went into remission, she began to teach. Now her goal is to be the master mentor to many yoga teachers."

I tilted my head. "She is in remission? Was it cancer?"

"Laura doesn't talk about it, so I'm not sure."

"Okay, well, I guess she has a right to her privacy, but I still don't understand. She's a yoga teacher without a studio?"

"Yes—well, yes and no," Sally said. "Her specialty is mentoring yoga teachers on how to run a more productive yoga practice. She teaches envisioning goals, marketing practices, and in general how to take their small businesses to the next level."

"Huh," I said. "And you work for her?"

"I'm a human resources consultant and a yoga teacher. So I work for Laura and many of her clients to help them hire the right people and get the right benefits in place. Simply because you love yoga doesn't mean you're a good business person. We all need a little help now and then."

We stopped to ponder a huge brass art sculpture. I was getting a feel for the group. The three yoga teachers hung out together. Sally and Amy were close, while Dan and Laura kept themselves aloof from the group.

Millie enjoyed the walk along the trails, sniffing strange smells and playing in the leaves. It was a perfect autumn day—the air was a clear, and the sky was a bright cloudless blue. The trail wound up hills and through trees. On our way to the prayer tree, we stopped at a rare magnolia and saw a stone amphitheater before checking out another sculpture. This one had a bell.

I had done my research and gave a pretty good guided tour. In the hills with the sun beating down on us, it got warm quickly, and we stopped often for water and to rest. I would point out interesting exotic trees and shrubs while Laura would continue to counsel them on breathing practice and mindfulness. All in all, I thought we worked well together.

That was, until we started back down the trail from the prayer tree. Laura sought me out. "This tour is fine," she said.

"Thank you?" I wasn't sure fine was a compliment or not. "It's just started."

"I think I could help you do a better job."

"Excuse me?" The criticism stung. After all, it was my first tour, and I thought it was going well. It was hard to hear she didn't agree. "Isn't your thing yoga?"

"Yes, but I know I can improve your business."

"Look." I tried to quash my feelings of affront. "I don't pretend to be a yoga expert, but I do know a thing about Sonoma."

"And I specialize in improving small businesses," she said. "There are things you can do better."

"Thanks, but I think I'll figure them out on my own," I said. "Excuse me, but I need to check on the rest of the group."

I turned to find the stragglers. It was hard not to be insulted. This might be my first tour, but I knew as much or more about marketing for small business. Sheesh.

I encouraged the stragglers to head back toward the picnic area. Laura sped up, and the group dispersed, each one going at their own pace based on their level of tiredness. I lost track of those in the front and made sure that Millie and I hung out with the ladies in the rear, ensuring that no one was left behind.

Then Dan sought me out. "Taylor," he said as he dropped behind the rest, "this has been a nice tour."

"Thank you," I said. "The botanical gardens are one of my favorite places in the area. Have you been here before?"

"No, but Rashida has," Dan said and pointed toward the yoga teacher with thick black hair. "She was telling us about visiting the gardens with her sister from out of town. It does seem to be a nice setting to promote well-being and a team approach."

"Well, the team seems to have fallen into a natural divide." I pointed out how everyone had broken into small groups that didn't seem to interact.

"We're aware," Dan said, his mouth a tight line, "but they'll loosen up as the day goes on. Listen, Laura and I were talking about how you could improve your business."

"What do you mean?"

"We've been studying marketing for small businesses for close to fifteen years, and Laura and I feel that you should consider taking our mastermind workshop. Invest your time and money with us, and we can greatly improve your business."

"I'm not a yoga teacher," I said, slightly confused.

"We want to branch out into other small businesses," Dan said. "Your business seems ripe for our training."

I didn't know if I was insulted or flattered. "I got my degree in marketing and advertising. I worked for Jacob, Epstein, and Bishop—San Francisco's premier marketing agency—for five years. I think I know how to market my own small business."

"If you were so good at it, why leave and take up guiding tour groups through Sonoma?" He sounded smug.

I stopped still and shook my head. "I left to take care of my aunt. She's getting along in years and needed family to be near her."

"We all know you can work remotely," he said pointedly. "Lots of people do."

"That might work for them, but I needed more time to help my aunt."

"So you started a small business," he pointed out. "Sounds like you weren't doing so well in San Francisco after all. Perhaps what you need is a refresher course in marketing. You know, something to revive your skills. Trust me when I say Laura can help."

I was flabbergasted. "I don't think I need to explain myself to you, and I most certainly don't need your or Laura's help."

"She tells me you have issues showing up to class on time. You seem a little scattered. Look at your group. I'm certain a lesson—"

"Thank you, but no," I said. "Now if you'll excuse me, I have a tour group to round up."

I hurried past him and tried to swallow my feelings of insult and anger. As a tour guide, you had to be calm, happy, and entertaining at all times. Especially in front of difficult people. My upset must have shown because when I reached the ladies a few feet ahead of me, they had words of sympathy.

"Don't let him get to you," Emma said.

"Did you hear us?" I asked, embarrassed and confused.

"He's a bit loud and a bit of a zealot," Rashida admitted. "We all follow Laura, but that doesn't mean her marketing methods are right for all businesses."

"I don't think he thought that through," Juliet said. "When it comes to Laura, the man is blind."

"It's fine," I said as we stepped out into the clearing with the picnic tables, across from where my van was parked. "Everyone, why don't you make a trip to the gift shop or use the facilities while I set out lunch?"

"Can I help?" Amy asked. "I'm usually the coordinator of these things, so I'm used to being put to work."

"Thanks," I said, and we went to the van. I opened the door, and Millie hopped inside to watch me rummage through the coolers and bags of food. We got out a long checkered tablecloth and spread it across two picnic tables that Amy and I moved together. Next I set out platters of cold cuts, raw veggies, apples, grapes, and melon. Everything was organic, non-GMO, and gluten-free per Laura's request. We had rice crackers, a variety of cheeses, lettuce to make wraps, and a loaf of gluten-free bread. There was something for everyone, including vegan butter and tofu.

Last were eight stemless wineglasses and three bottles of my aunt's wine. For some reason, I couldn't find my main corkscrew to open the bottles. Luckily I kept a spare in the glove compartment. I opened the passenger's side door and paused. Wait—the door hadn't been locked. That was one thing about using the older van. It didn't have automatic locks. I would have to remember to tell whoever sat in the passenger seat to lock the door when we left the van.

I grabbed my spare wine opener and opened the bottles as the group started to emerge from the gift shop. Plates and silverware were next. When everyone was seated, I heard Dan ask, "Where's Laura?"

"Perhaps she's still in the gift shop. I'll go check," I said. "Meanwhile, dive in and help yourself to some of my Aunt Jemma's famous wine."

I left Millie tied to a leg of the picnic table with a bowl of water and a plate of steamed chicken, then I went to the gift shop.

Laura was not inside. She also wasn't in the ladies' room. I stepped out and counted heads, thinking maybe she was back outside. There were only six at the table. When I walked out alone, Dan stood and came over.

"Where is she?"

"I'm not sure," I said. "Maybe she got sidetracked and is still on the trail."

"I don't like it," Dan said. "It's not like Laura to go missing from the group. I told you that you were a scattered guide. I'm going back up the trail."

"I'm sure she's on the trail somewhere. It's not so big that you can get lost."

"Then let's find her."

"Okay, I'll take Millie," I agreed. "You go up the front of the trail, and I'll backtrack from the other end. You have your cell phone?"

"Yes," he said.

"Great, text me if you find her, and I'll do the same."

I went to the table and unleashed Millie.

"Is everything all right?" Amy asked.

"Laura doesn't seem to have come back from the trail," I said. "Has anyone seen her?"

"I thought she was in front with Dan," Sally said.

"No, Dan was in the back with me at the end of the trail."

"Yes, that's right," Amy said. They both looked at me.

"Did anyone see her as they came down the trail?"

"I didn't," Emma said.

"I know I didn't," Sally added.

I started to get nervous when no one could remember when they last saw Laura. The gardens were twenty-five acres. Most paths were well marked, but I had noted other less well-marked paths wandering through. I figured you had to work at getting lost, but I couldn't help thinking that I should have counted heads when we first arrived back at the parking lot.

"Maybe she stopped to take pictures of the waterfall and the Japanese garden bridge," Juliet said. "She should be coming in soon."

"Where's Dan going?" Sally asked, shielding her eyes from the bright sun.

"He's going to take the trailhead to see if he can find her," I said. "Millie and I will go up through the back of the trail. She's probably taking pictures or meditating on a certain scene."

"Really, if Dan was with you, then Laura must have been as well," Emma said. "They are always together."

"No, only Dan," Amy said in my defense.

"Let's not worry. I'm sure she's fine," I said. "Everyone stay put. I've got my cell. Millie and I will go up the trail until we find Laura or meet Dan. Please stay here and enjoy the food and good wine. I'm sure it's nothing but Laura getting a little lost or distracted."

"That doesn't sound like our Laura," Sally said, her mouth a thin line.

"Come on, Millie," I said. "Let's go back on the trail." All I could do was hope that the rest of the group stayed put while Dan and I backtracked. The last thing I needed was for more than one of the group to go missing on my first tour.

Maybe Laura was hiding on me. I knew that sounded silly, even to myself, but Dan had pointed out that I was scattered and needed their help with marketing. Maybe this was their plan to make me think twice about turning them down.

Millie barked as I unleashed her, and she ran back and forth along the edges of the wide trail. We rounded a curve and came upon the stream. The sound of water bubbling was peaceful in the midst of my anxiety. "Laura," I called out. "Laura, are you okay?"

I stepped over the bridge and onto the other side of the pond. "Laura, can you hear me? If you can hear me, please say something."

As we started up the fairly steep path, I thought back to when I'd last seen Laura. After our sort of disastrous talk, I had dropped back. She was fit and had quickly taken the lead down the trail. It had been the last I saw of her.

Millie stopped where the trail curved and split. I paused and called Laura's name. There was no answer. At this point in the trail, the brush along the sides was over six feet tall. A post displayed the general warning about mountain lions in the area and what to do should you encounter one. I was certain Laura hadn't encountered one. Millie might have been a puppy, but I had no doubt that she would've alerted me if there were any big cats on the trail today.

Laura's absence was a puzzle. It seemed to me she couldn't have been that far ahead of the rest of the group. If she had been, surely she would have waited at one of the sculptures for everyone to catch up. What would cause her to disappear?

Millie and I hurried up the trail, which wound back into the woods with steep cliffs along the right side as you went. The trail was wide enough for two to walk side by side. There was no way she would have fallen. At least that was my assumption. I had kept a keen eye on some of the older women who seemed more fragile—yoga teachers or not, some were so skinny a stiff wind could have knocked them down. That was why I'd let Laura lead us down, but maybe that hadn't been such a good idea after all.

I was at a curve with a little bridge that went over a waterfall creek when Millie spotted her. Millie barked, and I let my gaze follow the dog's nose, which pointed over the edge of a cliff. Under the cliff was a small stream. I saw Laura lying near the bank, very still. Her arms and legs were in odd positions. "Laura?" I called her name to see if she was responsive. "Laura?" My first reaction was to rush down to her, but I tempered that impulse, checking to see if I had any bars on my cell phone. I had four bars, so I called 9-1-1.

"Nine-one-one. What is your emergency?"

"Hi, I'm on a trail at Quarryhill, and I've got an unresponsive, injured woman halfway down the cliff face. Can you send help?"

"I'm sending out a rescue crew now."

"I think I can reach her," I said. "Can I go down and check for injuries?"

"You said she was on a cliff face. I'd advise you not to go down. You could get hurt as well."

"It's pretty steep, but there are lots of trees to hold onto and make my way down."

"I'm sorry, but we prefer you stay on the trail and wait for help."

"Okay," I said. While I answered standard emergency responder questions about my location, I texted Dan: "Found Laura. She's by the pond and is hurt. I've called nine-one-one."

Dan texted back. "Where are you?"

"Near the waterfall where the pond goes down sharply."

"I'm coming."

I then texted Sally and the rest of the group.

"We're coming." Sally texted back.

"No!" I responded. "Safer to stay together near the van."

There was no answer, and I sighed. Sally was on her way whether I wanted her to be or not. I looked at Laura. Her curly blonde hair had twigs and bits of loam in it. "Laura," I called.

"Hang on. I'm on the phone with nine-one-one. Someone will be here soon."

Millie moved back down the trail and barked. Then Dan burst out of the trail, running toward me. "Where is she? Laura!"

I grabbed him before he tumbled down the cliff. "Easy. They said not to go down there."

He jerked out of my hands. "That's my wife." Then he scrambled his way down to her, rocks and loam flying everywhere. "Laura, my goodness. Laura!"

"What's happening?" the emergency response operator called through my phone.

"Her husband, Dan, is here. He just went down the cliff to her."

"Take a deep breath," the voice on my phone advised. "I need you to stay calm."

"I'm calm," I said. "When are they getting here?" I heard Sally and the group coming up the trail.

"We're here to help," Amy said. They all peered over the edge to see Dan kneeling over Laura, calling her name.

"A rescue crew is on the way," I said. "Ladies, please, like I said, it would be best if you all went back to the van. One of you can direct the crew up the trail."

"Okay," Sally said. "Let's go, ladies."

"Amy," I said, stopping her before she left, "can you stay on the phone with the nine-one-one operator? I really want to get down there and see what I can do to help."

"Sure," Amy said and took my phone and started talking to the operator.

I climbed down the edge of the hill. It was steeper than I had first thought, and I found myself sliding more than climbing. I grabbed trees to slow myself down. Finally, I made it to

Dan and Laura. My heart was racing, and my breathing was fast. Laura was on her stomach with her head to one side. There appeared to be a gash on the back of her head that had bled profusely. Her arms were at odd angles, and one ankle was clearly broken, as her foot was facing the wrong direction. "Laura," I said as I scrambled over to her. "It's Taylor. Can you hear me?"

Dan had tears running down his face. "We have to turn her over," he said. "Help me."

I put my hand on his shoulder to stop him. "Don't move her. You could injure her."

"She's not talking," he said, grief written on his face. "I can't get her to talk to me."

"It looks like she hit her head. It could be a concussion. We can't move her until we have a board to stabilize her neck."

He clutched her T-shirt in his hands, then rubbed her back over and over, rocking silent tears.

I ran through what I knew. First aid taught to first figure out if the person was conscious. I touched her shoulder and gently jiggled it. "Laura?" She didn't answer. Dan was right. She was unconscious. I found her wrist and checked for a pulse, but I didn't find one. My heart was pounding pretty fast, though, so if her pulse was weak, my own pulse might be overriding it. I reached over to her neck. "Laura? Can you hear me?" I carefully stuck two fingers into the space at the side of her windpipe just below the jaw. I didn't want to move her neck in case she had broken her spine as well as her ankle.

I still couldn't find a pulse, and a sense of panic went through me. I withdrew my fingers to find them covered in blood. She was bleeding from someplace other than the gash on her head. Dan's face went white as a sheet at the sight of blood on my hand. My first instinct was to wipe it on my pants. I didn't know what to do. She was facedown on the hill. Her hair and jacket hid any source of the blood. How could I help? Maybe stop the flow of blood by putting pressure on it? But if I turned her over, I could injure her further. I put my hand on her back, but she didn't appear to be breathing. If she was breathing, it was too shallow to detect. I tried to clear the earth away from her mouth and see if her breath moved the dust. Time slowed. Did she need CPR? Should I roll her over and start it? What if it made her injuries worse? I hesitated only a moment to make the call to turn her over anyway. Not breathing trumped a possible spinal injury. I would have to turn her.

"Is she all right?" Amy called from the trail, distracting me.

"I can't find a pulse," I said to Dan, who sobbed. I looked up at Amy. "I'm afraid to move her in case her neck is broken. But she needs CPR."

"I got a text from Sally. The paramedics are heading up the trail. They said don't touch anything."

"Okay," I replied. It was best to do what the EMTs said. I kept my hand on Laura's back and talked to her, trying to drown out Dan's sobs. "Did you hear that, Laura? The paramedics are almost here. They'll take good care of you and see that you're brought back up the hill safely." I patted her back and hummed a tune.

Finally, a pair of deputies peered over the trail edge. "Hello? Is everyone okay down there?"

I waved my hands. "Dan and I are okay, but Laura needs help desperately. I'm not sure she's breathing. Should I start CPR?"

"Stay put," the taller deputy with a square jaw and straight nose told me. "The paramedics are coming down now."

"Hurry!"

A man and a woman in paramedic gear looked over the cliff edge. The man had a rope hooked to his gear belt around his waist and half climbed, half slid down like I did.

"Are you okay?"

"Yes, I'm fine," I said and stepped away from Laura. "Dan," I said and gently pulled him back. "I was unable to assess the rest of the damage because I didn't want to turn her over and chance breaking her neck."

"I understand," he said and motioned to the woman and deputies above. They sent a stretcher down on the rope. He unhooked it, left the stretcher on the bank, and hurried to us.

He did the same thing I had—he first checked her wrist for a pulse and then her neck. "I'm having trouble finding a pulse."

Dan turned his head and lost his breakfast. The paramedic grabbed a blanket and covered his shoulders, forcing Dan to sit. "He's in shock. How long has she been down here?"

"We don't know exactly. She was leading our tour group down the trail, but when we reached the bottom, she wasn't there. So Millie—that's my dog—and I went back up the trail to find her."

By the time I finished speaking, he had a brace around her neck. The female paramedic was down with us.

"Help us turn her," he said. "Gently."

I carefully put my hands under her knees. The female paramedic expertly handled Laura's head. Laura rolled like a dead weight. Her eyes were open, but she was very pale. Her jaw hung loose. I could see that, even though I had tried to brush the dirt away, she had a mouth full of forest loam.

Dan sat with his head in his hands, rocking and moaning her name over and over.

The female paramedic carefully used a hooked finger to take the dirt out of Laura's mouth and clear her airway. The male held out his hand.

"Stop!" Everyone froze. "She's bleeding profusely." He pointed to a deep pool of blood on the ground where Laura had been. That's when I noticed Laura's face was ghost white, and a creepy feeling came over me. He carefully unzipped her jacket and pulled it away from her neck. A large corkscrew stuck out from underneath the neck brace. The handle dug into her collarbone, and it looked like the corkscrew was deep inside her.

"Triage," he said to his partner. He glanced up at us. "You need to let us do our job."

"Is she dead?" I asked. "That's too much blood."

"What! No!" Dan scrambled toward us. The paramedic was strong enough to hold him back. "Laura? Laura!"

The other paramedic hit the radio on her shoulder. "Deputy Pike."

"Roger that, Smith."

"Call detectives and the County Crime Scene Department out here. We're going to treat the victim, but she was definitely attacked. We don't want to further contaminate the scene." She looked at me. "Smith" was older than me by twenty years. Her dark-brown gaze showed the same look the principal would give me whenever I was called to the office for pulling a prank. "Don't move, lady. You're in the middle of a crime scene."

I held my hands up and planted my feet. The two paramedics bundled Laura onto a stretcher and pulled her body up to the trail.

Great, I thought and slowly put my hands down. My first wine country tour, and one of my guests may have been killed by a corkscrew. All that needed to be determined now was if it was an accident—she might have fallen on the corkscrew on her way down the cliff—or murder.

"Are you okay?" Sally called from the trail.

I looked up to see my entire tour group crowding the trail and looking down at me with curiosity.

"Are they with you?" Deputy Pike asked as we looked at the group of women.

"Yes," I said and sighed. "I'm their tour guide."

More police showed up and pushed the women back. Crime scene techs came, and I was photographed where I stood. My first tour was a disaster. I swallowed hard at the thought. Laura was badly hurt and, from the amount of blood on the ground, was most probably dead. I barely knew her, but I had been responsible for her well-being. Guilt flooded me. I looked at Dan, who had crumpled to the ground in grief when they asked him to stay put. My heart went out to him, but I couldn't move. Couldn't hold him and let him rest on my shoulder. I couldn't imagine having to wait while paramedics carted off someone I loved. No wonder he had lost it. I noticed my own hands shook, and I sat down, putting my head between my knees. The last thing they needed was for me to pass out.

Poor Laura. Poor Dan. I'd always wanted to run my own start-up. I never dreamed something terrible like this could happen. I wrapped my arms around my knees so that the police officers wouldn't see me tremble. I did my best to silently console myself. I'd never been in a situation this bad. That meant that things couldn't possible get worse, right?

Chapter 4

The climb back up the hill was harder than the tumble down. They took Dan up on a stretcher since he had no strength left in him to make the climb. They tied a rope around my waist, and I walked up the hill clinging to the rope. I sat down next to a tree, unable to walk any farther. Around me, the women in the group were all in states of shock. Some cried quietly. Others rocked back and forth. One sat in lotus pose with her eyes closed as if meditating.

"Miss O'Brian?"

I looked up to see a handsome man looking at me flatly. It took a moment for me to realize it was the county sheriff. He had neatly cut brown hair and gorgeous blue eyes that had seen too much. He wore a well-pressed khaki uniform over his broad shoulders. "Yes?"

"I'm Sheriff Hennessey. Can I ask you a few questions?"

"Sure," I said and stood. Someone had covered my shoulders with a green army blanket. Millie spilled out of my lap. I handed her leash to Amy and walked woodenly to the farthest corner of the clearing where the sheriff had stopped for privacy.

"I'm sorry to report that Laura Scott was pronounced dead on arrival."

"Oh, my goodness." I felt as if I'd been hit in the stomach.

"I understand you're the tour guide for the group."

"Yes," I said and hugged the blanket to me, suddenly colder.

He studied me for a moment. "Are you okay?"

"No," I said. "Nothing about this is okay."

He nodded and looked at a notepad in his hands. "Tell me what happened."

"When we finished the hike and sat down at the picnic tables to eat, Dan asked where Laura was. She wasn't with the group, so I checked the gift shop and the toilets but couldn't find her. While the rest of the group remained at the picnic area, Dan went up the trailhead, and I took the back way looking for her."

"I see." He made a note. "Who's Dan?"

"Laura's husband, Dan Scott. I'm not sure if you saw him. He was in terrible shock, and they took him up the cliff before me. I think the EMTs took him to the hospital to keep an eye on him. I know he wanted to go with Laura. I'm sure he's at the hospital. Oh, my gosh, does he know Laura is dead?" Now I was babbling. I closed my mouth.

"So the husband went one way, and you went the other."

"Yes. We were coming up the trail when Millie, my dog, stopped and barked. That's when I saw Laura. It looked like she had fallen down the cliff face. It's pretty steep. At first I thought maybe she'd stopped to take a picture and leaned too far over."

"But you didn't see a camera."

"Well, most people take pictures with their cell phones," I said. "I called nine-one-one and the operator told me to stay put, but Dan got here, and I couldn't stop him from climbing down to help Laura. When the other ladies arrived, I gave the phone to Amy and went down to see if I could help him."

"But you couldn't."

"There was so much blood, and I couldn't find a pulse." I shivered. "The ambulance crew came and turned her over. That's when we saw the corkscrew driven into her neck near her collarbone."

"Any idea where the corkscrew came from?"

"It looks like the one out of my van," I said, "but I don't know why Laura would have had it."

"You believe it was a homicide?" He raised his right eyebrow.

"I don't know. I think you know more about that than I would," I said truthfully. I didn't want to put ideas out there if they weren't true.

He narrowed his eyes at my response but didn't press the issue, switching his line of questioning. "Miss O'Brian, when was the last time you saw Laura unhurt?"

"We headed down the trail after hitting the prayer tree at the top, where Laura and I talked for a while. Afterward, I made my way to the back of the group to pick up the stragglers and ensure everyone's safety."

"And where was Laura while you were ensuring the others' safety?"

"I'm sorry?" I said, confused.

"You said you ensured everyone made it back safe, but Laura wasn't in the group."

"She had a tendency to lead, so I thought she was at the front of the group."

"Did anyone go with her?"

"Dan," I said. "He was with her for a while, but then he came to speak to me about taking one of their marketing classes.

I told him I didn't need to, and we had a few words before he left. I assumed he was going back to the front of the group with Laura. But I don't know for sure. I don't remember. Why can't I remember?"

"You've had a shock," he said. "Details will come back to you. So, you set up this tour?"

"Yes, this is my first tour for Taylor O'Brian Presents 'Off the Beaten Path' Wine Country Tours."

"And how did you arrange this group?" the sheriff asked.

"Well, I take a yoga class from Laura. She overheard me talking about my new tour business. She mentioned that she wanted to do a morale-boosting program for her team, so I suggested they try out my tour."

"So it was your idea to come hiking at Quarryhill?"

"Yes," I said. "I love this hike and thought it would be a great destination for my first wine country tour. When I told Laura, she agreed."

"And then she died here."

"It's so tragic and very strange."

"I agree that having a corkscrew pushed through your artery is unusual, Miss O'Brian," Sheriff Hennessey stated blandly. "Someone had to be pretty angry to come at her with the corkscrew. Looks like they used it like an ice pick. Whoever did it was either lucky or knew right where to put it to do the most damage."

I shuddered. "What a horrible way to die."

"Did you see anyone else at the gardens today?"

"Do you mean the tour members?"

"Besides them," he said. "Were you the only group out here?"

"I don't remember seeing anyone here but us. The garden is a hidden gem," I paused, horror rushing through me again.

"Wait, are you saying someone in the group may have murdered Laura?"

"If there was no one else on the trails . . ."

I covered my mouth and sat down hard. A quick glance over my shoulder told me the rest of the crew were being interviewed one by one. "Wouldn't the murderer be covered in blood?"

He gave me a look.

"What?"

"You have blood on your hands, Miss O'Brian."

It was then that I noticed I had Laura's blood on my hands and pants. "I helped turn her over. She wasn't breathing when I got to her."

"Dan is also covered in blood."

"He was distraught and had his hands all over her as well."

"No one else seems to be bloody."

"Well, *I* didn't kill Laura . . ." I stopped in terror. "There's no way Dan did it. He was devoted to her. I mean, the man was an emotional wreck when we got to her. Besides, we all saw him before we found Laura. No one saw any blood."

The sheriff looked at me flatly. His expression gave nothing away. He held up a bag with the bloody corkscrew in it. "You told me earlier you recognized this?"

I tilted my head and looked at it. "Yes, it looks like the kind of wine opener I brought. I don't know how Laura got it."

"And if we find your prints on it?"

"It's because it was my corkscrew—*not* because I murdered Laura. I was with the group every step of the way. I didn't do this, Sheriff."

"I didn't say you had," he said. "Here's my card. Call me if you remember anything else. Also, my team will be calling you to schedule a convenient time for you to give your DNA sample and fingerprints to rule you out."

"Okay," I said weakly.

"Do you need my help getting up?"

"No," I said and set my chin stubbornly. "I'll be fine in a few moments. You can go question someone else."

"It's not personal, Miss O'Brian. I'm just doing my job."

"Well, Sheriff, I hope you solve this soon. I hate to think I'm going to be driving a murderer home."

"I'll have a deputy escort you back to your place," he said grimly.

"Great," I said and pulled the blanket tighter around me. "Aunt Jemma will be thrilled."

*   *   *

"What happened? You look like you've been through a war," Aunt Jemma said as I unloaded the van. Everyone was weary and went back to their cars in a hurry to leave. I gathered up the remaining food and promptly tossed it in the garbage. No one wanted to eat food from a crime scene, even if it was hundreds of yards away.

"I feel like I've been through a war," I said grimly as I pulled the cooler full of wine out of the back of the van and tucked it away in the wine storage shelves in the garage.

"What happened? Were you in a car accident?"

Millie barked and raced around my feet. She was leash-free on the farm and enjoying every moment of it.

"Worse," I said. "You remember Laura?"

"The mean yoga instructor who asked you to take her team on this outing. Sure. Why? What happened? Is she okay?"

46

"No, she's not," I said and sat down on a bench outside the garage. "She was murdered, and apparently the murderer used my corkscrew."

"What? That's horrific. No wonder you look so bad."

I pointed with my chin toward the group members getting into their respective cars. "It's devastating for them. Laura's business was their livelihood."

"Who would kill her? And why?"

"Those are the big questions," I said as I watched the last of the cars disappear down the driveway. It was one of those fall days that was warm during the day but cooled with an early sunset. The vineyard faced the mountains to the west, so the sun went down fast, leaving streaks of red and orange in the sky.

"Come on. Why don't you shower, and I'll make you some tea."

"Thanks." I got up and called for Millie. She followed us into the semidarkness of the house. Aunt Jemma went to work in the kitchen while I went back to my apartment and showered. The hot water on my skin felt good, but I was still cold inside. Someone had used my corkscrew to kill Laura. That took a lot of strength or a lot of anger. She hadn't been the nicest person, but no one deserved to die like that.

I thought of all the people in the group. No one had been covered in blood. It didn't make sense. An act that violent would surely have left evidence on the murderer. Maybe they'd gotten lucky. Maybe she didn't bleed out until after they pushed her down the cliff. That was a morbid thought.

I wandered into the kitchen. Aunt Jemma had tea steeping in a pot and pulled down two blue ceramic mugs. "I made chamomile," she said, pouring. "You need something soothing. Did you eat today?"

"No," I said and climbed up on a barstool, wrapping my hands around the warm mug and resting my elbows on the table. "Laura was lost before I could eat lunch, and then after we found her . . ." I sighed.

Aunt Jemma patted my arm. She wore a floaty caftan made out of an orange-and-brown African print. She was the kind of woman who dressed however she wanted—styles be darned—so she bought many of her clothes from websites that sustainably supported weavers and craftswomen in emerging countries. Small businesses were her passion.

"Your hands are cold. I'll make you some soup."

"Thanks," I said. "Looks like we wore someone else out too." Millie was as tired as I was from the day. She curled up in the snuggly bed I'd bought her and was fast asleep near the breakfast bar.

"I fed her," Aunt Jemma said. "She ate and then went straight to bed."

"I forget she's a little pup."

"Any news on her owners?"

"No," I said, my smile fading. "I hope I don't hear anything, though. I'd love to keep her."

"Well, your business could use a mascot."

"That's what Holly said." I sipped my tea. It was warm and sweetened with honey. "Millie was a big help today in finding Laura. She was a good girl and stayed out of the way of the police and paramedics."

"I'd love for you to keep her, but I'm not sure what Clementine thinks."

My kitty had come out from her closet and given the sleeping dog a wide berth before leaping up onto the counter for attention.

"Clemmie will get used to Millie," I announced. Clem seemed to sneer at me and jumped back down to go to her box. "I'm hoping," I added and took another sip of tea.

"Tell me more about the day," Aunt Jemma said and pushed a bowl of thick potato soup toward me.

I told her everything that happened. "I don't know how anyone who was with us could've done this. Surely there'd be some evidence. But everyone seems to have an alibi since we were all together."

"Who else knew you all were going to Quarryhill?"

"Well, Holly, and some of my other friends. The Quarryhill staff, people at the next destination." I paused my spoon halfway to my mouth. "I used the itinerary as advertising for my business."

"So anyone who hated Laura could have lain in wait for her."

"But how would they know they could get her alone, and how did they get my corkscrew?"

"Did you lock the van before you hiked up the trail?"

"Yes . . . but it's old and easy to jimmy. Wait . . . you know what? Now that I think about it, I didn't have to unlock the passenger's side door when we got back. I remember thinking I needed to remind people to lock the van behind them, but then I was busy setting up the picnic. I've got to call the sheriff and let him know."

Aunt Jemma put her hand on mine as I reached for my cell phone. "Why don't you wait?"

"Because they say the first forty-eight hours are the most important in an investigation."

"They also say that witness recall is the most unreliable, especially after such a shock."

"What're you saying?"

"I think it'd be best for you to get a lawyer," Aunt Jemma said. "I'll call my friend Patrick Aimes."

"Wait, Patrick Aimes? The hot guy from high school?"

"He's defended some good, honest people in sticky situations."

"How am I in a sticky situation?"

"Let's call Patrick and let him explain," Aunt Jemma said and took my cell phone. "Eat your soup."

Great, Patrick Aimes was a lawyer and now he's going to know I'm in trouble. Could things possibly get any worse?

Chapter 5

"Oh, my goodness, Taylor, are you okay? Did you hire a lawyer?"

"Holly," I said. "It's eleven o'clock at night. I'm tired."

"I can't believe I had to call you. When did this happen? Why didn't you call me? Did you hire a lawyer?"

"Do you think I need a lawyer?"

"Of course, anyone who is involved in a murder investigation needs a lawyer. Don't you watch crime shows? They can make innocent people confess to crimes and stuff. You need to lawyer up."

I rolled my eyes and sat up in my bed. It was clear I was going to be on the phone for a while. Millie wiggled beside me as if my moving bothered her. "Hey, it's my bed," I whispered. Clemmie reached out as if to bat the dog as well, so I put my hand between them. "Stop it."

"Taylor, are you listening to me?"

"Yes, of course."

"Good because this is serious. Really I'm so offended you didn't call me the moment it happened. When were you going to tell me?"

"Tomorrow?" I sounded guilty to my own ears.

"Taylor!"

"What? I'm in shock. I can't unsee what I've seen today, Holly."

"Oh, poor girl," she said, sounding contrite. "Yes, okay, so just because I would've called you within the hour doesn't mean you're wrong for not calling me—"

"Holly!"

"We each react to shock differently."

"Look, I'm sorry. But the police kept us for hours. When I got back home, I wanted to shower. Then Aunt Jemma called a lawyer—"

"Who did she call?"

"Patrick Aimes."

"The young hot guy from Derrick's class?" Derrick was Holly's older brother. He and Patrick had been three years ahead of us at school. Derrick had been nicknamed "McDreamy" by me, and Holly had nicknamed Patrick "McSteamy." Yes, we'd stolen the nicknames from a television show. We'd been in high school.

"Yes."

"Then what happened? Go on . . ."

"You keep interrupting me."

"I'll stop. Go on."

I stared at the phone for a full minute.

"Taylor, I'm listening. Really."

"Fine. Aunt Jemma had Patrick come right over. He left about an hour ago, and I crawled into bed. I'm sorry I didn't call, but normal people don't call each other after nine o'clock at night unless something bad has happened."

"Taylor, something bad *did* happen," Holly pointed out.

"But it wasn't urgent."

"So you let me watch it on the news."

"The news?"

"Yes, the news. They're reporting Laura's murder and how she was on a corporate outing with Taylor O'Brian Presents 'Off the Beaten Path' Wine Country Tours."

"They said my name?"

"They said the name of your company, yes, so expect reporters to be calling all day tomorrow."

"Great, my first tour group, and I'm going to be forever associated with murder."

"It's fine," Holly said. "Any publicity is good publicity."

"Not if people think they might die on one of my tours."

"Maybe you could start some sort of mystery tour . . ."

"I'm not doing mystery tours. I'm doing 'Off the Beaten Path' Wine Country tours."

"You could turn them into mystery tours! People would love it. You could visit that winery where the proprietor chased the investor through the vineyard and shot him dead."

"I'm not touring that winery."

"Oh, and you could tour—"

"Stop it. I'm not doing it."

"It could be your niche," she pointed out. "Like ghost tours, only scene-of-the-crime tours."

"Holly."

"Fine, but when you see how popular you're going to be, you'll remember this conversation."

"Holly."

"And when you start doing crime tours, you have to call and tell me I was right and let me say 'I told you so.'"

"Holly, I'm not going to do scene-of-the-crime tours."

"Your loss," she said. "Is Patrick still steamy?"

"Is your brother still dreamy?"

"Ugh, he's my brother," Holly said. "How many times do I have to tell you it's creepy for me to think of him as anything other than stinky."

"Fine," I said. "Your brother—even though he's married now—is still dreamy."

"So that means that Patrick is still steamy. Is he married?"

"We didn't talk about his love life. We talked about the case and how the murder weapon came out of my van."

"What? Seriously?"

"Yes, but I'm pretty sure someone stole it while we were on the trail. I think Laura left her side door unlocked. Then we hiked for over an hour. Anyone could have come, taken the corkscrew, and left unseen."

"She was killed with a corkscrew? Yikes, that had to hurt."

"Holly."

"Fine, go on . . ."

"I wanted to go to the police when I remembered that the driver's side door was unlocked when I came back, but my aunt convinced me that my memory of things may have been affected by the shock."

"That's not like you. You're nearly obsessive about locking that silly van. As if anyone would want anything out of that hot mess."

"It runs fine, and it's a living piece of California history. People like it."

"Because it reminds them of the Scooby-Doo Mystery Machine. Hey . . ."

"No."

"It was a thought."

"Holly, I'm tired."

"What advice did McSteamy give you?"

"He said I should wait and have him go with me when I speak to the police about my van. They'd most likely want to search it and check for fingerprints and such. They can't do that without a search warrant or my permission. Patrick told me it'd go a long way if I give my permission to have it done."

"I hear fingerprint testing is pretty messy."

"Yes," I said. "But it'll be worth it if they can lift any fingerprints that don't belong to me or the group."

"But what if someone in the group actually did it?"

"Then they could have pocketed the corkscrew any time during the ride there. It's not like I hid it or anything. All the supplies were packed around them in the back."

"Oh, the plot thickens . . ."

"Be serious—a woman died today. You weren't there. You didn't see it."

There was silence on the other end of the phone. "You're right. I'm sorry. I guess I mostly called to see if you were all right. Do you need anything?"

"Some sleep," I said wearily. "Want to have coffee after yoga tomorrow?"

"Sure. I wonder who they will pick to teach since Laura's. . . . you know."

I fell back against my pillows, startling the animals. Clemmie darted off the bed, and Millie stood and licked my face. "I bet they cancel class."

"Let me come by and bring you coffee. We can talk at your place."

"I have an appointment to see Sheriff Hennessey at ten," I said. "What time are you coming by?"

"I'll be there at eight, and I'll bring gluten-free donuts."

"See you then." I hung up the phone and cuddled with Millie. It was going to be a long night. I was tired, but every time I closed my eyes, I saw Laura's lifeless body at the bottom of the ravine. It made me wonder: Who could do such a thing, and why?

Was there something I'd missed on the ride to the gardens? Or while on the trail? Could I have prevented this tragedy? I hadn't really cared for Laura, but that didn't mean I wanted her dead.

I closed my eyes and petted Millie. She smelled of puppy and warm sunshine. My first tour had been a disaster. How long could I stay in business if this murder didn't get solved? I was afraid people would always wonder if they were riding in a murder van. If someone they trusted would come after them with whatever weapon was handy . . .

* * *

The next morning, Holly arrived with the goods as promised. We were both trying to eat clean, but I had a hard time refusing sugar. Especially when I'd only slept a couple hours last night.

"You look gorgeous," I said. Holly wore a cute black jumpsuit that flattered her figure to perfection and maroon-red heels that added a pop of color.

"I figured if McSteamy was stopping by, I wanted to be ready."

"You're awful." I grabbed a coffee and sipped, letting the heat and caffeine infiltrate my system. "But beautiful. Can I be you?"

"Stop—you're lovely."

"Ha!" I snorted. I wore black slacks and a blue top that had a halter neckline. No high heels for me—I was running on so little sleep, I'd fall and break my ankle. My hair was up in a messy bun and my makeup minimal. "Next to you, I'm chopped liver."

"Oh, pooh," she said. We chatted for a while about yesterday and the horrible things that had gone wrong.

I nervously watched the clock until the doorbell rang. Millie barked, and Clemmie went running for her closet. I opened the door to a gorgeous dark-skinned man with a shaved head, brown eyes, and muscles from here to eternity. "Hi."

"Are you ready to go see the sheriff?" Patrick Aimes asked.

"Yes, let me get my purse."

"Hi, Patrick," Holly said. "Do you want some breakfast? We have coffee and gluten-free donuts."

"No, thanks," he said. "I'm watching my carbs. How have you been, Holly?"

"I've been good, busy with my business, and happy."

"Good to hear," he said with a grin. "You look great. Are you going somewhere?"

"Thanks, but I'm not going anywhere but work. I like the jumpsuit because it's so comfortable."

"Well, comfortable works for you," he said and winked at her.

I grabbed my purse. "We're going to take the van down for them to look over, right?"

"Yes, I'll follow you in my car, and then I'll drive you back home."

"What if they find something illegal?" I asked.

He gave me a look. "Do you have anything illegal in the van?"

"No, but the van lived through the seventies and eighties. Who knows what is hidden inside?"

"This isn't a television crime show. They aren't going to tear it apart," he reassured me as he held the door open. "The most they'll do is check for fingerprints and a cursory search."

"Well," I said as we walked to the van, "that makes me feel much better."

With Patrick following in his silver Audi, we drove to the station in Sonoma and walked in to meet the sheriff. "I have an appointment to see Sheriff Hennessey," I told the policewoman at the front desk. Her name tag said, "Officer Balder."

"Have a seat. I'll let him know you're here."

As Patrick and I waited, I couldn't seem to get my nerves under control. "Is it always so nerve-racking? I didn't do anything, and yet I still feel as if I'm waiting outside the principal's office."

"Don't worry. It'll be fine. I'm here to ensure everything goes well." He patted my hand.

Sheriff Hennessey came out from the other side of the reception desk. "Ah, Miss O'Brian, thanks for coming in. Please follow me."

We followed him through a crowded room full of cubicles and desks facing each other. "Do you want any coffee?"

"No, thanks," I said. The room smelled of old burnt coffee. "I already had some today."

He'd put us in an interview room with a small table and two chairs. I figured there was a camera somewhere and found it in an upper corner looking down on the chairs. "Have a seat. I'll be right with you."

We sat in the two chairs facing the door. Sheriff Hennessey came right back in with a manila folder. "So, Miss O'Brian, you brought your lawyer?"

"This is Patrick Aimes," I said. "He advised me it was best to have him present."

"It's your right, but it hardly seems necessary. We are still asking questions at this point."

I slumped with relief. "Good."

"I want to go over the events of yesterday. You've had a night to reflect. Have you spoken to anyone else who was there at the time?"

"No, I drove them home in shocked silence. They got into their cars and left the winery pretty fast. Not that I blame them. I took a shower and spoke to my best friend and my aunt, who suggested I hire Patrick, and here I am."

"I understand you brought your van in for fingerprinting?"

"Yes," I said. "I remembered last night that the passenger's side door was unlocked when I went to the van to put out the food. I thought it was odd because I always lock all the doors."

"You think the killer opened the door."

"It's a possibility," I said. "I know we all drove back in it last night, and I've touched the handle since then. So there's a chance you might not get any evidence, but I'm offering you the opportunity to go over it with a fine-tooth comb."

"Thank you," he said. "The county crime scene techs will be happy to see what evidence they can collect. I appreciate you coming in, but the van is not considered part of the crime scene."

"I want it to be noted that my client is acting with an over-abundance of caution," Patrick said.

"I'll note it in my file," the sheriff said. "But even if we find a partial print that doesn't fit, there's not a big chance we can use it in court since the van wasn't part of the scene."

"So you don't need it"? I asked.

"No, we'll still go over it. It could corroborate your story of how the corkscrew was obtained. I'm simply informing you that it may not lead to anything useful. Now do you mind taking a DNA test and fingerprinting?"

"I'll do whatever you need to rule me out."

"Good. I'll have a tech come and take care of that. Do you have a way home?"

"Patrick will take me."

"Great. If you think of anything else that seems relevant, be sure to let me know. Thank you for your time."

"That's it?" I asked.

"Do you have anything else to add?"

"No."

"Okay, then we're done here. I'll send the tech right in." He closed his folder and left the room.

I looked at Patrick. "Did that seem too easy?"

Patrick shrugged. "I think you're safe."

"Good." I slumped with relief. The tech came in with nitrile gloves on, took a swab of the inside of my cheek, and then used a digital machine to take ink-free fingerprints. "I'm leaving my van to be searched for evidence. Do you have any idea how long it will take before I get it back? I run my tour business out of it."

"We're a bit backed up," the tech said.

I shot a look at Patrick. "How backed up?"

"It could be a few days."

"As in a week or less?"

"Hopefully."

"But I have another tour scheduled for tomorrow."

"I'd get a loaner," the tech said, unbothered by my dilemma. "Your insurance should cover it. You're free to go."

Patrick and I walked out into the California sunshine. "I'm not sure my insurance will cover the cost of a rental van," I said as I got into his Audi.

"You did the right thing," he pointed out. "You're being helpful without admitting to anything." He patted my knee. "It's a good thing."

"A good thing that's going to cost me." I frowned. "I already had to pay your retainer."

"Five thousand dollars isn't a lot to ensure you stay out of jail."

"I know," I said and looked out the window as he drove me back to the winery. "But my emergency stash is disappearing fast."

"It's going to be all right," he said. "Once this is over, let's get a drink and catch up. It's been a few years since I've seen you."

I lifted my mouth in a half smile. It would make Holly crazy if I said no. "I'd like that. But first, let's get through this."

"I agree," he said and turned into the driveway. "How's your Aunt Jemma? I heard through the grapevine that you moved back because she was ailing."

"She's actually doing quite well," I said and shook my head. "I suspect she only gets sick when I mention moving back to San Francisco."

"You'd go back to the city?"

"I don't really know," I said with a shrug and opened the car door. "I own my own start-up. There's a lot of work involved . . . and risk. I'm hoping it'll start paying for itself before the end of the year."

"You could always get investors," Patrick pointed out.

"Who would invest in a small tour business? It's not like it'd be bought out by Priceline or go public for millions of dollars."

"Oh, you'd be surprised who would help out. There are quite a few people who want to keep the local economy humming." His expression made me think he might be willing to be one of those investors. "Think about it. Your business supports the wineries and other destinations in the area. Who wouldn't want to invest?"

"I hadn't thought about it that way," I said. "Thanks."

"You're welcome." He craned his neck to continue to look at me as I got out of the car and stood to close the door. "Call me before you interact with anyone on this case. Okay?"

"Why?" I asked. "The sheriff didn't say I was a person of interest."

"Let's not give them any opportunity to make you one."

"Right. Got it." I closed the door and waved good-bye, watching him drive away. Then I turned on my heel and opened the browser on my phone. I needed to find a rental van, and I needed a very good deal on it. My stash of start-up funds was quickly dwindling, and I didn't want to have to close down before I even got started.

Chapter 6

I decided to take Dan a casserole. I didn't really know him that well, but Laura had taken a chance on my tour business, and if nothing else, I owed him condolences. I made my best vegetarian lasagna with spinach, chopped broccoli, and vegan cheese.

I wrapped up the lasagna in case he wanted to freeze it and headed out to Dan's home in my rented minivan. Laura and Dan lived in a three-bedroom, two-story home on the corner of a cul-de-sac in a newer part of town. The small patch of lawn had been turned into a rock garden with an avocado tree in the center. I parked on the road and walked up to ring the bell.

Dan opened the door. "What do you want?"

I blinked back surprise at the anger in his tone. "Hello," I said. "How are you? I brought you a casserole."

Dan stood in the doorway. His face was red and tearstained. "I don't want a casserole from my wife's murderer."

"What?" I was stunned. "I didn't hurt your wife."

A woman who looked like a younger female version of Dan came to the door to stand beside him. "Is this the woman who killed Laura?"

"Yes," Dan said.

"No!" I said at the same time. I looked at Dan. "Why would you say that?"

"You were the one who found her. You were the only one who was alone with her. It was your corkscrew. You had her blood on your hands. Get off my property!" Dan took a step toward me, and I took a stunned step back.

"I didn't have anything to do with her death," I said. "I tried to save her. I called nine-one-one."

"Liar," he said and took another step toward me. From the look in his eye, I had a brief moment of panic. He looked as if he might hurt me.

I backed up. "I had no reason to kill Laura."

"The press reported that you took a lawyer with you when you went to the police station," the woman said. "A sign of a guilty mind."

"No," I said. "I was—"

"I don't care what your next lie is," Dan said. "You never liked Laura. You refused to let us help you. Leave my property."

"I'm calling the police," the woman said and pulled out her phone.

"Sheesh," I muttered. "All right, all right. I'll go. But I had nothing to do with Laura's death."

"Every murderer claims to be innocent," Dan shouted as I got back into the van. I drove away as the neighbors came out of their houses looking for a show. Why did he think I murdered Laura? Who was the woman—his sister? Their daughter? She seemed kind of old for a daughter. A police car rolled around the corner as I left the cul-de-sac. I drove another two blocks before he pulled me over.

A Case of Syrah, Syrah

I swallowed hard and opened the window. "Yes, Officer?" I knew I hadn't been speeding.

"I need to see your driver's license and registration, plus proof of insurance."

"Yes, sir," I said and got out the documentation, including my rental-car agreement. "What's this about?"

"I got a call that someone was harassing Dan Scott. You were seen leaving his home."

"It was a mistake, Officer," I said. "I went over to bring him a casserole. It's what my family does when someone dies. We feed people during times of grief." I pointed to the dish that was sitting, rejected, on the passenger's seat.

"His sister, Ivy Scott, claims you were harassing them." He looked at the documentation, then looked at me as if to verify everything. "Miss O'Brian, did you kill Laura Scott?"

"What? No. Why would I?"

"Are you stalking Dan Scott?"

"No."

"Did you go to his home and ring his doorbell?"

"Yes. Like I said, I brought him a casserole."

"I see, and are you and Mr. Scott friends?"

"I don't like your tone."

"It's a simple question."

"Have I done something wrong?"

"Ma'am?"

"It's a simple question," I said. "Have I done something wrong? Do I need to dial my lawyer?"

"No, ma'am. I think we're good here." He handed me back my documentation. "I suggest you leave the Scotts alone."

"Oh, no worries—Deputy Riley, is it?" I read his name tag.

"Yes."

"I won't be back."

"Good. I'm glad we understand each other. Have a nice day, miss."

I rolled my window up before I could say something not so nice. My first instinct was to drive away, so I did. I could feel the heat on my cheeks from embarrassment. I pulled into a parking lot outside of Vons grocery store. People were shopping as if it were a normal day. It was kind of comforting to see that life went on even when your world was spinning out of control. I called Patrick.

"Patrick Aimes."

"Hi, it's Taylor. Do you have a minute?"

"Sure."

"So I went to see Dan Scott."

"What? Why?"

Okay, not the reaction I was expecting. "Because his wife died, and I thought he might need a casserole. Don't you take food to someone when someone in the family dies?"

"It's a bit more complicated than that, Taylor. You found the man's wife dead. You don't think your presence would bring up more grief?"

"Well, when you put it that way . . ."

"What happened?"

"Why do you think something happened?"

"Why else would you be calling me?"

I sighed. "Dan accused me of murdering Laura."

"Why would he think that?"

"Because I found her. I was the only one he knew who was alone with her. And it was my corkscrew."

"That's serious."

"I told him it was ridiculous. I had no reason to kill Laura."

"Taylor, I told you to not speak to anyone—I mean anyone—about this if I'm not present."

"I didn't think it was a big deal," I said and rubbed my forehead and closed my eyes. "It's not, right?"

"That depends. Were you in his house when he accused you?"

"No," I said. "He barred me at the door. Then his sister called the cops on me."

"Why?"

"She said I was harassing them . . . I think it's all a bit of a crazy blur."

"Taylor, please tell me you left."

"I left," I said and glanced at the cold casserole. "But then a cop stopped me on the way out."

"I feel like a broken record. Why? Did you run a red light?"

"He said something about leaving the scene."

"Taylor, he had no reason to stop you."

"He asked me if I killed Laura."

"Taylor, please tell me you didn't say anything."

"I told him I didn't kill her."

He sighed long and hard.

"I know, I know. Don't say anything. But it's hard to think when you're in panic mode. It's why I stopped at Vons and called you."

"I'm glad you called me," he finally said. His tone was reassuring. "I know this is hard, Taylor. But you need to remember to only talk to people when I'm present. Can you do that?"

"Even Aunt Jemma?"

"It's best if you keep things to yourself. As your lawyer, it's my job to advise you."

"Sheesh. This is all crazy. All I wanted to do was bring over a casserole."

"I know this is hard."

"Darn right it's hard," I said. "I'm going to take my casserole to the soup kitchen and see if they can use it."

"You do that. And remember . . ."

"I know, I know. Don't talk to anyone about what happened. Thanks, Patrick."

"It's what you pay me for," he said.

*   *   *

My friend Jasper, a laid-back guy with a long ponytail, worked at the volunteer kitchen. "Hey, Taylor," he said. "Thanks for the casserole."

"It's vegan," I half apologized. "It was meant for someone who was vegan, but he refused it. So I figured you could always use it."

"Sure, it'll make a nice lunch. We have vegans who come eat with us," he said. "Sometimes it makes it difficult because the food is all donated, and people don't think about the poor or homeless being dairy intolerant or gluten-free."

"I'm glad you can use it."

"So it was for a guy, right? What happened? Were you looking for a date, and he turned you down?"

"I'm not supposed to talk about it," I said with a sigh.

"Then at least come have a cup of coffee. Tell me, what's been going on with you?"

"Don't you watch the news?"

"I don't," he said. "The Dalai Lama says to ask yourself if there is anything you can do to change it. Well, when it comes to national or even local news, the answer is usually no. So he says, why watch it if it bothers you?"

I smiled. It sounded like Jasper. "I like that idea."

"I know," he said. "I get that a lot." He poured me a cup of coffee, and I added creamer to it. "Now tell me what's been going on with you."

"I had my first wine country tour," I said and sipped.

"That's awesome. How did it go?"

"Someone died."

"No, don't kid like that. It's bad karma."

"Oh, I wish I were kidding," I said, "but it really happened."

"Was it a heart attack? You have to watch the older people."

"I can't talk about it," I said. "My lawyer advises that I keep my mouth shut."

"Okay, now I'm intrigued. Maybe I'll have to watch the news tonight."

I rubbed my face and sipped my coffee. "How are things here?"

"Oh, the usual," he said. "We have an uptick in clients, and the food shelves are low."

"Oh, I'll have Aunt Jemma start a drive at the winery."

"Thanks," he said. "Every bit counts, even if it's vegan. Hey, speaking of vegan, here's a guy you should meet." Jasper pointed to the deeply tanned man who'd walked into the kitchen. "Jack Henry Stokes, come meet my friend Taylor O'Brian. Taylor, Jack Henry is my right-hand guy."

"Hello," I said and stuck out my hand. "Nice to meet you."

"Miss," he said and shook my hand. He wore an old corduroy coat that had been patched, worn jeans, and boots, and he had shaggy hair.

"If you ever need any handiwork done or local gossip, Jack Henry here is your man," Jasper said with a twinkle in his eye.

Jack Henry tilted his head and looked at me like a cowboy from an old-time movie. "You're Jemma's niece. The one who started that tour business in the van."

"Yes," I said and felt my eyes grow wide with surprise. "How do you know?"

"Like I said, Jack Henry knows what goes on in Sonoma County," Jasper said. "Taylor brought us a vegan casserole. Are you hungry?"

"Certainly," Jack Henry said. "Mighty nice of you, ma'am."

"No problem," I said. "I've got to get back to the winery. Take care, Jasper. It was nice to meet you, Jack Henry."

"Try to come around more often," Jasper said. "Stay out of trouble."

"I will," I said. Although it might already be too late for the sentiment.

Chapter 7

My phone rang as I walked toward my car. I answered when I saw it was Aunt Jemma. "Hello?"

"Where are you? Are you okay? You need to come straight home." Aunt Jemma's tone meant business.

"I'm fine," I said. "I was at the volunteer food pantry—Jasper says hi. What's going on?"

"The place is crawling with reporters," Aunt Jemma said. "They can't come on the property without permission, but they're camping out on the street. I normally don't mind the publicity, but they're keeping the customers from coming in."

"What do the reporters want?"

"Someone told them that you killed Laura Scott."

"I didn't kill anyone."

"Well, I know that."

"I'll call Sheriff Hennessey and have him push the media back."

"I already called the police. Angus McCarty ensured me that he will send someone out to clear the road."

"Okay," I said. "I'm coming home."

"Be careful! The world is crazy."

"So I'm finding out."

I got into my car and drove home. Aunt Jemma was right. There were television vans and cars on either side of the road that wound around the vineyard. The entire drive was stop and go. Finally, a police car pulled around in front of traffic. Two minutes later, I saw that he had stopped to direct traffic. A second police car was there, and the officer was instructing the press to park on only one side of the road so that they weren't blocking anyone.

The traffic was beginning to flow fairly smoothly now, but I noticed that no one seemed to be stopping at the winery.

Finally, I pulled even with the deputy and opened my window when I saw it was Jason Elles. He'd been in the class ahead of me in school. "Hey, Jason, what's all the fuss about?" I knew what Aunt Jemma had said but couldn't believe this was all about me—an innocent woman.

"Someone got a tip that you killed Laura Scott," he said. "Did you?"

"What? No! How can you ask such a thing? I can't talk to you without my lawyer present." Sonoma was a small town, and I figured Jason thought he could make a stupid quip like that because he knew me.

"So you did do it?" He gave me the side eye. "Only the guilty lawyer up."

"Oh, come on," I said. "That's ridiculous."

"Had to ask," he said and grinned at me.

The driver two cars down from me honked and yelled out his window. "Can we keep it moving?"

I rolled my window up and waited until Jason waved me through. Then I turned into the driveway. I could see Juan and his brother, Julio, sitting on top of their cars guarding the vineyard. I waved to them as I passed by. Then I noticed that people must've realized it was me. They poured out of their vehicles and tried to walk down the driveway after me. Juan and Julio stopped them. I watched in the rearview mirror as the two men closed the big wrought-iron gates of the winery drive. We rarely had to gate the drive. The wrought-iron was mostly there for show.

Today, it felt a bit like prison gates closing behind me. I guessed that there'd be no wine tasting or club pickups today. Aunt Jemma was going to kill me.

Aunt Jemma and Holly came running out of the house toward me as I climbed out of the van. Aunt Jemma, in a colorful caftan, wrapped her arms around me and smothered me in a huge hug. "Oh, thank goodness you're home safe. I have no idea what they might've done had they found you in town. Why, that crowd of hungry newsmongers might've run you over."

"I'm fine," I said as I tried to breathe in her embrace. She squeezed harder and then let go only to hold my face and check it out for herself.

"They're likely to give me another heart attack."

"Aunt Jemma, I don't think the first episode was a heart—"

"Nonsense, my doctor is so glad you are here with me now to watch over me, and I'm glad I'm still here to watch over you."

"Are you okay?" Holly asked and gave me a hug. "I heard about Dan Scott calling the cops on you."

"How?"

"Sonoma is a small town," Holly said. "Word spread fast. Then the newspeople got a call saying you were trespassing on Dan's lawn, and people are saying that you killed Laura and tried to kill Dan this morning."

"Oh, for goodness' sake. I took him a casserole."

"Sheriff Hennessey is here to see you," Aunt Jemma said. "He's a handsome man, don't you think?"

"Aunt Jemma!"

"I'm just saying." She shooed me toward the house. "I've got him on the patio sipping iced tea. You go on out there and see what he wants. I'll bring more tea."

Holly locked her arm in mine. She still looked fabulous. "How can you have gone through the better part of the day and still look so put together?" I teased her.

"Pish, you're the one who has all these handsome men seeing you all the time."

"That's the problem. They aren't here for a personal visit. It might be different if I looked like you, but I don't."

"You look fine." She steered me into the house, through the great room, to the open patio doors, where Sheriff Hennessey sat at the patio table. He rose when we came out.

"I was keeping the sheriff company while we waited for you," Holly said with a wink. "Did you know he owns a couple of horses? I love horses."

"Good afternoon, Miss O'Brian."

"Taylor, please," I said. "Sit. Had I known you were here, I would've tried to get through the crowd outside a little faster."

"I came with the guys who came to help regulate the traffic," he said.

"It's a madhouse. It took me twenty minutes to get from one side of the vineyard to the other. The frontage is only a half a mile wide."

"My officers are moving them along," he said.

"So what can I help you with?" I asked as Aunt Jemma came bustling out with a big pitcher of iced tea and glasses for me and her.

"I'm concerned about you," he said, his blue gaze showing a hint of heat. "I heard you went to see Dan Scott this morning."

"I did," I said and tried not to blush. "I went to bring him a casserole. I don't understand what the big deal is."

"He's asked that you stay away from him until this is all cleared up."

"Okay," I said. "No worries. I'm not going back."

"Good, good," he said. "Where did you go afterward?"

"Why do you need to know?" I felt defensive.

"I'm looking out for you." His expression was genuine concern.

"That might be true," I said, "but my attorney keeps telling me I shouldn't talk to anyone without him present."

"Goodness, even me?" Aunt Jemma asked.

"Even you," I replied. "People keep taking things I do or say out of context. I mean, it was a casserole, not a gun."

Sheriff Hennessey took a sip of his drink. His intense gaze did not leave me. For some reason, it had my heart beating faster. "It might not hurt to lay low for a while," he advised, "until we figure out what happened that day on the hike."

"Oh, for goodness' sake . . ."

"He's right," Aunt Jemma said. "It's probably a good thing to lay low."

"But I have a tour tomorrow. My second 'Off the Beaten Path' tour."

"Honey, you're going to have to postpone," Holly said. "You can't guide a tour with the press popping out of the bushes."

"But I have to work."

"And the winery needs to be open," Aunt Jemma said. "Yet here we are." She patted my knee. "What's done is done. You need to listen to the handsome sheriff."

"Aunt Jemma!"

"Listening can't hurt," Holly said.

"Okay, now you all are ganging up on me."

The sheriff rose. He nodded at Aunt Jemma, who looked like she wanted to swoon. "Thanks for understanding. You ladies have a safe night."

"Let me walk you out." Aunt Jemma jumped up, nearly knocking her chair back. "You're welcome any time, Sheriff . . ."

"Unless he's coming to arrest me," I muttered when they left through the patio door.

"He's good-looking," Holly teased. "He could arrest me any day."

"What happened to your date the other night?"

"That didn't work out."

"And your crush on Patrick?"

"I don't think he'd do more than flirt with me if I tried. Unlike the good sheriff, who seems totally into you."

"Oh, for goodness' sake," I repeated.

"Trust me. I know guys."

"You are incorrigible."

"You need to think about dating again. How long has it been? Three months?"

"Six," I said, "and I'm not ready."

"I'd point you in the direction of my online dating profile, but you don't need one with that hunky sheriff."

"Stop." I had to laugh at her antics. "Both Patrick and the sheriff are involved in this investigation. The last thing I want is to be involved as well."

"Well, honey, I think it's a little too late for that."

Chapter 8

Things went from bad to worse. Turned out I didn't have to postpone tomorrow's tour since they called to cancel. The group spokesperson called me after dinner. "Hello, thank you for calling Taylor O'Brian Presents 'Off the Beaten Path' Wine Country Tours," I said. "This is Taylor. How can I help you?"

"Hi, Taylor, it's Stephanie Osborne."

"Hello, Stephanie," I said. "How are you?"

"I'm all right," she said. "Listen, I hate to do this, but the group has voted to cancel tomorrow's tour. We know it's last minute, so you can keep the down payment."

"Okay," I said slowly. "Is there a problem with the date or time? Shall we reschedule?"

"I think it's best if we skip the tour this year, given all that you have going on," she said. "How are you holding up?"

"I'm fine," I said. "Good, actually."

"Oh, that's good." She sounded relieved. "Then you're okay with us not coming? I thought it might be a bit of a hardship."

"Really, I'm fine."

"Great, then we'll talk later, okay? Gotta go. Bye, now." She hung up.

I stared at my phone. Darn it. Another opportunity lost.

"How are you doing, sweetie?" Aunt Jemma stood in the doorway of my office. She held two steaming mugs. "I brought you some apple cider tea."

"I think I'd prefer a glass of wine."

She chuckled. "Me too, but I don't have anything open at the moment, and if I don't get customers in, I'm going to have to try to sell everything online."

"Well, that's terrible. I'm sorry."

"What are you sorry for?" she asked as she glided over to my desk, set down the mug, and then sat across from me. "You didn't do anything. And that's what I've come to talk to you about."

"What do you mean?"

"Let me guess. That was tomorrow's tour canceling on you." She nodded toward my phone.

"Yes," I said with a sigh.

"So you're out of work for a few days, and so am I." Aunt Jemma sighed. "Just like my poor dead brother, Hank. Your uncle couldn't hold down a job for longer than three months."

"I'm not Uncle Hank."

"No, dear, you're not." She paused. "It's too bad you are an only child," she said.

"Why?"

"Because a person can always count on their siblings to help them out in a pinch." She looked off into the distance. Aunt Jemma was the last of her siblings that was alive. She had been the pampered baby of her family. My grandparents—her parents—had died when she was only eighteen, and Hank and my mom, Sybil, had always seen to her every need. My heart pinched. She must miss her family. Now that I was the only remaining relative, I could understand why she clung to me. Losing business was not something Aunt Jemma had encountered before in her life. Unfortunately, I'd worked with enough start-ups to understand how quickly new businesses failed.

"What?" I asked.

Aunt Jemma had a gleam in her eye that made me suspicious.

"What are you thinking?" I repeated.

"I think we should figure out who really killed Laura and get our businesses back," Aunt Jemma announced.

"Wait—what?"

"We're as good at detecting as any private investigator."

"Where did you get that idea?" I asked and drew my eyebrows together in confusion.

"Well, you were always good at puzzles, and you have an investigative degree."

"Aunt Jemma," I said, "my degree is in journalism. In *advertising*, not in investigation."

"You still had to do basic reporting classes and learn how to dig up clues, right?"

"Yes, I took reporting one and two, but—"

"Look, we don't even have to leave the house. We can do some digging online and—"

"Digging into what?"

"Into who Laura was and who might have wanted to kill her, of course. We should also look into the backgrounds of her employees. You never know. Someone—like Dan, for example—might be getting a big chunk of change from her death. That might be why he's so crazy about accusing you. They say killers like to involve themselves in the investigation."

"Which is what we'll be doing, if we do what you suggest."

"Not really," she said and leaned forward, her fingers hugging the mug. "We're not involving the police. We're taking some time to figure out who, besides you, might have killed Laura."

"I don't know . . ."

"Look, you have to be proactive in your life. Your mother and I both taught you that. You can't lie down and let them accuse you, maybe even railroad you straight to prison for something you didn't do."

"Wow, you really think it'll go that far?"

"Not if we're investigating," she said. "Look, let's do some digging online. It might help and certainly can't hurt."

"Unless the police charge us with interfering with an investigation."

Aunt Jemma laughed. "It's only interfering if you hide it from them. We'll tell them the minute we discover anything."

"Fine, let me sleep on it," I said.

"Sleep on it if you want, if you can. But I'm telling you, someone is framing you for Laura's murder, or the press wouldn't be knocking at our door. If you want to stop it, we have to act *now*."

"I'm not being framed."

"Says the girl who is losing business and is trapped in her own home by paparazzi." Aunt Jemma stood. "Some people need to be hit over the head with a situation before they act."

"Hey, that's not fair. I came here for you, remember?"

"And stayed even after figuring out that my heart is as healthy as a horse." She winked at me. "Doesn't mean it'll be healthy tomorrow, but if we both want to survive, I think we need to do some digging. I'll check in on you in the morning and see what we can find out. Good night, sweetheart."

"Ugh," I muttered to the air and sipped the apple cider tea. After a few moments, I opened up my computer browser. "I do have to do some work on my website, so I guess it wouldn't hurt to read the news."

The headline for the local paper read, "Local Yoga Instructor Killed. Tour Guide May Be a Person of Interest in the Case."

I sat back. "I'd better not be the only person of interest. In fact, I shouldn't be a person of interest at all."

Maybe Aunt Jemma was right. Maybe I needed to do a little investigating on my own.

*　*　*

The next morning, I woke up at my desk. I had fallen asleep at the computer, and drool pooled beside the pad where I rested my head. I sat up and stretched. My neck was sore from spending the night at such an odd angle. I probably needed a massage and yoga class to work the kinks out.

"Rise and shine, sunshine." Aunt Jemma strolled in with a mug of hot coffee in her hand. "We have two groups coming out for tasting and one corporate picnic."

I rubbed my gritty eyes. "Wait, I thought this was ruining your business?"

"It seems people are interested in getting a look at a murderer firsthand."

"What?"

"Kidding . . . not really. The point is that people are coming today. So get up. Let's get going."

"Oh, good, I think . . . That should help with yesterday's bad business, anyway. Is Juan still out at the gate?"

"He and Julio camped out there last night. Mary told me that she had a few scoundrels try to sneak in through her property last night, but Juan was onto them. He and Julio caught a few people climbing over the fence, but mostly the press went home around eleven—after the late news."

"Do you think they'll be back today?"

"Let's hope not," she said. "I'd love to pick up a few stragglers coming for a tasting and not simply rely on the buses today. I mean, the more the merrier, right?"

"Right." I grabbed the coffee and took a deep sip, glad for the rush of caffeine.

"So did you discover anything interesting last night?" Aunt Jemma asked.

"How did you know I was looking?"

"Because you're my niece," she said with a grin. "What did you find out?"

"Laura ran a couple of seminars a year teaching a mastermind class on yoga marketing," I said. "Her website offers promises of increasing wealth and reaching more people to help them heal, lose weight, and better their lives."

"Sounds magical," Aunt Jemma said.

"I know, right? Next is Dan. He's a new-age marketer and is pitching a program that's supposed train your brain to make new connections based on listening to a daily series of tones."

"That's weird. How does it work?"

"I'm not exactly sure," I said. "I signed up for the first thirty days free. I was listening to the tones when I must've fallen asleep last night."

"Can I hear?"

"Sure," I said and gave her my earphones, which had been hanging around my neck. I got up and stretched, letting her take my chair.

"So the sounds move from ear to ear and high to low," she said loudly.

"You don't need to shout. I'm right here and can hear you fine."

"Sorry," she said. "The tones are strange." She took off the headset. "How is this supposed to retrain your brain?"

"It stimulates growth by getting you to pay attention to different sounds and frequencies," I said. "At least that's what the website claims."

"I wonder how many people use this?"

"I don't know," I said. "I think it's relatively new, but they're using the same seminar and subscription marketing as her yoga business."

"Do you think an angry customer could have killed Laura?"

I shrugged. "Why go so far as to kill her? They have a money-back guarantee. And at a couple thousand dollars for personal service and one-on-one time with Laura for six months, I wouldn't think anyone would be that angry."

"So it probably wasn't a disgruntled customer."

"We didn't see anyone else out at Quarryhill."

"That doesn't mean someone wasn't waiting in the wings."

"What do you mean?"

"You did use the itinerary as an example of possible tours on your website."

"So you think someone read my website and went out there looking to kill Laura?"

"Did you list on your website who your first tour was with?"

"Oh, gosh no," I said.

"Then maybe Laura wasn't the initial target of the murderer."

"Wait, are you saying whoever killed Laura might have actually wanted to kill me? Whatever for?"

"Who knows," Aunt Jemma said and sipped her coffee. "You can't rule anything out at this point."

"Trust me, my website did not give an exact time or date of our tour. There is no way a person was waiting in the wings, as you say, to kill anyone."

"Did you check Twitter?"

"What?"

"People tweet where they are going all the time."

"That's crazy," I said. "If you tell people where you are, you invite stalkers."

"Now wait—don't blame the victim."

"I wasn't blaming anyone," I protested. "I meant—for safety—people shouldn't tweet where they are when they're there. Everyone should know that. It's like removing the place and time stamp on your pictures before you upload them. There are crazy people out there, and you need to be as safe as possible."

"I see. Well, then you need to call everyone in the yoga group and see who else might have known your group was at Quarryhill."

"Oh, right, and have them accuse me of blaming them? No, I think that's something I'll leave to the police."

"Don't leave anything to the police," Aunt Jemma said. "According to the newspaper, the sheriff is looking at you as the murderer."

"Sheriff Hennessey said they were collecting evidence and asking questions. Does that sound like I'm the number-one suspect?"

"He won't tell you if you are," she said. "If there is even a small rumor you might have done it, then you are a person of interest. Trust me, it'll be easier to put you away than someone no one knows about."

"Stop. You're scaring me."

"I'm not trying to scare you," Aunt Jemma said. "I want you to understand that this is serious. I don't want you to simply rely on the goodwill of others. Or think that people will go out of their way to prove your innocence. It's not their job."

"Fine. I'll work on figuring this out. Maybe you are right. Someone else could have been there. It is a public place. I got along well with Amy," I said. "I'll call her today and go for coffee. Maybe she can help me figure out if anyone tweeted the time and place."

"Good girl," Aunt Jemma said. "Now go shower and get dressed—we have a busy day today."

"Yes, ma'am," I said and walked to my bathroom. I sent a quick text to Amy, "Are you doing okay? Do you want to meet for coffee?"

"Sure," came the answer.

"How about one?"

"Perfect. Abuelo's?"

"I love their coffee," I texted back. "See you then." Maybe, just maybe, Amy could help shine some light on what was going on inside Laura's team.

* * *

After the first busload left the winery, I grabbed my car keys and headed out to Abuelo's. Unfortunately, the press was still camped out at the foot of our drive.

Someone recognized me as I turned onto the road, and everyone jumped into their cars and vans and followed me. There was no way I could have a private conversation with this kind of tail.

I lost half of them at the first light into town when I turned right, then left, then right. It was weird, but watching television had taught me a little bit about watching out for cars following you. I decided to park five blocks from Abuelo's. Then I ducked into the back of Stacey's dress shop and came out the front. I found my way into Sonoma Hardware and slipped out the side door, where I took two more alleys, went up to the second-floor vintage shop above the donut shop, and left by the back door.

Finally, I sneaked in the back of Abuelo's. "Hey, Austin," I said to the barista. "I'm meeting someone here. Can I slip through to your far corner?"

"Sure," he said and waved me in through the kitchen. I ordered a latte and took the far table with my back to the wall and my vision squarely on the front door. He brought me my drink. "What's with all the cloak-and-dagger?"

"I seem to be the news item of the day," I said. "I'm hiding out from the press."

"Awesome. What'd you do?"

"Nothing," I insisted.

Austin, a thin blond guy with a beard that was darker than his hair, was two years younger than I was. Surfing and the coffee shop were his life. "Dude, is this about that woman you killed?"

"I didn't kill anyone," I protested.

"Cool," he said with a grin. "Was it, like, gory?"

"It was not cool or fun," I said. "A man lost his wife."

"Dude, sorry," he shrugged.

"Keep my presence a secret, okay? For me?"

"Sure, whatever," he said and went back to his station behind the counter. Five minutes later, Amy walked in. I watched as she looked around until she spotted me.

Amy was a nice girl with rounded features and dark-brown hair. She had deep-green eyes and wore jeans and a T-shirt. "Hi, Taylor, how are you?" she asked as she gave me a hug.

I waved Austin down. "I'm buying."

"I'll have a chai tea latte," Amy said and took a seat.

"Coming right up," Austin said.

"How are you holding up?" I asked Amy.

She sighed long and hard and put her elbows on the table with her chin in her hands. "I left an emergency employee meeting at Dan's house. He's all fired up."

"I know. I tried to bring him a casserole yesterday, but he refused it and accused me of murdering Laura."

"I know. He was really upset today. So strange. He's normally such a nice guy. I once saw him give a homeless man the shirt off his back and his lunch."

"Wow."

"Yeah, he works nights helping poor kids sharpen their reading skills so that they can go further in school. He once gave the school five grand to cover any outstanding lunch bills. He's that kind of guy." She sighed. "You know, the classic really nice guy with the intense woman."

Austin brought over the latte. "Are you hiding out from the press too?" he asked.

Amy shook her head. "No, why?"

"You're sitting with the undercover girl." He nodded at me and left.

"What is he talking about?" Amy asked.

"Someone called the local news channel and said that I murdered Laura."

"That's ridiculous," Amy said. "You were with someone on the trail the whole time."

"Except when I took Millie to find Laura," I pointed out. "At least, that's why Dan's sister accused me of murder."

"That's ridiculous."

"Yes, well, I agree. So the question is, who did do it?"

"I have no idea," Amy said. "Laura was really intense and that rubbed some people the wrong way. But there are things you don't know about her. She was a very private person. A control freak, yeah, but you should've seen her at her workshops. She was really magic. She had twenty yoga instructors who were part of her mastermind group. Our goal was to stretch that to twenty-five this year."

"So who found her intense?" I asked. "I mean, besides me."

"Well, I worked closely with her at her home for the past year. She would say things without thinking them through whenever she was stressed."

"Like what?"

"Like how she couldn't trust anyone to do anything right. How we were all incompetent without her. How if we only did everything she said, nothing would ever get messed up—and trust me, *everything* we did was messed up in some way. Really, it was nothing that I would kill anyone over, but she was intense. There were times when it was superinsulting."

I put my hand on hers. "I'm sorry to hear you had such a harsh boss."

"The thing is that she didn't even pay me until I'd worked for her for six weeks."

"What? That's nuts."

"Well, she paid monthly, but if your first payday fell within your first two weeks of working, you had to wait until the next one to get a check. So I had to borrow money to cover my living expenses until I got my first paycheck. I'd asked Laura for an advance, but she said it wasn't in their policy to cover it. I should have had better control of my finances."

"Wow, that's crazy."

"But nothing to kill someone over," Amy said.

"Oh, I'm not accusing anyone of murder," I said. "I wondered who you thought might have done it. I mean, it seems that everyone in our group has an alibi. We watched each other hike down the hill."

"Well, Laura did go down the trail by herself."

"Do you think someone was lying in wait for her? Do you know if she had a stalker?"

"As far as I know, she didn't. It would've taken some planning to find us, isolate Laura, kill her, and then get out—sight unseen."

"I know," I said, "and the killer had to be covered in blood. That corkscrew hit her artery."

"See? None of us could have done it and gotten cleaned up in time to drive home with you in the van."

"Then someone was ready and waiting for her," I concluded. "It's the only thing that makes sense. Who all knew where we were?"

"No one."

"Did you tweet or mention our location on Facebook?"

"Oh, wait, yes, I did tweet and Facebook it. The goal was to get people to see that we were team building. Being a strong team is the best thing we can do for the business. We wanted to show the group bonding, working hard, and playing hard. So I took pictures and posted them on Facebook."

"Did anyone else post or tweet?"

"You'll have to ask them. My posts went to the official accounts, not my private account."

"You were her assistant—do you know if she got any bad mail or threats?"

"I told the police the same thing I'm going to tell you." She leaned in close. "There was a nasty letter sent without a signature a week or two back. Laura was creeped out by the note."

"Do you know where it is now?"

"The cops have it. It bothered Laura enough that she asked the police to look into the incident."

"Did she get many such notes?"

"Your average number of death threats." She smiled at me and sipped her chai latte.

"Average number? You mean she got more than one?"

"She was a public figure. Whenever you put yourself out there, you put a target on your back, especially marketing through the Internet. Laura wasn't a big corporation. She was the face of her company. Let's face it—there are a lot of strange people out there looking to bully and hate."

"Yes, well, the police will say I'm reaching if I try to find some random hateful stranger who murdered Laura. It's safer to assume someone she knew did it. Is there anyone else on staff who didn't get along with Laura? Anyone who would have sent that letter?"

"Oh, we all had our tiffs," Amy said. "Laura was a difficult boss, but I think it's because she was so nervous about everything."

"Funny, but I would have thought she would have been more Zen."

"Why? Because she teaches yoga?"

"Yes. She meditated too, right?"

Amy sent me a look. "She meditated because she needed to. Trust me, down-to-earth, gentle people don't *need* to meditate."

I frowned. "I wasn't the only one who didn't get along with Laura."

"No." Amy leaned in again. "Now that I think about it, a few months back, Laura got a few threatening e-mails. When that happened, she nearly hit the roof. She and Dan saved them all and started a police file. The thought was that, with enough complaints, it would eventually lead to an investigation."

"You mean the police didn't look into it at all?"

"No, they said there was nothing they could do until a crime was actually committed."

"I've heard it's difficult to get stalkers to go away." I sat back, sad to think of Laura having a stalker.

"Well, my sister tells me that you can eventually get a restraining order, but they are hard to enforce."

"Did Laura get a restraining order?"

"No." Amy shook her head. "It never went that far. She collected the e-mails. There were about four or five of them, and they all seemed to come from different sources. The odd thing was, the threats all sounded the same."

"Maybe they were from the same person," I mused.

"What do you mean?"

"I mean, if you're good enough with computers, you can make various fake e-mail addresses that are tough to track down."

"Do the police have this ability?"

"I don't know," I said and shrugged. "Did you tell them about the e-mails?"

"Yes," Amy said. "Sheriff Hennessey sent them to their cyber unit."

"Hopefully, they aren't swamped and can look at this mail soon." I tapped my chin. "I could look at it faster," I said. "I know a guy."

"Do you think it'll help capture Laura's killer?"

"I do," I said. "Can you send me a copy?"

"Sure," Amy said. "As Laura's assistant, I have access to her e-mail account." She picked up her smartphone, entered Laura's e-mail account, and sent me a link to the files.

I knew a guy at Google who could track anything. If these came from the same person, I'd have a point of reference to start my investigation. "Thanks."

"Listen, Taylor," Amy said and touched my hand, "I know that yesterday was horrific for you. It had to have been a shock to find her. Take care of *you*. Know that I know you didn't do anything bad."

"Thanks," I said. "If you think of anything else, can you let me know? I want to get to the bottom of things before I find myself in jail."

"You should never even get close to jail."

"Yes, well, tell that to the court of public opinion," I said. Suddenly a news crew came into the coffee shop. "Oh, no, I've got to go. Thanks for your help." I dashed through the back before anyone had time to see me. All I needed now was for the news crews to get tired of waiting for me to give them a statement.

Chapter 9

"My life is over," Holly said and dramatically flopped on the couch in front of me. I sat at my computer, e-mailing the links to Mike, my contact at Google. Hopefully he could figure out where Laura's threats originated.

"What's up?" I asked.

Holly looked at me with wide eyes. "I'm stopping online dating for good."

"Is this about the guy you saw the other night?"

"Yes and no." She sat up. "Yes, he was another dud in a long line of duds. But my life isn't over because of him. He simply brought to my attention how pathetic I am."

"He better not have called you pathetic," I said.

"No, no, he spit when he talked, and he didn't kiss all that well."

"Then what's ending your life?"

"Someone stole my identity."

"What?"

"Yes, from the dating website. It seems they hacked me through the site, and since I have all my information on there, they were able to get credit in my name and run up a bunch of bills."

"Wait, aren't those sites supposed to be secure?"

"They are, but this one was breached last week. I got a notice this morning, and when I checked my account, I saw all kinds of charges I hadn't made. So I contacted my bank and the credit card company. My bank told me I have to call and cancel all of the cards, change all my passwords, and stop using my banking apps."

"Ouch." I winced. "This sounds serious."

"It is, and I was so stupid to include my phone number and date of birth and everything on that site."

"Any site is hackable to the right kind of hacker," I said. "It's why we get identity-theft insurance."

"Yes, well, I don't have that."

"What?"

"I thought it was a bunch of people trying to get money out of me by scaring me about something that happens only to people I don't know."

"Oh, no," I said and stood up to give her a hug. "What now?"

"I've been advised by my bank to get an identity-theft lawyer and start writing a ton of letters to begin reestablishing myself."

"That's horrible." I hugged her.

"Do you think I should contact Patrick and ask him to recommend a good lawyer?"

"You most certainly should," I said and pulled out my phone. "Here's his number."

"Thank you," she said with a sniff. "I'm kind of in shock. I don't know what to do first."

"Did you shut down all your cards and freeze your bank account?"

"Yeah, it took me four hours," she said. "Everyone puts you on hold, and you have to listen to this terrible music. I've heard it can take years to get your credit back to normal."

"Are you getting bills?"

"Not yet."

"Keep an eye out for them," I said. "If the criminals are smart, they used your address."

"Ugh, why didn't I get identity-theft insurance?"

"Don't beat yourself up," I said and gave Holly a hug. "I guess there's a lot of identity theft going around these days."

"Oh," she said and wiped her eyes with a tissue from the box on the end table, "just FYI, there's still a crowd of reporters outside your door. They're trying to equate Laura's murder with the crazy vineyard murderer from two years ago."

"What? I'm not crazy, and I had no reason to kill Laura."

"There's speculation that she refused to pay her bill."

"Oh, come on, then you call a bill collector. You don't kill someone."

"Also, you were having an affair with Dan and wanted him all to yourself."

"That's ridiculous! Dan is thirty years older than me."

"It's California, dear," she said and patted my knee. "Rich older dudes date girls our age all the time."

"But Dan? Ew," I said. "He's the one who originally accused me of killing Laura."

"He's the one who called the cops?"

"No, his sister did."

"So she might be a suspect," Holly mused.

"Why would she kill Laura?" I asked and shut my laptop.

"Well, Laura was controlling. What if Dan was her favorite sibling?"

"That's a weak motive. Besides, she wasn't at Quarryhill."

"So let's look at who all was there," Holly said and waved her hand in the air.

"I talked to Amy today." I left my desk and climbed into the chair beside the couch.

"Who?"

"Laura and Dan's office admin. She told me she knows I didn't do it."

"Well, that's something," Holly said and sat up. "Why does she know that? Did she do it?"

"Holly!"

"I'm playing devil's advocate," she said, putting up her hands in defense.

"Amy didn't do it. I could see her on the trail, and then I left her with everyone else in the group when I took the trail back to find Laura."

"There goes another possible suspect. What about the others? You said that Laura was a micromanager and a control freak. Did she bother anyone else?"

"That's what I asked Amy. She said they were like a big family. They all had their little tiffs but then worked to fix them. That's why Laura planned a corporate retreat day. She wanted everyone to have positive experiences to help flush out the negativity that had gotten into their work environment."

"So there was conflict in her little business. Are you sure no one else could have done it?"

"Sheriff Hennessey agreed the killer most likely would have had blood on their hands, if not their clothes. Everyone else was clean, and before you say anything"—I held up my hand—"they were all wearing what they arrived in. At least, I'm pretty sure."

"Trust me. You were so worried about everything going on, you could've missed something. Do you have any before and after shots?"

"What?"

"Group pictures," she clarified, "to see if anyone changed their clothes."

"No one took any pictures once we found Laura. People were in shock, crying, and hugging each other."

"Did you take any before pictures?"

"Yes," I said and opened my cell phone. "Here's one of the group that morning." I zoomed in on the picture so we could see people's clothes up close. "Huh," I said.

"Huh, what?"

"See that green Windbreaker jacket Rashida is wearing?"

"The one around her waist?"

"Yes," I said. "I don't remember her having that when we got back to the house." I looked at Holly. "A Windbreaker could've shielded her from arterial spray. Right?"

"Sure. They repel wind and water. I got mine from the hiker's superstore."

"I wonder what happened to hers." I studied the photo. No one else had a protective garment.

"Does she have any issues with Laura?"

"I don't know. I can ask Amy."

"Or we can ask around about Rashida," Holly said. "They all must be out of work right now, right?"

"Don't they all work at Divine Yoga?" I asked.

"Yes, but Laura's business was their main source of income."

"That means Laura was the glue that held the company together." I looked at Holly. "So if it was one of her employees, the killer had to know they were risking their livelihood when they took Laura out."

"Maybe it was premeditated."

"Why use a corkscrew? That had to have been a weapon of opportunity."

"What was a weapon of opportunity?" Aunt Jemma asked as she came into the house through the back door.

"The corkscrew," I said. "It's a tough thing to plan to kill someone with. Why didn't they use a hunting knife or switchblade?"

"Oh, good question," Aunt Jemma said as she took the chair across from the couch. "Are you trying to investigate the murder like I told you to?"

"Yes," Holly said.

"No," I said at the same time and sent my friend a look, which she promptly ignored.

"Taylor had coffee with Amy today. Amy told her while everyone who worked for Laura felt like a family, there were times when things were not so hunky-dory."

"I figured as much," Aunt Jemma said. "Some small business owners are crazy protective of their ideas and products. So you think one of her own did the deed?"

"It feels like a crime of passion."

"Because of the corkscrew?" Aunt Jemma asked. "But even then, it might've been easier to pick up a rock and smash her head in than drill a corkscrew into her neck."

I pursed my lips. "True."

"So was it a crime of passion or a deliberate form of torture?" Holly asked. "When you bash someone's brains out, it's quick and messy. But a corkscrew—it seems like that would take planning to find the perfect place to stab it for it to do that kind of damage. I vote for premeditated murder. Maybe even a few turns of the screw just to make sure the deed was done."

"Gosh, we're getting gruesome," I said.

"Ladies, the second tour bus is arriving. So why don't you girls go down to the tasting barn and help Juan and Cristal out, please? It'll be good to think of something else for a while instead of your problems."

We both got up. I slipped my arm through Holly's and walked out the back door with her. "So do you need any help with the letters for the creditors?"

She looked at me and smiled. "You'd do that for me?"

"Sure. That's what friends are for," I said.

"You're the best," she said and kissed me on the cheek. "We can get started tonight after dinner."

I smiled back. The scent of grapes and loamy earth filled the air as we crunched our way over the gravel path past the wine bar to the tasting barn. It was a warm fall day, and the sun was low over the mountains. The bus had pulled to a stop, and seniors were unloading step by slow step. They laughed and teased each other. Clearly we were their last stop for the evening.

I had forgotten briefly what it was like to be so carefree.

Chapter 10

The next day, I got up at dawn, grabbed a cup of coffee, and took Millie for a walk the length of our driveway to see if the press had moved on. Julio was snoozing near the locked gate.

The weather was fair and lovely. The scent of fall vines filled the air. The leaves were turning on the grapevines and would soon be shed. Then the workers would mulch the vines by tilling the leaves into the dirt. The grape skins and leftover pulp that were filtered out of the fermented juice would be made into compost to nourish the roots of the vines.

Millie playfully barked and ran to Julio. "Good morning, miss." He took off his hat with respect.

"Hi, Julio," I said. "How's guarding going?"

"Better today. No one tried to sneak in through the grapes."

"Seriously? Someone climbed the fence and came up through the vines?"

"That happened the first day. We had one or two news-hounds, but today only two vans remain."

I glanced over his shoulder to see that he was right. "Good. I'm turning into an old news item."

"Why did they think you killed that lady, anyway?" Julio asked.

"Someone said I was a person of interest because Millie and I found the body. But I didn't kill her."

"No, miss, you wouldn't do that. I've seen how you can't stand it when we butcher the chickens for Sunday dinner."

"Ugh, poor chickens." I made a face. "It's hard to eat anything with a face."

"But God put those animals on this earth to nourish his people. You should eat the foods he gave you."

"I eat plenty of plants," I pointed out.

"And the occasional burger." He winked at me. "I've seen you sneak them."

"They are yummy," I said.

"Cows have faces," he pointed out.

"But they aren't as sweet as chickens," I added.

Millie sat and watched us, her head turning from me to Julio and back as if she were watching a tennis match. Suddenly she jumped up, barked, and rushed by us. I turned to see that one of the news vans had its door open, and a camera guy rolled out, yawning and filming Julio and me in the driveway.

I turned my back on the camera. "Come on, Millie. Let's go home. We have a lot to do today. Thanks for your help, Julio," I said, then walked back up the hill. So this is what it felt like to be a prisoner in your own home.

My cell phone rang as I walked. "Hello?"

"Taylor O'Brian?"

"Yes?"

"Sheriff Hennessey," he said. "Do you have a minute?"

"Do I need my lawyer?"

"Do you think you do?"

"That's not an answer to my question. So what's up?"

"Can you come down to the station?"

"I have a tour today that starts at ten AM and goes until six PM. I can come in before if that works for you."

"It does. I'll see you at nine?"

"Sure, but don't be surprised if the news crews follow me in as I've still got a few trucks camped out outside the winery."

"You'll be fine."

I went into the house, made some oatmeal, and got ready to go into town. First I checked my e-mail to ensure that today's tour group hadn't canceled. So far so good. I planned a trip to the Di Rosa Outdoor Sculpture Exhibit. It was an exhibit of Californian art that was located on acres of a local vineyard. I loved the Di Rosa. Inside the buildings was the largest collection of Californian art in the world.

Today we would simply sip wine and tour the outside collection, then move onto the winery to taste the new Syrah, and finally end up at Aunt Jemma's for an outdoor dinner. My friend Alison was catering with some classic California picnic food—guacamole and chips with fresh Mexican enchiladas and tacos.

I had gone against my plan not to mix our businesses. The news crews made it nearly impossible not to use Aunt Jemma's winery. It was the only place where they couldn't come to harass me and my guests. Now not only was I hosting the picnic on the grounds, but Aunt Jemma would provide the wines in hope of selling memberships to her wine club.

Thankfully no one had contacted me looking for Millie. So far she was still mine. As each day passed, I became more relaxed. Before heading out, I poured Millie some kibble for breakfast and gave her fresh water. Then I ran to my van. Perhaps I'd draw the last of the news guys away from the winery.

I headed out with a wave to Julio as he opened and closed the gates for me, then went to town, where I parked in front of the sheriff's department. Inside, Deputy Blake was at the reception desk. "Good morning," I said. "I'm here to see Sheriff Hennessey. He's waiting for me."

"You're name?"

"Taylor O'Brian."

"Have a seat. I'll let him know you're here."

I went to the plastic chairs and sat, waiting for him to call me. There was nothing much to do, so I used my phone to research new tour sites.

"Miss O'Brian?"

"Yes?" I looked up to see Sheriff Hennessey sticking his head out of the door between the waiting room and the rest of the department. "Hi, how are you?" I asked as I followed him to an office in the far corner of the building.

"Thanks for coming in. I have some things to ask you," he said as he closed the door. "Take a seat."

I sat down. "What's up?"

"We found a small SD card on Laura's body."

"Okay."

"It had your information on it."

"What do you mean?"

"I mean, it had your address, social security number, and bank account details. It also had your friend Holly's information on it, along with data from fifty other people."

"Holly said someone stole her identity, created credit cards in her name, and racked up hundreds of dollars in debt. But how did they get my name?"

"It seems we found a motive for whoever killed Laura."

"What do you mean?"

"She has your identity and Holly's identity, which she most likely sold."

"So you think I killed her to wrench back my identity? That's crazy. I have identity insurance."

"Hold on—I didn't say anything about you killing anyone. She had your information. Perhaps she was blackmailing you or someone else on the list."

"For what? I'm an open book." I waved my hands wide to demonstrate my openness.

"So you had no idea that she had your social security number? Bank account info?"

"No," I said with a shake of my head. "Should I be worried?"

"No," he said with a slight frown. "I wanted you to know so that you can cancel your accounts and protect yourself."

"You wanted to know if I knew she'd stolen my identity," I pointed out. "You wanted to see my reaction. Well, you got it. I had no idea Laura had anything."

He studied me for a moment. His handsome face unnerved me a little, and I crossed my arms to protect myself. If I wasn't being investigated as a criminal, I might have reversed my thinking on dating. The man's eyes could captivate.

"I'd recommend that you contact your financial institutions and your identity-theft company to share that your information has been compromised."

"Okay," I said. "Anything else?"

"Anything you want to tell me?" he asked.

I got up. "Thanks for the info," I said and turned to leave, then stopped. "You would tell me if I were still a person of interest, right?"

"There is one other thing," he said. "I wasn't going to bring it up, but there is an eyewitness who saw you arguing with Laura the day before the tour."

"Arguing? Where?"

"At the yoga studio," he said. "They told me it was pretty heated."

"Not that heated." I put my hands on my hips.

"What was the argument about?"

"She didn't like that I was late to class," I said with a shrug. "She told me she wouldn't have second thoughts about kicking me out of her yoga class if I was late again."

"Sounds like she didn't care for you much."

"She didn't."

"Then why did she hire you to do the tour?"

"I'm still figuring that out," I said. "Who was the eyewitness, anyway?"

"An even better question is, did Laura pay you for the tour? I mean, don't people prepay for those things?"

"Usually," I said. "I give a discount if they prepay. Laura chose not to go that route."

"So you didn't get paid." It was more statement than question.

"I got a third down payment, but no, I didn't get the rest of the money. Laura died before she could pay me."

"That had to make you angry," he said. "Is that why you went to see Dan? To ask for the money?"

"Of course not."

"Just checking," he said and sat up straight. "Have a nice day, Taylor."

Right, like that was going to help things. I used my phone to dig up the contact information to my identity-theft insurance company. I walked out of the police station and made a phone call on my way to the van. I had a nice talk with Priti about my problem, and she assured me that they'd handle everything for me. I got into my van and saw that I needed to get going. My clients would be arriving at the winery in fifteen minutes.

This tour group was from the Sunshine Senior Assisted Living Center. I kept my tour groups small for a reason. It was more personal, I thought, and allowed me to have more one-on-one time with every member of the group.

I pulled into the winery parking lot as the ladies were disembarking from the home's minibus. It only took me a minute to put my van into park and reach for my tour clipboard. "Welcome, ladies," I said. "I hope you wore your walking shoes. We have an outdoor sculpture tour today."

"Oh, we're ready for the exercise," the first woman said.

I glanced at my clipboard. "Are you Irene?"

"That's me," she said. Irene wore a turquoise tracksuit, and her blue-gray hair was caught up in a short ponytail. "Thanks for hosting us today."

"It's my pleasure," I said. "Let's do a roll call as we get into my van."

"Oh, I thought you had that fun and funky old VW bus."

"I did, but it's out of service for the week," I said.

"I hope nothing is terribly wrong."

"Oh, no, it's being inspected." I was coy with my answer as I didn't want to freak anyone out.

"Are you the one who found that dead girl the other day?" the second woman, who identified herself as Debbie, asked. She was shorter with a shock of white hair and a lovely tan.

"I'm sorry?" I said.

"The dead girl at Quarryhill," she said and turned to the third woman off the van, who wore yoga pants, an athletic jacket, and a fanny pack around her waist. "Isn't that what you said, Shelly? Our tour girl was the one who found the dead body?"

"Yes," Shelly said. "It was you, right? We're so excited to see if you find any dead bodies on our tour."

"We love a good crime to solve," Debbie said.

"Yes, I found her," I admitted with a small smile, "but I hope to never have that experience again."

"Darn, I was so looking forward to something of interest," Shelly said.

I shook my head. "Come on, ladies. Let's get into the minivan and buckled up. Di Rosa is waiting for us."

Along the way, I told some local stories about the art movements in California, both past and present. I came to learn that Debbie and Shelly ran the cozy-mystery book club for the senior center. Irene, Mary, Gladys, and Barb were also members—which was why the ladies hadn't canceled today's tour. They wanted to know all about how I had found Laura and who I thought had killed her. The ladies quizzed me more than the cops had.

"But seriously, who do you think killed Laura and why?" Debbie asked one more time as I pulled up to the parking lot of the museum site. I parked and turned around.

"All I can say is that I didn't do it," I said. "Now, ladies, I've got your tickets to get in. They'll take us from the parking lot to the farm in a trolley, and we'll walk from there. I'll open some wine during the ride and pour you each a glass. We'll have an hour to view the outdoor sculptures. After that, I'll serve more wine and tapas before we head over to the winery for our picnic."

"What do we do if we find a dead body?" Shelly asked.

"You won't find a dead body," I reassured her.

"Unless one of us dies," Debbie chuckled.

"Please don't die," I said. "I've got enough problems without that."

"Well, we'll do our best not to die, honey," Mary said. "But we're old, so we don't make promises." She laughed at my expression of horror.

"Stop," Debbie said. "You're going to make her afraid to tour with people over fifty."

"How old was the yoga teacher?" Shelly asked.

"I'm not sure," I said. "She looked like she was in her early fifties."

"See, I told you she was going to get paranoid about older people," Debbie said with a grin.

The ladies turned out to be full of stories from their glory days. We walked the grounds, looking at a sculpture of a glass house made from bottles and another of a man lying on his side.

"This would be a great place to find a dead body," Mary said.

"Stop," I protested.

"No, really, who do you think did it?"

"It couldn't have been anyone in the group," I said. "Surely the killer would have had blood on their clothing. No one but Dan and I had any blood on them, and that's because we ran down to check on her."

"In books, the sleuth goes over every person. Let's do that. You said there were three yoga teachers there."

"Yes," I said as we dodged a peacock and walked toward a red metal sculpture. "Emma, Rashida, and Juliet."

"What connection did they have to Laura?"

"They all took her mastermind classes and spread the word."

"So they were her evangelists," Mary said. "One of them could've done it. For that matter, all three could have and then alibied each other."

"Ooh, that's good," Debbie said. "One could have stabbed her, the other twisted the screw, and the third tossed her down the hill. Then they all cleaned up and covered for each other. I mean, who would suspect yoga teachers?"

"What could Laura have possibly done to make them so angry?" I had to ask.

"Maybe she was a tyrant and they were too scared to leave," Debbie suggested.

"Maybe she was blackmailing them," Irene piped up.

"What could she possibly have on them to blackmail them with?" Shelly asked.

I thought about the list of identity information. Laura would have gotten their social security numbers because they worked for her. Maybe she was collecting the identities of all her seminar attendees and selling them on the black market. No, I shook my head and dismissed the thought as farfetched. "You know, Rashida had on a Windbreaker when we started the hike, and it was missing when we ended the hike."

"Oh, Rashida could have used the Windbreaker to keep arterial spray off of her when she plunged the corkscrew in and twisted."

"Now that's gruesome," I said.

"She could have had a lot of built up rage," Shelly said. "I know I did right after my divorce. Hey, did Rashida just get divorced?"

"I have no idea," I said. I supposed I needed to ask her. "Ladies, let's keep walking," I said as we approached another piece of art. "I'm sure that Sheriff Hennessey has the investigation well in hand."

"What about Sally?" Shelly said. "She seems like the least likely suspect. Sometimes the least likely suspect turns out to be the killer. You know how they always say the serial killer next door seemed like such a nice man?"

"Oh, so she's less likely than me to have killed Laura?" I teased.

"Less likely than the others in the group," Shelly said with a blush. "We know you didn't do it."

"How do you know that?"

That stopped them short for a moment. I laughed. "I did *not* do it."

They all laughed with relief on their faces. I shook my head. Who knew that old people could be so morbid? I started thinking about all three yoga teachers taking part in the murder and then alibiing each other. If that were the case, someone would crack sooner or later. Right?

Chapter 11

Tour complete, I thought long and hard about what the seniors had said. It was a quick decision to call Rashida. Unfortunately, I got her voice mail. "Hello, Rashida, it's Taylor O'Brian. I was calling with a question. If you could call me back today that would be great."

I had a few minutes before I was supposed to have a phone meeting with my Google friend over tracing the e-mails Laura received. Maybe if I went to the yoga studio, I could talk to Rashida or one of the other two ladies. Holly had told me that the yoga classes had continued as a way of keeping the community together after Laura's death.

The car ride there was filled with dodging crazy traffic. I arrived just as a class was starting. I could see them gathering in the biggest studio. I got out and went inside.

"Excuse me," I said to the receptionist. "Is Rashida teaching today?"

"She called in sick," the receptionist said. "We have Tandy, our substitute from Turtles Yoga, filling in for her today. Wait—aren't you Taylor O'Brian?"

"Yes," I said and stepped back, expecting her to kick me out.

"Did you want to talk to Sally or Juliet? They're both here and were on your tour."

Surprised, I nodded. "Sure."

"Hang on, and I'll get them for you."

Five minutes later, I wondered if I should just leave. Why was Rashida not answering her phone? Maybe if she was sick, she was sleeping. I could go and see if she needed anything. I had no idea where she lived, but one of the other ladies might tell me.

"Taylor?" Juliet said as she stepped inside the lobby. "Is everything okay?"

"Sure," I said and gave her a hello hug. "How are you?"

"Well, things have been a little nuts," she said and stood a foot away and studied me awkwardly. After a few moments of silence, we both started talking at the same time. "What brings you here?"

"I wanted to ask about Rashida."

"Oh," Juliet said and gave an awkward laugh. "Go ahead."

"I came to see Rashida," I said. "I know you three went down the hill together that day."

"Yes, we did," Juliet said. "We didn't see anything."

"I saw in a photo that Rashida had a Windbreaker-type jacket on at the start of the hike, but she didn't have it by the end. Do you know what happened to it?"

"Oh, gosh, I don't remember a jacket. Sorry," she said and pursed her lips.

"Someone suggested that the coat might have been used to prevent the killer from being covered in blood."

"Oh, that's terrible," Juliet said and covered her mouth. "Who would do that? Poor Rashida—to think that her jacket might have been used by a killer. Wait, do the police think this really happened?"

"Oh, no," I said. "It wasn't the police."

"I see, so it was you who was speculating how the jacket was used?"

"I—"

"Do you have any evidence that it was used?" Her eyes narrowed.

"No—"

"And you came here to do what? Confront Rashida?" Her chin went up, and her hands curled on her hips.

"I—"

"I think you should leave."

"Right," I said and let my mouth form a thin line. "For the record, I wasn't pointing any fingers. I just wanted—"

"To pin the murder on one of us," she said. "Well, our alibis are tight. If I were you, I'd let the police do their job. Good-bye, Taylor." She turned on her heel and left in a big huff.

I winced and thanked the receptionist on the way out. She sent me a puzzled look, but I decided I'd done enough talking for now. Whatever had happened to Rashida's jacket, it was clear that Juliet wasn't about to change her alibi. Which meant that most likely the ladies were as innocent as I was.

Without any evidence, there wasn't any reason to think otherwise.

I sighed and got into my car in time to call my Google friend. "Hey, Mike," I said. "What did you learn about the source of the e-mails threatening Laura?"

"I followed them as deep as I could," he said, sounding disappointed. "There's no proof they're not just what they seem to be—random e-mails. Sorry I couldn't come up with anything more definitive."

"It's okay," I said. "I appreciate that you tried. I'll owe you dinner next time I'm in town."

"Sure thing," he said, and I could hear the grin in his voice. "Take care, Taylor."

"You too," I said and hung up. So the threats turned out to be a dead end. If Laura had a single stalker, he was too good to leave an electronic trail.

*   *   *

"Here's to your first successful tour." Aunt Jemma raised a glass of wine to toast me. We sat with Holly out on the patio of the winery later that night and watched the stars come out. Clemmie sneaked around under our chairs, while Millie sat at my feet chewing a rope bone. I had to admit that the puppy was doing very well with her potty training. It really helped that we spent a lot of time outside at the winery.

"Thanks," I said.

"And they weren't concerned by the murder?" Holly asked.

"Apparently it was precisely because of the murder that they wanted to see me. The ladies like to think of their book club as a detective agency."

"Like I said, murder tours is a good marketing hook," Holly said.

"No, thank you," I said. "I'm not willing to go down that gimmicky alley. I like what I'm doing. There are so many hidden gems in Sonoma County. How's the art gallery going?"

Holly shrugged. "The latest exhibition hasn't been that great. I don't understand it. Hanson's work is pure eclectic northern

Californian art. People usually line up for that kind of thing, but I think I've sold one piece in the last three weeks."

"Maybe you need to find a different marketing hook," I teased.

"First I need to restore my identity," Holly said. "I learned today that someone in Georgia tried to take a mortgage out in my name."

"How can they do that?" Aunt Jemma asked.

"All they need are fake identity papers and collateral," Holly said.

"Wait, you said *almost* took out a mortgage. What stopped them?" I asked.

"The mortgage company saw the flag on my credit report and stopped. They called my bank and discovered I was still in California. My bank contacted me."

"Good save," Aunt Jemma said. "What would've happened if they'd succeeded?"

"I guess I'd have to go to court to get my name back and the mortgage terminated."

"Court fees are expensive. Wow," I said. "Did you call Patrick?"

"Yes, thanks," she said with a smile and sipped her wine. "He gave me the name of this guy in northern San Francisco who specializes in identity theft. I can't believe that dating site got hacked like that. I was stupid and should have never posted that information. Still, I don't know how the thief got my social security number."

"Did you know that Laura had your info on a memory card, along with mine and several other people?" I took a sip of wine.

"No, I didn't." Holly drew her eyebrows together. "What was she doing with my information?"

"I suspect she got mine when I did some advertising work for her. It's how we first met."

"Wait—I did some contract work for her as well," she said. "Dan asked me to redo their logo. I don't usually do things like that, but the extra money was good. Or so I thought."

"Does Sheriff Hennessey think that Laura was selling the information?" Aunt Jemma asked.

"Why else would she have a memory card on her at our tour? She had to have been planning to meet someone and give it to them," I said.

"Why not e-mail them?" Holly asked.

"Using the card means the government can't track the information back to Laura's IP address," I replied.

"Why do you think she was selling our information?" Aunt Jemma asked. "I thought her business was going well."

"It was," I said, "but apparently for the wrong reasons."

"So whoever she met might have killed her."

"I don't know," I said and pursed my lips. "If they killed her, why didn't they take the SD card?"

"Maybe they couldn't find it. Or maybe she changed her mind and couldn't go through with the sale." Holly took a gulp of wine.

"But your identity was stolen. So she had to have gone through with the sale."

"No, remember, I got a notice from the online dating website that they'd had a breach. My identity might've been stolen even before Laura got a hold of it."

"Or maybe she wasn't selling the information at all," Aunt Jemma mused.

"What do you mean?"

"I mean that the SD card may not mean anything," Aunt Jemma said. "She might have been transferring information from one computer to the next and forgot it was in her pocket. We simply don't know."

"But Sheriff Hennessey thought it was identity theft," I said.

"I'm playing the devil's advocate," Aunt Jemma said.

Holly sighed. "I hate that I'm going through this and you're still a person of interest."

"But at least today's tour was a success," Aunt Jemma said. "When's your next one?"

"Tomorrow. It's a group of writers in from the crime fiction conference in Oakland."

"That should be fun."

"I'm sensing a theme here," Holly teased.

"The one after that is a family reunion," I pointed out. "So no theme, just coincidence."

There was the sound of glass breaking, and we all stood and looked at each other. Then more glass broke even closer to us. "What was that?" Aunt Jemma asked.

"Are Juan or Julio around?" I opened the patio door, and we went into the house. Millie ran by me, but I was quick enough to grab her. If there was broken glass in the house, I didn't want her paws in it.

"No, they've been working around the clock lately due to the press," Aunt Jemma said. "So I told them they could have the evening for their families."

I was the first to see it. The front window was smashed, glass was everywhere, and a large rock rested on the floor inside. I turned on a light, handed Millie to Holly, and stepped carefully toward the rock.

"I'm calling the police." Aunt Jemma picked up Clemmie as she dialed.

I grabbed a tissue and picked up the rock. It was huge, and there was something written on it.

Murderer.

"What does it say?" Holly asked.

"Murderer," I said with a slight tremble. The house sat a good quarter mile from the road. That meant whoever threw the rock had to have come over the fence and through the vineyard. I looked out the window. The outside floodlight was not lit. It must have been bashed as well because it was usually kept on at night. Which meant they could be outside now. Even worse, they had been out there when we were on the patio.

"That's horrible," Holly said.

"The police are on their way," Aunt Jemma said. "They said not to touch anything."

I put the rock back down where it had landed and cautiously stepped back out of the glass. "There was someone out there when we were outside."

"Why didn't Millie bark?" Holly asked me and looked at the dog in her hands. "Are you hard of hearing, baby?"

"We were all talking. Maybe she was sleeping and didn't hear anything. We certainly didn't hear anything." I took the pup and hugged her. She squirmed at the attention.

"Maybe she knew who it was," Aunt Jemma said. "Who has Millie met?"

"Well, you, me, Holly, Juan, and Julio," I said. "They wouldn't do that to the window."

"She also met everyone on your first hike," Holly reminded me.

"So it could've been someone from Laura's team." I frowned. "Most likely she didn't hear anything. If it were someone she knew, she would have gone to greet them, don't you think?"

"Whether she heard anything or not, I don't like the idea of anyone getting that close to my home. Tomorrow I'm getting cameras and motion-sensor lights," Aunt Jemma said.

"They'll go off and on all night when the raccoons come by," Holly pointed out.

"Better to be safe than sorry," Aunt Jemma said and absently put down the cat. "The police are on their way. I'm calling Juan and Julio next."

Clemmie sneaked toward the glass-covered area. I handed Millie to Holly and scooped Clemmie up before she could hurt herself. "Oh, no, kitties and doggies need to go into the bedroom to be safe." Holly and I took them to the bedroom. I opened the closet for Clemmie to get to her favorite box, and then we put Millie in her kennel. "It's for your own safety, girls."

The police had arrived when we came back into the great room. Juan and Julio weren't far behind them. Four men checked the premises while a fifth took pictures of the damage, bagged the rock, and took our statements.

"So you heard nothing until the glass broke," Deputy Angus McCarty said. He was about five foot nine with gray hair and brown eyes, and his muscled frame filled out his uniform. He was older and put off the aura of someone you could trust in a tight spot—like Holly's brother, Derrick.

"We were out on the patio having a drink," I said. "The patio is on the opposite side of the house, so we couldn't really hear anything."

"Even the dog didn't bark," Holly said.

"Do you think it was someone she knew?" I asked.

"Who does she know?" Angus asked.

"Well, whoever left her in my vineyard," I said, "and she knows my aunt, Holly, Juan, Julio, and the people on my first tour."

"The people on your first tour?" Angus repeated.

"Yes, everyone who was there from the yoga mastermind group."

He scratched his head. "Isn't that the group where the boss lady got killed?"

"Yes," I said, "but I don't think they would do this. I mean, maybe Dan or his sister, but not the other ladies."

"That you know," Aunt Jemma pointed out. "One of them may have killed Laura after all."

"I'm pretty sure they didn't—none of them were bloody."

Deputy Jason Elles came into the house with Juan and Julio behind him. "We found some tracks. I took photos and called the crime scene unit to come check it out."

"Is it okay to stay here with the window broken?" I asked. With tracks outside, it seemed clear that sleeping in a house with a gaping picture window might not be the safest.

"Why don't you come stay in town with me?" Holly asked.

"It might be for the best," Jason said. He was taller than Angus, with dark hair and wide shoulders.

"But I don't want to leave my home," Aunt Jemma said.

"I'll have a crew out here for a few hours, and then your men can board up the window," Jason suggested. "We can call you when it's done."

"You should stay with me. I'd feel better about your safety," Holly said. "Bring Millie and Clemmie."

Just then Sheriff Hennessey walked in. The red-and-blue police lights flashed around the living room, sparkling on the broken glass. "What happened?" he asked, an expression of concern on his face. "Are you all right?"

"Someone threw a rock through my window," I stated the obvious. "We think it was someone we know because Millie didn't bark."

"Where's Millie now?"

"We kenneled her and put Clemmie, my cat, in the bedroom so they wouldn't get hurt."

"So everyone is okay," he said and put his hand on my forearm and gave it a comforting rub.

"We think this has something to do with the murder," Holly said.

"Show him the rock," I said to the deputy. He pointed the sheriff toward the evidence bag on the table.

"Looks like some sort of stunt," he said. "Someone trying to intimidate you."

"Or someone trying to really hurt us," Aunt Jemma said.

"I think they could have done a lot more than throw a rock through your window had they meant to really hurt you," Sheriff Hennessey said.

I wasn't liking him too much right now. "A rock through our window is enough."

"I'm not downplaying the incident," he said and held out his hands to calm us. "I'm simply asking that you stay vigilant, but not fearful. You've had the press following you around for a couple of days now. I'm sure it brought undue stress and attention to you."

"Undue is right since I didn't do anything," I said and put my hands on my hips.

"The department didn't release any statements about persons of interest—no matter how tempting."

"What does that mean?"

"I think that's a double entendre," Holly said with a wink and a grin. Sheriff Hennessey blushed.

"Holly!" I nudged her, shocked. "She's a kidder," I told the sheriff. "Don't let her get you flustered." I sent her a look. She smiled and shrugged.

"Are you saying you don't think this is related?" Aunt Jemma piped up.

"I'm saying, don't worry too much," he said. "You've been in the news. People get strange ideas and play pranks."

"Are you going to have the winery watched more carefully?"

"We'll send a patrolman down once or twice a night. I recommend purchasing motion-sensor lights and an alarm."

"Is that the advice you give all your murder suspects?"

"Sonoma rarely has a murder, so I've yet to give any advice to anyone connected to one, let alone the suspects."

"So I am a suspect . . . ?"

"Taylor," he said and shook his head, "get some clothes, and go into town for the night. When you come back in the morning, things won't feel so scary."

"I'm not afraid in my aunt's home," I said, lifting my chin.

"Someone put a rock through your window. It's okay to feel threatened and afraid."

"I suppose you deal with this every day."

"No," he said and shoved his hands in his pockets. "Most of my homicides don't involve people like you."

"Like me?"

"People who want to help the investigation."

"I see," I said.

"Come on, Taylor," Holly said and put her hands around my arm. "Let's get out of here and let the cops do their jobs. Okay?"

"Sure," I said and went to get my things while Holly collected Millie and Clemmie. I was still dealing with the zing I felt when Sheriff Hennessey looked in my eyes and said, "People like you."

Chapter 12

I sat up in bed after I remembered something Dan had said. "Rashida had been to Quarryhill before." Rashida was the one who had brought along a plastic coat. Rashida, who didn't have her coat when we came back home.

"What's going on?" Holly asked as she peeked out at me from under her eye mask.

"Nothing," I said. "Go back to sleep." I waited until she'd fallen back to sleep to get up and go into the living room, where I turned on my laptop. I spent the next two hours learning everything there was online to know about Rashida Davis.

After a while, Holly came into the living room and opened the curtains. I blinked as the sunlight poured in. "Have you been on the computer since you woke me?" she asked.

"Yes," I said and sighed. "I thought I had an idea of who to investigate for Laura's murder, but I didn't find all that much information online."

"Who?" Holly asked as she made coffee.

"Rashida Davis," I said. "She was one of Laura's yoga crew."

"Isn't she the one with the missing jacket?"

"Yes," I said and closed my computer. "At one point, Dan told me Rashida had been to Quarryhill before. She was the only one besides me familiar with the gardens."

"That's interesting," Holly said and brought me a mug of fresh brewed coffee. She sat at the dining room table with me.

Holly had a small two-bedroom apartment with a great room, which she had made into two spaces: a small dining room and a living area with couch, two club chairs, and a television the size of her wall. Okay, it wasn't *that* big, but it was big and curved, and she swore she'd bought it to attract more men in her life. I secretly suspected that she enjoyed the surround sound for her movies.

"The problem is that it doesn't seem Rashida had any reason to kill Laura. As far as I can tell from her social media and online stuff, she adored Laura."

Millie whimpered at my feet, wanting to go out. I got up and slipped my shoes on. "I'll be right back." I leashed Millie and took her down the two flights of stairs to the park across the street. Our walk was uneventful—I only saw two joggers and a man reading a newspaper on a bench across from Holly's place.

When I walked by, he waited a moment and got up. After last night's incident, I was a little spooked about things. I walked faster and noticed that he walked faster. I scooped up Millie and sprinted to the apartment complex. I went around the corner but waited and let Millie explore the grass a bit. The man didn't come around the building. Heart still beating fast, I took a roundabout way to Holly's door. The man was gone.

"That was an adventure," I said as we came inside and I unleashed Millie. She went and drank some fresh water, then found the spot of sunshine to curl up in. I assumed that Clemmie was still in her carry case because everyone knew how hard it would be to get her back inside once we let her out.

"What happened?" Holly asked.

"I'm not sure, but I think I was followed. There was this guy sitting on a bench and reading a newspaper, facing your complex. When we walked by, he got up. I went faster, and I swear he sped up too. So I picked Millie up and ducked around the building next door."

"Did he follow?"

"I thought I heard footsteps, but he never showed. So I circled around three buildings before I came back here."

"I don't like it. We should call the police."

I went to the window and looked out. The park was empty, and no one was near the sidewalk. "I think he's gone."

"I still think we should call the cops," Holly said.

"And say what? A guy was walking behind me suspiciously?"

"Did you recognize him?" Holly asked.

"No," I said.

"What did he look like? Maybe he's always in the park," Holly said.

"Oh, that's good. Let's see. He was a little taller than me and stocky. He wore a dress shirt with short sleeves and jeans. I think he was wearing dress shoes. They weren't sneakers."

"He sounds kind of nondescript." Holly frowned at me.

"He was dark haired," I said. "I didn't catch his eye color. He did have a darker complexion. Indian, maybe?"

Holly laughed. "I live in little India. There are a lot of Indian people here. Can you be more specific?"

"No," I said and frowned. "I was scared. He weirded me out is all."

"Okay, I'll take your word for it," she said. "Come on, I made breakfast. Have some more coffee and take a seat."

I washed my hands and sat down at the table. "Maybe it was nothing," I said and sipped my coffee. "I think my imagination is working overtime because of the rock."

Aunt Jemma came out of the smaller bedroom wearing a bright-blue-and-green caftan. "Good morning, lovelies. How did you sleep?"

"I slept fine," Holly said. "Taylor, on the other hand, was up at four AM."

"Poor baby," Aunt Jemma said and hugged me. "Where's the coffee?"

"There's a pot to the right of the stove," Holly said. Clemmie took the moment to streak into the second bedroom. "We're going to have to search for your cat."

"I thought we agreed not to let her out?"

"Oops, I wanted her to sleep with us last night," Holly said sheepishly. "I figured we could get her back in her carrier. We can, right?"

"Clemmie will come out if you rattle a treat bag." Aunt Jemma sat down with us and sipped her coffee. Holly had a spread of fresh fruit, coffee cake, and yogurt.

"Fine, you two can get her back in her carrying case," I said, "but don't say I didn't warn you."

"What were you worried about that you were up at four AM?" Aunt Jemma asked.

"I remembered something about the day Laura died," I said, "but it didn't really pan out."

"You need to meet with Amy and see if she remembered anything new. You know Amy has all the dirt," Holly said.

"Sally should have the dirt. She's the human resources lady."

"No one tells HR anything," Aunt Jemma said and popped a grape into her mouth. "Everyone knows that."

"That's ridiculous," I said.

"But true," Holly added. "Call Amy, and see what she thinks. Ply her with wine, and she might share some juicy gossip."

"Have you seen anyone from that day besides Amy and Dan?" Aunt Jemma asked.

"No," I said. "I didn't really get to know anyone else but Sally, and she's been quiet since that day."

"Maybe she has something to hide," Aunt Jemma suggested. She grabbed a plate and put a slice of coffee cake on it. "Holly, dear, you are a gem. This breakfast is to die for."

"Let's hope no one does that, okay?" I said. "I've had enough of that lately."

"What makes you so sour today?"

"Taylor thought a man may have tried to follow her to my place," Holly said. "I think she should call the police."

"There's nothing to call about," I explained yet again. "He weirded me out is all. He was in the park facing the apartment complex and reading a paper. Who does that anymore, anyway?"

"Lots of people read papers," Aunt Jemma said.

"People usually look at news on their phone," I pointed out. "Anyway, when we walked by, he got up and walked behind me, which was creepy. So I sped up, and he did too. I picked up Millie and hurried. It felt like he hurried too until I ducked around a building. Then he slowed back down."

"She lost her tail by circling around three buildings to get here," Holly teased me and forked up a chunk of coffee cake.

"Stop," I said, feeling the heat of a blush rush up my neck and into my cheeks. "Maybe I am paranoid, but I found a dead woman. Then someone trespassed on the winery and threw a rock through the window. I have cause to be a little paranoid."

"Oh, honey, I'm sorry. I shouldn't tease you so much," Holly said. "But seriously, who would know you were staying with me? And why would he sit outside in the park and wait to follow you?"

"Maybe he recognized Millie," Aunt Jemma said.

"What?"

"Maybe he knew the puppy," Aunt Jemma repeated. "Have you called the vet lately to see if they were able to get ahold of the owners?"

"Oh," I said and slumped in my seat. "I didn't think of that."

"Much less dramatic than having a killer follow you, I know," Aunt Jemma said. "But still sad if Millie has to go home."

"Let's hope that isn't the case," I said and made a note in my phone to call the vet. I had to admit that I'd been procrastinating. I wanted to keep Millie for myself. I was growing fond of the little brown fur face, and the last thing I needed was to lose my new puppy.

Chapter 13

With worries about safety at the winery, I rescheduled my tour for the following day. There was no sense in trying to pretend I wasn't shaken up by the events of the past week and needed time to steady my nerves. Instead of going to Cornerstone Gardens with a tour, I stayed at the winery and supervised the workmen putting boards up over the window.

I had to admit, I felt safer with boards up instead of more glass. At least until the murder was solved or the person who threw the rock was found. The deputies said they had discovered footprints. They looked like they'd come from a male shoe.

I left Clemmie at Holly's and brought Millie home with me. The cat would have been freaked out by all the workmen. Besides, Holly hadn't figured out how to get Clemmie back into her carrying case yet. Millie, on the other hand, loved all the attention from the crew. Every workman had to scratch her ears or her chin. After the work was done and the living room was darkened by plywood, I did the right thing and called the vet.

"Petside Paws," said the receptionist.

"Hi, this is Taylor O'Brian. I'm calling regarding the micro-chipped cocker spaniel I found and brought in a few days ago. Were you ever able to get ahold of her owners?"

"The number had been disconnected," the receptionist said. "We sent a letter to the address. It might take a while. Is the puppy still doing well?"

"She is, and I love her," I said, "so I'm not in any hurry to give her up."

"Well, she will need her shots since we don't have shot records on her. So let's make an appointment for two weeks from now. Okay?"

"Sounds good," I said and made the appointment. That lightened my heart a bit. Surely if the owners hadn't responded by then, it would mean they weren't going to, right? Then maybe, just maybe, she would be mine forever.

* * *

Later that afternoon, Aunt Jemma had a tour group come in for some wine tasting. We were busy at the barn for an hour. Afterward I called Sally.

"Hi, Sally, it's Taylor," I said. "How are you doing?"

"I'm having a rough time," Sally said, sounding teary. "I can't believe this is happening. I can't believe anyone would hurt Laura. It's devastating. I go from anger to sorrow and back again."

"Do you know if anyone on the team had any problems with Laura?"

"No, we all worked very hard to understand each other. Listen, Laura knew she could come on strong, but she was working on that. Everyone knew she was working on that. She listened if you took the time to tell her what you were feeling."

"She sounds like she was trying to be a good person," I said soothingly.

"She was," Sally said. "I worked with her for almost ten years. She was always trying to improve."

"And yet she was sometimes rude and often mean, you have to admit. Even I felt that."

"I would say she was intense, yes, but well meaning," Sally said. "Like I said, everyone tried to understand Laura. Besides, why would we hurt her? She was our employer. Now we all have to find new jobs. That's no small feat at my age. I'm going to have to do more independent small-business work. Luckily Dan said he'd give me a good reference."

"Oh, that's very nice of him," I said. "I'm so sorry for your loss. What about the others? I spoke to Amy, and she seems to have some prospects, but what of Emma, Rashida, and Juliet?"

"The ladies are devastated. They've been asking me if I can recommend any other yoga teachers they can continue with. I've given them the names of a few of Laura's mentors. Maybe one of them will know someone else on Laura's level."

"I certainly hope so," I said. "Are you sure no one was upset with Laura?"

"What are you suggesting?" Sally asked, sounding a little affronted.

"Sheriff Hennessey told me that Laura had an SD chip on her with all our personal information. Do you know why she'd have that?"

"I have no idea," she said and paused. "Wait. I take that back. Laura was making a copy for me. I had a computer virus meltdown of my hard drive. I asked Laura to give me the information she keeps on her backup hard drive. We didn't want to send it over e-mail since that is easily hacked."

"So the SD card was for you?"

"Yes," she said. "I'm pretty sure."

"That's a relief," I said. "I didn't like to think that perhaps Laura was trying to sell our information."

"What? No! She would never do that. There is no way she would've sold out her team. After all, she staked her reputation on them."

"Thanks, Sally," I said. "I understand there'll be a memorial the end of the week?"

"Yes, at Admen's funeral home. Dan said Laura had wanted an outdoor ceremony. It's at four PM on the hill."

"Thanks. I'll be sure to send flowers," I said. With the way Dan felt about me, I thought it was best I didn't attend.

After talking to Sally, I called Amy and made plans to have her come over for dinner and drinks later. She might be able to shed more light on Rashida.

Meanwhile, I continued my research. Rashida's website and social media presence told me that she was a yoga teacher and a fitness guru. She counseled people on physical, mental, and emotional health through diet and exercise. Her website was stunning. All in all—at least on paper—she looked like she wouldn't hurt a flea. Could she have done this alone? Or did the group of three do this together? It was an interesting question. Maybe if I dug into the others as well, I could answer a few lingering questions. I went back to my computer and did some background checking.

"How's the sleuthing going?" Aunt Jemma asked as she walked into the house.

"How did you know I was—never mind," I said with a sigh. There was very little that got by Aunt Jemma. "The new window glass is ordered, but we're stuck with plywood for a week to ten days."

"Good. That feels safer," she said and got coffee from the pot. "Now what are you researching?" She sat down across the table from me.

"I was renewing my efforts to look into Rashida's background," I said. "She seems legit. But you know, I was thinking: What if Laura insulted these ladies like she did her other staff members who quit?"

"She insulted other staff members?"

"Yes, Amy said that Laura tended to speak without thinking. Apparently she had a habit of screaming that she couldn't trust anyone to do anything right."

"Ouch."

"Right? Overreact much? Anyway, some members of the team took it as a huge insult and quit."

"They quit?"

"Yes, they cited micromanaging as a huge issue. I know Laura could bulldoze her way into getting what she wanted at any cost. She was not fun to work with on the tiny tour we took." I shrugged. "But that didn't mean I wanted her dead. It could be that none of the people on the tour wanted her dead."

"I don't know," Aunt Jemma said. "Still waters run deep and all that."

"That's why I invited Amy to dinner and drinks," I said. "I want to pick her brain again. Surely everyone wasn't happy working with Laura if I had trouble working a small event with her."

"Best of luck there," Aunt Jemma said. "Do you have a tour today?"

"No, I pushed it back to tomorrow," I said. "How about wine tastings?"

"The weekdays aren't as good as weekends," Aunt Jemma complained. "The boys are mulching the vines today. I'm going to my mah-jongg group."

"So Millie and I are home alone?"

"The boys are outside," Aunt Jemma said. "You'll be fine." She paused. "What if Amy is the killer? What if you are inviting the killer into our home?"

"Amy is not the killer," I said with confidence.

"Maybe that's what she wants you to believe."

"Oh, Aunt Jemma." I got up and kissed her cheek. "Thanks for being so special."

"You're welcome," Aunt Jemma said. "Someone has to think things through for you."

Chapter 14

"My life is a living nightmare," Holly said as she came into the tasting room. "Every time the mail comes, I cringe at the next notice of payment due."

"I'm so sorry."

"It's really frustrating." She sat on a stool, and I poured her an ounce of the nice petite sirah that was open. "Apparently they went down the five and hit every gas station, big-box store, and convenience mart between here and Los Angeles. Bogus checks are popping up left and right. I know the bank woman personally now. 'Hi, Francine, how are the grandkids?'"

"Oh, honey." I went around and gave her a hug.

"Then they sold the ID because not only did they try to get a mortgage in Georgia, but someone bought a used car in Alabama, and don't even get me started on the Internet charges."

"But you've frozen everything, right?"

"Yes, of course." She swigged the wine and sent me a harried look. "But bad news keeps coming. I have collection agencies after me. I send them to my lawyer—who is costing me a fortune, by the way—but they're still calling. I have to get a new phone number, but I can't because I froze my accounts."

"What? Surely you can—"

"No, I needed to freeze my credit reports so that no one can open a new account, not even me."

"That's ridiculous."

"So are the mountains of paper work and e-mails and phone calls I've been getting. Luckily I haven't had to pay anything yet, but my name is trashed. It'll take years to remove this from my credit report. Did I tell you I called the police and filed a report? I demanded that when they find these guys, they prosecute to the fullest. They looked at me and said, 'Yes, ma'am.' But I could tell they didn't have much hope."

"So they aren't going to find them?"

"No." She pouted and tapped her wineglass. I poured her another tasting ounce. "My lawyer says they probably moved on the minute I started to get notifications."

"Now you have alerts set up, right?"

"Oh, yes. When they call and ask me if I'm in Austin, Texas, buying a round for the bar, I tell them no!"

"What?"

"Yes, that happened. Also, they rang up thousands of dollars in international phone calls."

"Now you're being ridiculous."

"I wish I were," she said with a sigh. "It'd be easier if I changed my name and started all over again."

"But people in the art world wouldn't know you," I pointed out.

"True, my name and reputation for fine art sales is still good, thank goodness."

"This too will pass," I said.

"Not fast enough," she groused.

"Want to have dinner with Amy and me?"

"Sure. Who's Amy again?"

"Amy Hampton is—was—the coordinator for Laura's yoga mastermind business. I want to ask her a bit more about the three yoga teachers who were on the retreat."

"I thought she said no one would hurt Laura."

"Yes, well, now that she's had time to think about it, that might've changed. I want to ask her some new questions."

"Ask who some new questions?" Amy asked as she walked into the tasting barn.

"Hi, Amy," I said and went around to give her a hug. "This is my friend Holly Petree. Holly, Amy Hampton. Holly's going to have dinner with us as well."

"Cool. Nice to meet you," Amy said and shook Holly's hand. While Holly was tall and thin, Amy was short and round, but they had the same sparkling personality. I poured Amy some wine.

"Holly had her identity stolen," I said.

"Oh, I'm so sorry," Amy said. "That happened to me too. In fact, everyone at yoga mastermind had it happen at one time or another. It's a real mess."

"That's strange, don't you think?"

"Not really," she said with a shrug. "We were a small business, and the firewalls weren't what they should be. There are hackers everywhere these days."

"That's crazy," I said.

"Laura and Dan had to get us all identity-theft insurance. That way we were all pretty well contained. What did the thieves get from you? Your bank account?"

"And my social security number and my address. It's crazy. I hope they enjoyed their little crime spree on the five."

"They hit everything down the highway?"

"Yes, then they sold my numbers to some giant list because I keep getting notices from different states about big-ticket items. I can't wait to see what small items start popping up. You know, things too small to trigger alerts."

"Set your alerts for a dollar," she suggested. "It's what I did."

"Wow," I said and poured us all another bit of wine. "I didn't realize how common it was."

"I know," Amy said. "You think that those things only happen to someone else until it happens to you."

Holly put her elbow on the bar and held her cheek. "Did you change your name? I'm thinking about changing my name and starting over."

"Ha!" Amy laughed. "No, silly, it still follows you. Think of it as a life moment. That's what Laura always said."

I finished fiddling with my phone and cut into their banter. "I've called us an Uber to go to Stan's Diner for dinner. I hope that works."

"It does," Amy said.

"I'm in," Holly agreed.

We kept up the small talk until after our meal of gluten-free veggie pizza.

"The wine here isn't as good as your aunt's," Amy said.

"Thanks," I said and saluted her with the wineglass. "Didn't you say that everyone at Laura's business had had their identity stolen at one point or another?"

"Yes, like I said, I didn't really think anything of it. We went through a spurt there where every week it seemed like a new member was having their information stolen. Then Laura paid to have an IT expert put in stronger firewalls and got everyone identity-theft insurance."

"Did you know that the police found an SD card on Laura that had a list of members with all their account numbers, social security, et cetera?"

"No," Amy looked horrified. "No, Laura would never put that all in one place. The lengths she went through to protect our identities cost her too much for her to undo it all like that."

"Is there anyone else who might've taken the information and put it on an SD card?" Holly asked.

"No," Amy said.

"But Sally told me that she and Laura did it to pass information back and forth."

"Well, I don't know why Sally said that, but I can promise you Laura would never be so careless with that kind of information as to bring it on a retreat."

"Maybe someone gave it to her on the retreat," I suggested.

"Maybe someone was trying to steal the information," Holly said. "Laura caught them, took it away, and they killed her for it."

"Wow, creepy," Amy said. "We were all pretty upset about the identity theft. Laura would've become unhinged if she discovered someone in the group was doing it."

"This takes my thinking in a whole new direction," I muttered.

"Why? What were you thinking before?" Amy asked.

"Did you notice that Rashida started out our hike with a jacket, and yet it wasn't with her when we left? She didn't mention losing it."

"So you think it was evidence she destroyed?"

"I'm not sure," I admitted, "but I was wondering if Rashida and Laura really truly got along?"

"As I told you earlier, we might not have always got along, but overall we were still like family. I mean, we all had our tiffs now and then . . ."

"What about the other two ladies?"

"Same thing," Amy said. "Although all of the yoga teachers were upset because Laura and Dan decided to increase the cost of their services by nearly double. They were trying to make a profit this year. They had some outstanding bills."

"So the ladies were unhappy."

"Emma, Rashida, and Juliet got a deep discount as members of the team, but that was ending in January. Laura wanted to only offer them ten dollars an hour to act as mentors. Meanwhile, they'd have to pay thousands to stay in her mastermind classes."

"I don't understand the logic. Why would she do that?" Holly asked.

"Well, Laura figured she had other yoga teachers who'd love to make a little extra cash by being her mentors. So the ladies had to either suck it up or let it go. There was quite a bit of conflict there."

"Enough for all three to murder Laura?"

"All three?"

"Well, they alibied each other," I said. "No one mentioned the jacket. I only realized it was missing because of the photos I took on my phone before we started."

"I suppose they could have done something like that," Amy said. "So why kill Laura? Because she was cutting their pay?"

"When I was researching online, I noticed that the ladies posted notices to Laura's clients offering their services now as lead mentors," I said. "Their websites and e-mail newsletters are full of condolences and stepping in to fill the void."

"So not only would they get rid of Laura and her new policy, but they'd retain their clients and keep the fees for themselves?" Holly asked.

"Exactly," I said.

"Do the police know about this?" Amy asked.

"I need more evidence before the police will act," I said. "I was hoping you could tell me more, and you did."

"But you're going to the police, right?"

"Yes," I said. "I'm serious about solving this thing."

"Why are you taking it so personally?" Amy asked. "It's not like you did it. Right?"

"Someone threw a rock through Aunt Jemma's front window last night."

"Oh, no!"

"The word 'murderer' was written on the rock," I said. "I need to clear my name and ensure nothing bad happens to my family."

"I certainly hope you do that soon."

Me too.

Chapter 15

Patrick woke me up by calling my cell phone. "Taylor, we need to talk."

"What's going on?" I asked and sat up in my bed. A look at the clock told me it was six thirty AM.

"I got a heads-up from the sheriff's department. There's been a new development in Laura's murder case."

"Okay," I said, "and it has to do with the rock that was thrown through my aunt's window?"

"No," he said and sounded firm. "No, some new evidence has been brought to light, and you are officially named a person on interest in Laura's murder."

"What? No, I didn't do anything."

"They are having a warrant issued for your arrest," Patrick said. "I haven't read it yet, but I think we should head this off at the beginning and have you turn yourself in."

"Turn myself in? For what?"

"Once the warrant is issued, they can take you into custody. I was given a heads-up so that you can walk in on your own."

"Walk in on my own?"

"That way they won't make a scene and cuff you in public," Patrick said. "I told them we would come right down. I'm getting dressed now. I suggest you do the same. I'll pick you up at your aunt's house in twenty minutes. I want to get ahead of this before the press wakes up. Okay?"

"Okay," I said and hung up. I stared at my closet door for a moment. What the heck do you wear to get arrested? I settled on a blue blouse and dark wash jeans. I hoped blue showed I was trustworthy. I let Millie into Aunt Jemma's place, and she immediately got my aunt out of bed.

"What are you doing here?" Aunt Jemma asked as she sat up and rubbed Millie's ears.

"I hope you don't mind if I leave her with you," I said as I leaned against her doorjamb. "I got a call from Patrick."

"Oh, no. What's going on?" She got up and pulled on a long kimono-type dressing gown. It covered her floor-length nightgown made of pale-blue brushed cotton. Her hair was pulled back.

"Oh, I didn't mean for you to get up," I said and put out my hand.

"I was awake anyway," she said. "Let's make coffee while you tell me what is going on."

"Right," I said and followed her to the kitchen. "It seems there is a warrant out for my arrest."

"Oh, my goodness! No!" She stopped in her tracks and came around to hug me. "What are you going to do?"

"Patrick is on his way here. He said it was best if I came in voluntarily. It helps build my innocence." I gave her a quick hug and checked my phone. "He should be here right now. Please watch Millie for me. I'll let you know the minute I know anything."

"Okay," Aunt Jemma said and wrung her hands while I stepped to the front door.

"It will be okay," I said and gave her another quick hug. "Try not to worry."

"All I can do is worry," she said. "Please keep me posted."

"I will," I promised and went outside to find Patrick pulling up in his car.

Ten minutes later, we turned into the sheriff's station parking lot. My hands were cold as I clutched them tight.

"I told you not to speak to anyone about the case when I wasn't present," Patrick chided me as we entered the building.

"Is this because I was talking to people?" I asked. "It shouldn't be. I didn't say anything. I was simply asking questions about the other members of the tour," I said. "It should have in no way given anyone a reason to declare me a person of interest. In fact, someone else should be arrested for throwing a rock through my window."

"What did you ask? What did you tell them? Wait, don't answer. I don't want to know. Let's go inside and see the judge."

"I've got to see a judge?"

"It's part of being processed, Taylor."

"What am I being charged for?" I asked.

"Taylor O'Brian, come with me for processing," a female officer with the name tag "Wolfe" said.

"Patrick, what am I being charged with?"

"Don't worry. As soon as the judge signs the warrant, I'll get a copy. We'll know for sure where to go from there," Patrick said. He looked so attractive in his high-end charcoal suit. But right now his handsome face was marred with concern.

"This way," the officer said. She took my mug shots and filled out paper work. They already had my fingerprints and

DNA sample from the time I came in and offered them. The rest—well, I got a nice orange jumpsuit when they took all of my possessions.

"When will I see my lawyer?"

"Come with me," she said. "I'll put you in a holding cell until your lawyer calls for you, and then you see the judge."

"None of this makes any sense," I said.

She didn't seem to care—it was as if she'd heard a thousand pleas. She stuffed me in a small room with a chair and a table, cameras, and a two-way mirror so people I couldn't see would be able to watch me like they did on television. I sat down and hugged my stomach and studied the floor. What happened? Last night, I was having dinner with my friends. Now I was sitting in the sheriff's office uncertain of my future.

Hours later, the door opened, and Patrick came in. "They're charging you with manslaughter," he said, his tone serious. "I want you to plead not guilty."

"I *am* not guilty."

"Your Aunt Jemma will post whatever bail the judge sets for you. I'll argue that you're not a flight risk, and the judge shouldn't ask for anything too crazy."

I tugged at my hair. "I don't understand. What evidence do they have that's strong enough to arrest me? I didn't do anything."

"It seems a witness has come forward."

"A witness? Who?"

"Don't worry. I'll find out who. But for now, I know that the witness claims to have seen and heard you arguing with Laura earlier on the trail."

"That's a lie! We only talked about her wanting to mentor my business. I told her I wasn't interested, and she left. If I argued with anyone that day, it was Dan because he was pressuring me to try out their marketing class. I turned him down because he was insulting. But the other ladies should be able to confirm that Laura wasn't even present for that conversation." I sighed. "That's not enough to charge me with manslaughter."

"The witness claims they saw you throw Laura down the hill."

"That witness is making this up," I said.

"It was enough to get probable cause."

"Seriously?"

"You *were* covered in Laura's blood."

"I tried to help her, and Dan was covered in her blood too."

"It was your corkscrew."

"This is nuts."

"We'll take it one step at a time."

"I want to see Sheriff Hennessey."

"No," Patrick said firmly. "As your lawyer, I'm telling you not to say a word to the sheriff from here on out."

"But—"

"No." Patrick was firm. "Now let's go over what'll happen in court tomorrow."

"Tomorrow? I have to spend the night in jail?"

"Unfortunately, yes," Patrick said, "but the good news is that I got you the earliest available time in court."

"Great. I have to stay in this orange jumpsuit?"

"Taylor, focus. They're charging you with manslaughter because they can't prove premeditation."

"I didn't do anything."

"We can deal with manslaughter. The repercussions are not as big as murder one."

"So they're saying I accidentally killed Laura and then threw her down the cliff?"

"It's better than the alternative."

"But I didn't do it."

"And we'll get our day in court to prove it. Now let's go talk about how to look and when to speak."

*   *   *

It was the worst twenty-four hours of my life. At least I had a cell alone.

Finally, they gave me breakfast and brought me a suit to wear to court. Being handcuffed and walked to court was humiliating. At least Aunt Jemma and Holly were there when I entered the courtroom. They sent me a thumbs-up and a smile.

My heart raced when the charges were read. It was terrifying to think I could actually go to prison for years for a murder I didn't commit.

"How do you pled?" The judge asked.

"Not guilty," I said. It was all I was allowed to say, according to Patrick. It was hard not to shout out to the court that they had the wrong person. That I'd never dreamed of hurting anyone. How could an innocent person be in this situation?

"Trust me," Patrick had said. Fine. I had to trust that Patrick knew more than I did. After all, he was a trial attorney, and I had never before set foot in a courtroom.

"The prosecution would like to recommend that bail be set at one million dollars," the district attorney said, and my heart dropped to my feet. Who had that kind of money?

"Your honor, my client has never been accused of a crime before. She is not a flight risk. Bail should be set at one hundred thousand dollars."

"Your Honor, the charge is manslaughter."

"Not murder one," Patrick pointed out. "She is not a danger to the community."

The judge slammed down his gavel. "Okay, gentlemen, I've heard enough. Since Miss O'Brian only recently moved to Sonoma, she is—in the court's opinion—more of a flight risk. Bail is set at one million dollars."

"But I grew up here," I said.

Patrick shushed me and I crumpled in my seat. That was a lot of money. How was I going to raise it? We all stood as the judge left the courtroom.

"Don't worry," Patrick said. "Your Aunt Jemma can use the winery as collateral. You'll be free in a matter of hours."

I looked at my aunt while the bailiff handcuffed my hands behind me and put his arm through mine to guide me out.

"I love you," Aunt Jemma said.

Holly stood beside Aunt Jemma, her expression stricken.

My gaze went to the other side of the courtroom. Dan and his sister stood there, angry and shooting daggers at me with their gazes. The bailiff took me back through the crowded hallways. I could feel the heat of embarrassment rush over my face as I was dragged back into a holding cell. The cuffs were removed, and I was left in silence to ponder my fate.

Someone was framing me. Why? Who was the witness who claimed to see me do something I didn't? Why would they say such a thing?

How in the world would I get out of this mess?

* * *

"I have to cancel all my tours," I said with a moan. I was finally back at Aunt Jemma's house. My cell phone had to be turned off because of the constant calls from the press for interviews. I used Aunt Jemma's phone to call my insurance company after I had gotten an e-mail notification of cancelation of policy. "The insurance company won't insure me since I've been charged."

"I could do the tours for you," Holly offered.

"I still couldn't get the proper insurance," I said. "Besides, you have enough on your plate between trying to regain your identity and the art gallery."

"I could do them," Aunt Jemma said. "It could be fun."

"I really don't think the insurance would cover you," I said. "I'm going to have to shut down before I even really get started."

"Let me do them," Aunt Jemma said. "I've got my own insurance for the vineyard. Plus, Millie can help me."

"Are you sure?"

"Sure."

I caved. "Then let's try one and see what you think. Tomorrow is a small writer's group that wants a tour of Cornerstone Gardens and then to catch wine tastings at two of the nearby wineries. They will end up with dinner at a local diner—and wine, of course."

"I can do that."

"I'll organize dinner if you handle the tour."

"I wish I could help," Holly said.

"We need to figure out who really killed Laura," I said.

"I thought Patrick told you to stay out of it."

"My entire life is on the line," I said. "There's no way I can stay out of it. We have to find out who the witness is. Someone is lying."

"Oh, I have a friend in the county court system. Maybe she can find out for me."

"Perfect!" I was starting to have a little hope that I could keep my business and restore my life. "Did you see Dan and his sister in the courtroom? They were so angry with me. I wonder if they know the witness who is framing me."

"Did Patrick find out who it is yet?"

"No, the DA said they are processing all the evidence and will get us our copy in due time."

"We need to find out who the witness is and why they seem to think you did this," Aunt Jemma said. "I'm guessing Dan and his sister know something about it."

"I'm on it," Holly said. "I'll do a little door-to-door soliciting at Dan's and see what I can find out."

"Oh, gosh no," I said. "I don't want you to get in trouble for hampering a murder investigation. My being out on bail is bad enough."

"Amy would know," Aunt Jemma piped up. "Don't you think?"

"You know what? She might," I said and gave Amy a quick call.

"Hello?"

"Hi, Amy, it's Taylor."

"This isn't your usual number."

"I'm calling from my aunt's home phone. I had to turn off my cell phone. I wanted to ask you—"

"I can't talk right now," she interrupted me.

I frowned. "Why?"

"I'm not allowed to talk to you until after your trial."

"But—"

"Dan hired a lawyer, and the lawyer said that I'm not supposed to talk about that day, and neither is anyone else who works for Dan."

"But—"

"Good-bye, Taylor." She hung up. I stared at the phone.

"What?" Aunt Jemma asked.

"Amy said Dan hired a lawyer and doesn't want any of his employees to talk to me."

"Why?"

"I don't know. Darn. How do I investigate when no one will tell me what they know?"

"We'll have to get sneaky," Holly said.

"Oh, right, I can't talk to her, but maybe you can?"

"My guess is that they have all been advised not talk to *anyone* about it," Aunt Jemma said. "Sorry, kiddo, looks like your investigating days are over."

"No!" I said. "No, no, no. I'm not going to prison for something I didn't do."

"Don't worry, honey. We won't let that happen."

"I certainly hope not." How was I going to investigate when no one would talk to me?

Chapter 16

"You know I didn't do this, right?" I said to Sheriff Hennessey the next morning. He had come out with backup to take care of the traffic and bring my van back from processing.

Since my plea, reporters had returned in droves to squeeze back into the small space at the mouth of the winery. This time, they were more aggressive. It was harder for Juan and Julio to keep them out.

Aunt Jemma had called the police to evict the reporters who didn't respect the winery's boundaries.

"I can't comment," Sheriff Hennessey said. "I only came out to bring back your van and ensure you were safe."

"What did you find on my van?"

"There was a partial print, but ultimately there wasn't anything to use in the case. That's why I returned it. I see the press is back. Would you like us to leave a police presence in the vicinity?"

"That would be perfect."

"I don't want you to think we're holding you hostage."

"But you are," I said. "I can't do my job. I can't talk to anyone to investigate what really happened. I'm stuck here with nothing to do but sweat. I hate having my hands tied."

"My hands are tied as well. The DA is convinced that you are the strongest suspect," he said. "Come on, Taylor, you know the wheels of justice are already set in motion."

"You are the law. Figure out who the real killer is, because it's *not* me," I insisted. "What about the three yoga ladies? Did you ask Rashida what happened to the jacket she was wearing at the beginning of the day? Did you ask them about how they were collecting Laura's students for their own? Did you know that Laura was cutting their pay and charging them more for their classes? It seems to me that their motive, means, and opportunity are stronger than mine."

"They all have alibis."

"Yes, each other," I pointed out. "What if all three of them did it, and they're each other's alibis? The only thing I haven't figured out is why they would frame me for the deed. I mean, they didn't even know me. Was I the closest person?"

"There's no evidence that all three did it, Taylor," he said dryly.

"What about the missing Windbreaker?"

"I can ask about the jacket."

"You can?"

"I will," he said. "I'll look into Laura's pay cuts as well, but it doesn't mean anything. You're grasping at straws."

"You're grasping at straws too. By arresting me, you're letting the real killer get away with murder."

"Taylor . . ."

"What about the SD card with all the identity information on it? What if someone was angry because Laura was selling his or her identity? Sally claimed she had the card because of her computer failure, but Amy said that Laura would never be so careless with customers' data that way. Maybe that's suspicious too! Did you know that everyone in her organization had their identities stolen at some point over the last year? You need to look into that."

"Taylor . . ."

"What?"

"I *am* looking into things."

"Then why have me arrested? Why put me through booking and a hearing?"

"Because we have an eyewitness."

"Who is lying," I said. "You're not listening to me."

"I think you're the one not listening. Look, we'll have hourly patrols to ensure that the press and anyone else you don't want stays away from your property."

"Don't you think that'll keep out the wine tasters Aunt Jemma depends on?"

"No," he said plainly and stepped to the door.

"Wait," I said.

"What?"

"What's your first name?"

"Why?" he asked.

"I just want to know," I said with a shrug. "You know mine."

He had the grace to blush. "Ron. When this is over, you can call me Ron."

"Only if I'm declared innocent."

"Be safe, Taylor." He left, closing the door behind him.

"Why? So you can prosecute me for something I didn't do?" I shouted at his back. I doubt he heard me. I slumped in a chair. How was I going to get out of this one?

A Case of Syrah, Syrah

Aunt Jemma was blushing and her eyes were sparkling when she returned from the tour.

"How was it?" I asked.

"Wonderful," she said. "See that handsome man over there?" She pointed at a chubby gray-haired guy with a beard. He had twinkling green eyes. *Oh, no.* Twinkling eyes. Blushing aunt. Hmmm.

"Yes, what's his name?"

"That's Milo, and he is so sweet." Aunt Jemma was all aflutter.

"What does he do for a living?" I asked, concerned. My aunt was a beautiful woman with money, and there were a lot of so-called retired guys in the area looking for a woman of substance to finance their lifestyle.

"Oh, he's a consultant in mergers and acquisitions," she said. "Isn't that nice?"

"Very nice," I said, trying not to squash her joy. "Is he married?"

"Divorced," she said. "He's been single for five years. Why all the questions?"

"I'm curious," I said and shrugged.

"Well, keep your curiosity to yourself, missy," Aunt Jemma said. "He's a nice guy, and I'm having fun."

"Good. You deserve to have fun," I said.

"I'm glad you agree." She seemed genuinely excited. "Since we're back, I'm going to go spend some time with Milo."

"Of course, go." I made a shooing motion with my hands. "Have fun."

The tour group left quickly, and Milo and Aunt Jemma went into town for coffee. I tried not to worry about her too much. She was a grown woman after all.

Instead, I went inside the tasting room and pulled up my schedule of tours on my laptop. How was I supposed to get my business going when I couldn't do anything for the next few months, if not years if I end up going to prison for this crime I didn't commit? I mean, innocent people got convicted all the time, right? There was nothing for it. I was going to have to close my business within the first month of opening it.

"Hey, there," my friend Tim said as he entered the tasting room. Tim owned a winery south of us. He often popped in when he was in the area scouting out the competition.

"What brings you by?" I asked.

"I saw the press outside when I drove by and thought I'd come check on you," he said. Tim was a tall guy with a slender build and blond hair. "Why do you look so gloomy? There isn't gloom in the wine business. Only happiness."

"I think my business is over before it starts," I said. "Ever since I was arrested, I can't take any tours. The insurance is too high. At least I got my van back."

"I always did love that VW van you have. I'm surprised you were able to find one after all these years, and a working one at that."

"Aunt Jemma knew someone who was storing it in their barn," I said.

"Good old Aunt Jemma," he said and went behind the bar to grab a cab and a bottle opener. "Let's drink to her."

"Fine," I said and went to sit with him. He put down two glasses and poured. I'd started a fire in the wine-tasting barn's fireplace. The doors were open, revealing a clear star-filled night.

"Here's to us," he said. "The best people we know."

I clinked his glass and took a sip of really good wine. Syrah was one of the darkest full-bodied red wines. Aunt Jemma's wine held dark fruit flavors of sweet blueberry, licorice, and chocolate that ended with a spicy peppery note in the aftertaste. I loved the darker wines for their antioxidants and full flavors. Millie came over and jumped on me, begging for a scratch behind the ear.

"So how's everything? I mean, besides all the doom and gloom."

"Well, Aunt Jemma might have a new boyfriend."

"Really?"

"She met him on my tour group today. She volunteered to take the group around for me. My last tour, and she finds a boyfriend."

"Meanwhile, your love life . . . ?"

"Is what it has been since I moved here," I smiled at him. "Salute." I toasted him with my glass and sipped again. "No one is going to want to date a murder suspect."

"I'm sorry this is happening to you," Tim said, then leaned forward. "So tell me, did you do it?"

"No, I barely knew her. Whoever killed her had a lot of rage."

"What's it like in jail? Did they make you wear an orange jumpsuit?"

"First of all, it's nothing like television," I said. "Second, yes, I did have to wear the jumpsuit until the hearing."

"How was it?"

"Scratchy."

He laughed and leaned closer. "Tell me, did you have to make friends with the biggest girl to stay safe? Did anyone hurt you? Are they all like rabid dogs like they show on television?"

"No, no, and no," I said and laughed at his antics. "I was processed and went in front of the judge for a bail hearing within twenty-four hours. There was no time to make friends. Besides, I was in a cell by myself."

"Too bad," he said and waggled his eyebrows. "I would love to hear your prison stories."

"Stop it," I said and smacked his arms. "It's not funny."

"But now you're free."

"Not exactly," I said. "Aunt Jemma put up a million dollars in bail money, and I can't run my business because insurance won't cover the liability of having a murder suspect for a tour guide."

"Darn, no juicy gossip."

"No juicy gossip," I said. "How are you? What's up in your love life?"

"I've been stirring the vats every twelve hours, so there is no love life," he said and sipped his wine. "You know how much time wine making takes in the fall. You have to punch the vats every six hours. I do have a real nice batch of zinfandel going this year. I mixed two parts of my grapes and one part of bought grapes from La Montague. The sugars are good. It should be amazing."

"It's all chemistry to me." I wrinkled my nose. "Not my favorite subject."

"That's why you don't have a love life."

I smacked his arm. He chuckled.

"So who do you think really did it?" he asked.

"Ugh, I've hashed it over a million times and have no proof of who it could be. Now I can't really investigate because Dan's lawyer is against me talking to anyone else who was there."

"That's awful," Tim said.

"Give me the town gossip. What are they saying about me?"

"That you did the world a favor and got rid of a horrendous person."

"They are not," I said, horrified.

"No, that's me," he teased. "Truth is, everyone is shocked that you were arraigned. The word is that the mayor is being pressured to get this under control quickly. The tourists are our livelihood, and no one wants to have to a killer on the loose. I'm sure they're jumping the gun due to political reasons."

"Well, while they're doing that, the real killer is going free."

"Is there anything I can do?"

"Yes, keep your eyes and ears open," I said. "You're tuned into the local gossip. Let me know if anything seems strange."

"You mean if I hear anything about Laura, Dan, or the people who were there?"

"Yes, or the people who weren't. What do you know about Dan's sister?"

"Ivy?" Tim said. "She is as big a force as Laura was. I guess Dan married what he knew. You know, he was one of those quiet guys who picks the mean girl and champions her."

"Did Ivy like Laura?"

"Rumor is that Ivy hated Laura. She thought she was taking advantage of her brother's good nature. Dan put his career on hold to support Laura and her yoga business. Did you know that before he met Laura, he was a neuroscientist with a staunch reputation for doing great work in his field? But when he got with Laura, he went all metaphysical and started studying energy and such. When he started marketing the metaphysical technology, he was denounced by his community."

"Seriously? I thought he was a new-age marketing guru."

"It's the new age angle that got him denounced as a quack," Tim said. "It was Laura's idea to put her yoga business together with his brain-wave techniques. It made Dan the laughingstock of his community."

"That's terrible."

Tim shrugged. "Word is that Dan didn't mind at all. Laura and he were touting his new listening device. The sound was supposed to solve depression and anxiety, help you stay focused and meet your goals, and increase energy."

"Sounds like meditation."

"In a way," Tim said. "Not that I'm into all that. The rumor mill has been all abuzz since Dan broke away from the scientific community and entered Laura's metaphysical world. When it first happened, everyone was sure Ivy was going to pop her cork. She was spreading rumors about Laura and trying to discredit her instead of Dan."

"So she had motive to kill Laura."

"But she wasn't there, was she?"

"No," I said with a shake of my head. "I can't prove she was there."

"That stinks."

"I know, right?" I sighed. "Listen, I can't investigate, but maybe you can. Can you look into Ivy's whereabouts the day Laura was killed? I mean, Quarryhill is twenty-five acres. She could have parked somewhere nearby and waited on the property for an opportunity to get Laura alone."

"But how would she get your corkscrew?"

"I left it in the van," I said. "I remember that when I got back after the hike, the passenger's side door on my van was unlocked. She could have gotten in and stolen the corkscrew."

"Did she?" His eyes were wide.

"I don't know if she did or not. I thought if I took it to the police, the CSI people could tell."

"And could they?"

"No," I said with a small pout. "The results were inconclusive. But, unlocked or locked, she could've somehow gotten in and searched the van for a weapon and then gone up the end of the hiking route and gotten Laura alone. After all, Laura was marching ahead of everyone else at the time of her disappearance."

"Okay, look, if there is proof Ivy was there, I'll find it. Meanwhile, you sit tight and keep yourself safe. Okay?"

"Okay," I said and gave him a hug. "You're the best."

"You're welcome," he said. "Now let's have another drink."

As if wine could make it all go away.

Chapter 17

"Hey, I'm having a gallery showing tonight," Holly said on the phone. "Why don't you stop moping on the farm and come out. It might do you some good."

"Who's the artist?"

"Anna Fran," Holly said. "She is a modern plein air artist. She has some really gorgeous landscapes of the area. I think tourists will love them and buy them as souvenirs."

"Isn't that sort of commercial for you?"

Holly usually showcased the more bizarre art that came out of San Francisco and northern California. She liked to think of her gallery as one that specialized in edgy pieces.

"Her mother is a friend of my mother's," Holly said. "They got together and pushed this."

"Oh, no," I said in sympathy. Holly's mother, Cookie, was such a wonder. When she got an idea into her head, there was no getting it out. The best way out was like a whirlpool. Simply let go and let her suck you in, knowing that you'll come out the other side a little wiser for the journey.

A Case of Syrah, Syrah

"It's okay. The art is really good," Holly said. "I like Anna. You'll like her too. Come on. I'm serving your aunt's wine and some really great local cheeses."

I opened the door to let Millie out. It was dark, but there was a light on in the back. "I don't know," I said. "I'm afraid everyone will be talking about me and not the art. I mean, it's not every day you meet or know a suspected murderer."

"Stop it," Holly said. "We all know you didn't do this."

"Except for the police and the prosecutors."

"Come out," Holly said while I watched Millie sniff around. "If nothing else, news of you being there will draw a crowd, and Cookie"—Holly always called her mom Cookie—"and Anna's mom will see that I did all I could to showcase Anna's art."

"Oh, I see. You want to use me."

"Did I say that?" Holly sounded falsely innocent.

"Fine," I said. "I'll be there by eight."

"Yay!" Holly hung up as Millie barked and ran away.

"Millie," I called. "Millie, come back here." No answer. Her bark was farther away. Darn it. I slipped on a pair of boots and grabbed a flashlight. The winery was big. There were a lot of places to lose a puppy. "Millie!" I called and tromped out into the darkness. The moon wasn't out, and the stars shone in the clear sky. There was a fogbank rolling in over the mountains. The ocean was a mere twenty miles away.

"Millie," I called and whistled. "Come here, girl."

There was a happy excited bark in the distance. She was moving away from the road and to the right of the house. There were neighbors in that direction, but they were at least a mile away. What would cause her to run out here? A rabbit, I suspected. Unfortunately, rabbits were also prey for local coyotes and mountain lions. Millie was a puppy. Any one of those big predators could do away with her.

Her barking was getting closer. I came around the corner of the vines to see Millie eating out of the hands of a strange man. It suddenly occurred to me that I was alone outside. A shiver ran down my back.

"Who are you, and what are you feeding my dog?" I demanded, wishing I had a gun or a stick or something. I didn't suppose that I would have known what to do if it were a mountain lion or coyote that had drawn Millie's attention. In fact, right now I felt pretty silly for having gone after her with nothing but a flashlight in my hand. At best I could blind him.

The man raised his hand to protect his eyes. I could see that he wore an old corduroy coat that had been patched. He wore jeans and boots and had shaggy hair. "I said, who are you, and what are you feeding my dog?"

"This here's my dog," he said, his voice gruff. "Not yer dog."

"Millie, come," I demanded. But she simply sat down at the feet of the man and wagged her tail at me.

"So ya named her Millie," he said, "after my best girl." He stood up, and I recognized him from the soup kitchen.

"Jack Henry? How? Why are you here? What are you doing?"

"Just my usual," he said. "I've been wandering these parts for my entire life."

"Did you abandon Millie in my vineyard?"

"I didn't abandon her. She's free to come and go as she pleases, like me."

"I see," I said. I didn't step closer. I was acutely aware of the danger of being alone in the middle of nowhere with a man I hardly knew. Sure, Jasper had introduced us, but that was before someone had thrown a rock into Aunt Jemma's window. "Did you have her microchipped?" It seemed weird that a wanderer would microchip a puppy.

"Got her that way," he said. "The folks who gave her to me said the pet store did it in case she got lost."

"Well, she did get lost, and we couldn't get ahold of anyone to return her," I said. "So I adopted her."

"She was never lost," he argued. "I knowed where she was the whole time. She asked if it was okay to stay with ya, and I said sure."

I looked down at Millie. "She asked to stay with me?"

"She did," he said. He looked me up and down. "She likes the vineyard. She likes you. You better treat her right, or I'll be taking her back."

"I'll treat her right," I said.

"Good," he said. "Oh, one more thing." He reached into a bag he carried. I stepped back out of reflex. "It won't hurt ya." He pulled a jacket out of his bag. "I do some general gardening work for Quarryhill. I found this jacket half buried near the waterfall. I figured since you took people out to tour the place, you might know who it belongs to."

"What? Why are you giving this to me?" I asked, suddenly feeling confused.

"I know a lot of what happens around here," he said. "I'm always around. Ain't got no TV or nothing to distract me from what's going on in real life." He shook the jacket at me. "I think you need this. Are ya going to take this, or what?"

"This is the jacket from Quarryhill?"

"Yes."

"Why didn't you take it to the police?"

"I don't like police. Do you want it or not?"

"Thank you," I said. I reached into my pocket and pulled out a tissue, then carefully took the jacket from him so that I wouldn't get my prints on it.

"I see what ya done there," he said. "Smart. Now I'm gonna say my good-byes to Millie here. You take good care of her and know I'm watching to see that you do." He bent down and patted Millie on the head. She licked his face, and then he stood. "Good night, now." Jack Henry disappeared into the darkness.

I stood still for a moment and tried to put together what happened. Jack Henry Stokes had given me not only his dog but a piece of evidence that could clear my name in this murder. I juggled the jacket and the flashlight to pull out my cell phone.

"Sheriff Hennessey. Leave a message at the beep."

"Hello, Sheriff, this is Taylor O'Brian. I have what might be a crucial piece of evidence from the crime scene. I think you need to come collect it." I hung up, and then I dialed the number I probably should've dialed first.

"This is Patrick."

"Hi, it's Taylor."

"What's going on, Taylor?"

"I had a run-in with a guy called Jack Henry Stokes."

"I know Jack Henry," Patrick said. "Where are you?"

"I'm at the vineyard. He came to visit me and brought a jacket he said he found at Quarryhill. I think it might be Rashida's missing jacket. It could have blood on it."

"Don't touch it!"

"I'm using a tissue."

"Taylor—"

"I already called Sheriff Hennessey and left him a message about it."

"Was anyone there with you to see Jack Henry give you the jacket?"

"No," I said as I came up to the patio. "Is that a problem?"

"It would've been better if he'd given it to the police and not you. It looks suspicious."

"He said he didn't like the police," I said. "I'll leave it on the patio table."

"Good idea," he said. "I'm on my way to you. Don't talk to the police without me. I mean it. I heard you talked with the sheriff without me when he brought your car back. Please, please, Taylor, trust me on this."

"I trust you," I said and blew out a deep breath. "I'll be out on the patio waiting." I hung up and looked around until I found a plastic bag from the recycle bin. I pulled the bag inside out on the patio table so that anything left on the outside wouldn't contaminate the jacket, and then I placed the jacket on the bag to keep it from touching any of my surfaces. Jack Henry might have not collected it properly, but I wasn't going to add to that mistake. Millie played at my feet. "You," I said to the pup. "You didn't tell me you had another owner. I almost lost you." I reached down and picked her up. "With everything else going on, I couldn't lose you, little girl."

She licked my cheek as if to reassure me that she'd never leave me. I laughed. Then I heard a car pull up the gravel drive. I walked around to the front of the house to see Aunt Jemma and her new boyfriend laughing. I waved to them, and they sobered up a moment as they got out of the car.

"Hi, dear," Aunt Jemma said. "What brings you out to greet us?"

"I'm expecting company," I said. "I'll leave you to your good nights. I'm out on the patio, so you have your house."

Millie barked in my hands. "Millie says, 'Don't do anything she wouldn't do.'" I waved good night to my aunt and hurried back to the table. The jacket was still where I'd left it. It occurred to me that I had let it out of my sight, and that would not bode well for chain of custody.

Ten minutes later, I heard another car, but this time I waited for my aunt to show whoever it was around to the patio. It was Sheriff Hennessey.

"Hello," I said from where I sat. Millie raced up to bark at him and beg for pets. I had started a fire in the fire pit, and it was warm against my skin. The lights out on the patio were soft string lights meant to give it a fairy-tale feel.

"You said you had a key piece of evidence in the Laura Scott case?" He looked from me to the table. "What is it? Where did you get it?"

"Don't say a word," Patrick said as he came around from the other side of the house. "I want your notes to show that my client voluntarily called when this piece of evidence came into her possession."

"It will be so noted," Sheriff Hennessey said and put on a pair of nitrile gloves. "Where did you find the jacket?"

I looked at Patrick, who nodded. "It was given to me by a man named Jack Henry Stokes."

"Where?"

"Millie found him in the vineyard. He told me that Millie was his dog but that he was letting her adopt me."

"So Jack Henry Stokes was Millie's previous owner."

"Yes," I said and raised my hand. "I don't want any charges put up against him."

"For what?"

"Abandoning an animal, general cruelty, and such," I said. "He explained that she saw me and wanted to be part of my family, so he let her go."

Sheriff Hennessey raised an eyebrow. "Did he, now?"

"Yes, then he said that he had been doing some work at Quarryhill and had discovered a jacket that might be of interest to me." I pointed to the jacket. "I held it with a tissue covering my fingerprints and placed it on the table."

"Why would he bring the jacket to you?"

"He said I'd know what to do with it. It looks like the jacket that Rashida was wearing at the beginning of the hike at Quarryhill. The jacket she was *not* wearing when we came back home."

"And how is that key evidence?"

"I need you to have it checked for blood and DNA," I said. "I suspect the real killer wore the jacket when they attacked Laura, then discarded it to hide any evidence."

He took a couple of photos of the jacket and used a pen to spread it out a little. "There are a few dark stains, but I can't tell if it's blood. Arterial spray has a distinctive look. I'm not sure this fits." My heart sank as he pulled an evidence bag out of his pocket. He placed the jacket in the bag and sealed it, then turned to me. "Listen, this may or may not be Rashida's jacket. If it is, there's no evidence that she murdered anyone."

"Unless you find blood on it, right?" I asked and turned to Patrick. "If it has Laura's blood on it, you have to consider Rashida and the other yoga teachers as viable suspects. I mean, they could have all three been complicit."

"Because they alibied each other?" he asked.

"Yes," I said.

"My client has said enough," Patrick said and stood beside me. "Please take the jacket and have the lab test it."

"It could be months before they get to it," Sheriff Hennessey warned.

"Good night, Sheriff."

We waited in silence while Sheriff Hennessey took the evidence bag and left. I walked Patrick to his car.

"You know, they may throw out the jacket as evidence due to the suspicious way you got it."

"It might be a little unconventional, but I wouldn't label it suspicious," I argued. "Call Jack Henry to the stand. He can testify as to where he got it."

"Hopefully it won't come to that," Patrick said. "With any luck, it'll throw enough suspicion on the yoga teachers that they'll drop the charges against you. Now go get some rest." He unlocked his car and opened the driver's side door. "Be careful, okay? Don't go rushing out into the dark by yourself anymore. Remember, the killer is still out there."

"Okay," I said.

He touched my cheek. "People care about you, Taylor. Don't forget you're not alone in this. Okay?"

"Okay."

"Good night."

I watched him drive down the long driveway. Laughter came from inside the house, and I walked around the back way to the pool house. Maybe, just maybe, the jacket would prove to be the saving piece of evidence.

Chapter 18

"Hey, you didn't show last night. What happened?" Holly asked as she picked me up for yoga class.

"Oh, man, I completely forgot about your showing. How'd it go? Did you sell a lot of landscapes?"

"Now, see, that's how you deflect a question," Holly said as she drove toward town. "You stood me up, girlfriend. That's not like you."

"It's a bit of a story," I said.

"I've got nothing but time."

I told her the details of last night's strange visitor.

"Huh, Millie is this man's girlfriend's name? Strange."

I laughed. "Is that all you can say about what happened?"

"No, I want to know if you are going to let Patrick take you out."

"What? Why would he want to take me out?"

She pulled into a strip mall with a low-hanging tiled roof. Palm trees were strategically placed to make the mall look more tropical. "Because he's hot, and clearly he likes you."

"Seriously?"

"Are you blind?"

I considered her comment as we went and signed in for class. "I'm sorry," the receptionist said and looked directly at me. "We can't have you in class."

"Excuse me? I'm paid up for the next three months."

"Your presence is too disruptive to the class," the receptionist stated. "The instructors have asked me to ban you from coming."

"But—"

"We will gladly refund your money."

"You'd better," Holly said and put her arm around my shoulders. "Refund mine while you're at it. Seriously, what happened to innocent until proven guilty?"

"What's going on?" The manager of the yoga club where Laura and her students taught, Angela Maggs, came out of the office.

"She said that my friend Taylor is banned from class even though she paid."

"Please come into my office," Angela said. "Let's not disrupt the classes."

"So it's true?" Holly's voice went up an octave.

"Holly," I said and put my hand on her arm.

"No," Holly said. "This is an outrage."

"Please, come into my office." We were ushered into the manager's office and out of the lobby, where others had gathered. "Now," she said as she went around her desk, putting it between us, "I want to thank you for your business . . ."

"I sense a 'but' coming . . ." I said.

"We can't have you here. It's too distracting to our community."

"I didn't kill Laura."

"Taylor, you're being tried for her murder."

"Technically I'm being arraigned in a potential manslaughter case," I interjected.

"Pot-ay-toes, pot-ah-oes," she said. "We have a lot of people who are sensitive to negative energy."

"My energy isn't negative."

"We need you to leave the premises."

"But I've paid through the next three months."

"We have your refund check here." She pulled out a check from her top drawer. "We appreciate your business, but we are unable to continue having you on our campus."

"Well, drat."

"I won't come if she isn't coming," Holly said and put her arm around my shoulder.

"That's fine," the manager said. "I'll write you a check right now for your membership as well." She pulled out a checkbook and started writing.

"But we've been coming here for over a year."

"And we thank you for your business." She ripped a check out of the checkbook. "Here you are. Now please leave quietly. I don't want to have to call security." She stood and waved toward the door.

"Hold onto your hat. What's your hurry?" Holly muttered as she stomped to the door, dragging me along with her.

"It's all good," I said as we walked out into the California sunshine. "We can start our own classes on the winery grounds." We got into Holly's car. "We can do 'Wine Down Wednesday' with an hour of yoga and wine and cheese after."

"Oh, I like it. Who will you get to lead the class?"

"I know a few people," I said. "Let's go get coffee."

"I'm on it," she said and drove us to Abuelo's. "I still have some landscapes left if you want to see what you missed at the show."

"I'd love to." We chatted with Austin for a moment, then picked up lattes and went to Le Art Galleria. Holly held the door open for me. During the day, the galleria was open from nine to five and staffed by Miss Finglestein. Miss Finglestein was close to ninety years old and wore black cigarette pants and a colorful peasant shirt. She smoked cigarettes with a stem and waved her hands as she talked to display her wild nail polishes.

"Ladies, ladies, ladies." Miss Finglestein floated over when we entered the foyer. "Come in, darlings. What brings you around? I thought you had a yoga class."

"Not anymore," Holly said and waved her check. "We've been paid to leave."

"Well, I never," Miss Finglestein said.

"Neither have we," I replied and gave the old woman an air kiss on each cheek. "Holly tells me you had quite the showing last night. Show me this fabulous collection."

"Darling, let me tell you how lovely this collection is—all pastels. They are the freshest thing on the market today. Such a departure from the graphic colors and lines of the latest midcentury modern fad."

"I didn't know there was a new midcentury modern fad," I said.

"Pay attention, darling," Miss Finglestein said. "Now come with me." She floated across the gallery to where there were large and small pictures in soft pinks, oranges, and yellows highlighting the California coastline, vineyards, and sunsets. "Ta-da!"

"Wow," I said. "These are gorgeous."

"Thanks!" A young woman with short sandy-blonde hair came around the corner.

"Taylor, this is our plein air artist, Anna. Anna, this is my best friend, Taylor," Holly introduced us.

A Case of Syrah, Syrah

"Nice to meet you," I said and held out my hand.

"A friend of Holly's is a friend of mine," Anna said and gave me a big hug and air kisses. I patted her on the back because her warmth was a little awkward for me.

"Anna studied in Paris and Rome," Miss Finglestein declared. "Right there in the same spot as the masters."

"I bet that was cool," I said.

"Très chic," Anna said with a wave of her hand. She wore cropped distressed jeans and a plain white T-shirt, but she made them look like they were top-designer elegant.

"I'm sorry I missed last night's show," I said. "I heard it was a huge success. After seeing these paintings, I can see why."

"I thought it went well," Anna said with a smile. "I really try to capture the local flavor in the pictures. I want people to take a bit of California home with them."

"Well, this series looks as if it was drawn at Quarryhill," I said and waved at the waterfalls.

"It was!" Anna clapped her hands. "I'm so glad you recognize it. I spent a month at Quarryhill doing sketches."

"This series is so successful that we're thinking of creating a group of numbered prints."

"Wow," I said. "That would be something."

"I think the success is because of the rare wild Asian plants," Anna said. "The setting and rarity of the plants makes people want to take a picture home to remind them that they sat in the garden. If enough prints sell, we might even get a coffee-table book commissioned."

"Sounds ambitious," I said and looked at Holly and Miss Finglestein as they nodded. Their faces were filled with joy at the prospect. "I'm excited for you."

"Thank you," Anna said.

"Listen," I began as I leaned in close to her. "While you were working at Quarryhill, did you happen to meet Jack Henry Stokes? He said he'd done some gardening work for Quarryhill."

"Jack Henry? Yes, he's a nice guy, if a bit of an odd duck. He could appear and disappear like a ghost. Spooked me until I got used to his coming and going. I swear there isn't anything that doesn't escape his intent eye."

"So he was there a lot?"

"The month I was there, I saw him at least twice a week. I think he lives in nature and is a bit territorial about his places."

"What makes you say that?"

"I came to the conclusion that he has a circuit he works. Quarryhill is his Tuesday to Thursday job. I think he works somewhere else the other days. Probably doing similar work in the vineyards."

"That makes sense," I said. I looked at Holly. "My tour was at Quarryhill on a Tuesday. I wonder if he might've seen who killed Laura."

"A witness?" Holly said. "Is this the same guy who brought you the jacket last night?"

"Yes," I said. "If I can prove he's a regular, perhaps I can convince Sheriff Hennessey to question him. At the very least, I can get Patrick to call him to the stand and testify about what he saw that day. You never know. He might be the answer to everything."

That was my first big hope in a long time. I saluted Anna with my latte cup and took a sip. Her paintings were gorgeous. Perhaps I could talk Aunt Jemma into purchasing one or two for the tasting barn. After all, she might have saved my life. The least I could do was support a local artist.

Chapter 19

"We have a problem." Patrick's voice came through my cell phone.

"What now?" I asked. I was in the tasting barn, helping Aunt Jemma with her latest group.

"They found Laura's blood on the jacket you gave Sheriff Hennessey."

"That's good, right? Now they'll have to look at the yoga instructors like Rashida."

"No."

"No?"

"No, you gave them the coat. They want to use it as evidence that you killed Laura."

"What! But Jack Henry Stokes gave it to me. Call him to the stand as a witness. He can tell them where he found it."

"Most likely they'll throw out that piece of evidence. In fact, Taylor, we want them to throw it out. It is darn suspicious."

"I don't understand. Sheriff Hennessey said he wanted proof that someone else could have done it. I gave him that proof."

"It's not up to the sheriff. It's up to the prosecution, and they want to use it against you. I'm going to have them throw it out."

"But—"

"It's for the best."

"How can I solve this if I can't talk to anyone and I can't present evidence?"

"It's not for you to solve, Taylor," he said. "We're simply trying to keep you out of jail at this point."

"But I didn't do anything."

"I understand, but we're in the middle of a fight for your life here. Trust me."

"I have to trust you," I said and tried not to sound bitter. "You hold my life in your hands."

"I'm going to see that nothing happens to you," he said.

"I didn't do this."

"I know."

I hung up and sat down to wipe away the tears.

"What's going on?" Aunt Jemma asked.

"They aren't going to use the jacket to pursue other suspects in Laura's case," I said. "It's because I gave the jacket to the police. They can link me to the jacket even though it's Rashida's. It has Laura's blood on it."

"That's crazy."

"I know that, and you know that, but the prosecution is trying to build a case against me, not anyone else."

"What will it take for them to drop the charges?"

"At this point, the only thing I can imagine is if someone else admits they did it."

"But no one is allowed to talk to you," Aunt Jemma said.

"I know," I said.

"Then we'll have to make them talk to me," Aunt Jemma said and put her hands on her hips. "Whoever did this needs to be brought to justice. I'll help you clear your name."

"You would?"

"Yes, of course," Aunt Jemma said. "Holly and I will take you to dinner tonight, and we'll figure out what we can do to clear your name."

"Thanks, Aunt Jemma."

"Why don't you take Millie and go on up to the house and rest?"

"I think I'll take a walk. Come on, Millie," I said and called the pup from her bed behind the bar. We walked out into the quiet California evening as the sun was hitting the mountains. The air was moist, and the loamy scent of the grapevines turning for the fall tickled my nose. The best thing about wine country was that you could walk for miles through the grapes. It was sort of meditative—but this time, I had my phone on me and a small can of pepper spray to be safe.

I went over the suspects in my head again as I walked. Clearly if there was blood on the jacket, Rashida could've been wearing it when she assaulted Laura. Jack Henry had said he'd found it partially buried. I wished that he had taken it to the police instead of me. But I had a feeling the prosecution would have used it against me either way.

I found myself dialing Rashida. I had the phone number of everyone who had toured with me so I could call them with updates on the tours.

"Hello?"

"Rashida?"

"Yes?"

"This is Taylor from the—"

179

"Yes, what do you want, Taylor?"

"Your jacket was found by a gardener at Quarryhill," I said, trying to get some response from her.

"My jacket?"

"The one you were wearing the morning Laura died."

"Oh, that jacket. I thought I'd lost it for good. I think I took it off as we walked because I got hot. I thought I'd tied it around my waist, but it must've come undone. Where did they find it?"

"Half buried near the waterfall."

"That's odd," she said.

"It had Laura's blood on it."

"What?"

"It was given to the police, and they found Laura's blood on it. It was suggested that the killer may have been wearing it to keep their clothing clean when they killed Laura."

"Oh, my gosh, that's horrible." Rashida sounded truly shocked and surprised. I frowned. She didn't sound like a person caught in a lie. What if her story were true?

"Rashida, do you remember if you gave your jacket to anyone? Did you see anyone pick it up?"

"No," she said. "Honestly, I didn't realize I didn't have it until I went to put it on the next morning. I guess I was in such a state of shock over Laura that I didn't realize it was missing."

"You think it fell off of you?"

"Yes," she said. "The material is slick, and I didn't knot it very well. It's happened before. Are you saying someone picked it up and wore it to kill Laura?"

"That's a possibility," I said.

"Surely if it were one of the staff members, they would've given it to me."

"Unless they wore it to kill Laura and incriminate you?"

"Incriminate me? I—is that possible? Who? Maybe I shouldn't be talking to you. Isn't that what Dan's lawyer said?"

"So I've heard," I said. "I wanted to let you know it was found and see if you knew anything about it."

"I don't." For the first time she sounded worried. "I've got to go. Bye." She hung up on me. By now, the sun had set behind the mountains, and damp fog had started to roll into the depressions.

"Come on, Millie," I said after catching a sudden chill. "Let's go home." When I was a kid, everyone used to say that when a chill ran down your back, someone was walking on your grave. The last thing I wanted was to find out who.

* * *

"So Rashida didn't know her jacket was used in Laura's killing?" Holly asked as she, Aunt Jemma, and I sat around the fire pit and sipped wine.

"No," I said, "and I believe her."

"That means anyone who was in the park that day could've picked it up, used it to incriminate Rashida, and then buried it."

"Yes," I said. "Anyone in the park."

"Except Rashida," Holly said. "We're ruling her out. Which means that the other two yoga teachers probably didn't do it either since they were all each other's alibis."

"Yes." I frowned. "That leaves me with Sally, Amy, and Dan."

"It could have been someone who was there but not in your group," Holly suggested.

"Like who?" I asked.

"Jack Henry Stokes," Aunt Jemma said. "He *is* the one who gave you the bloody jacket."

"We need to find him and ask if he was there," I said. "He might have seen who did it."

"Didn't Anna say he made regular rounds?"

"Yes, she said that the month she was at Quarryhill with her artwork, she saw him on the same days of the week."

"So let's plan a trip to Quarryhill," Holly said. "We can try to find Jack Henry."

"And we can re-create the events of the day," Aunt Jemma said with excitement. "I can be Dan, and Holly can be Amy. We can test the theory that one of them had something to do with it."

"What about Sally?" I asked.

"We'll say she was with Amy for now."

"Okay," I said. "Let's go tomorrow morning."

"I'm in," Holly said.

"Are you?" I asked Millie.

She barked and wagged her tail. Hopefully a reenactment will bring us closer to the truth.

Chapter 20

No one was at Quarryhill when we pulled up. It seemed like most of the visitors came during the weekend. I was glad we had the place to ourselves. It would be difficult to reenact a crime with a bunch of families discovering the botanical gardens. I got a map of the gardens from the gift shop and spread it out on the picnic table. "Okay," I said to my gathered troops. "We all started here." I pointed to the beginning of the trail. "We took the trail up and looped around at the prayer tree before heading back down by the waterfall. We'll walk it again today and re-create the moment of finding Laura. Okay?"

"Got it," Holly said.

We started up the trail. I used my pictures from that day to help re-create moments. "After this sculpture," I said, "Amy was behind me with the other yoga teachers. Sally was talking with me. Dan and Laura were ahead."

The two women positioned themselves. "Were we out of sight?"

I bit my bottom lip. "Yes, I think it was Millie, Sally, and me at this point. Laura and Dan were power walking, Amy more strolling." We separated and walked until we reached the next sculpture point in my pictures that proved we were all together.

"How long did you have to wait for me to arrive?" I asked Aunt Jemma.

"Five minutes," she said. "But Laura was here, right?"

"Yes," I said, "but they could've had a fight, and no one would have known."

"Oh, I think you would have felt the tension," Holly pointed out.

"Yes, true." I chewed on my lip and then took out my water bottle to take a swig. "Did anyone see Jack Henry?"

"No."

"Not yet."

"Okay, keep your eyes peeled. Aunt Jemma, meet us at the prayer tree. I think you'll be there at least five minutes before I show. Holly, Amy, and I walked this route together. Sally was behind me with the other yoga teachers. Aunt Jemma, take Millie with you this time. I'm nervous about you being so far ahead by yourself."

"Okay, come on, pup. Let's power walk." She moved ahead of us on the trail.

"I don't think this is working," I confided to Holly.

"It's early yet," she said. "We don't know. Maybe Aunt Jemma will see Jack Henry and have time to talk to him."

"I can't imagine it being Sally, Amy, or Dan. Think about it. The killer had to get the corkscrew from my van. You're both too far away to get it while I wasn't watching."

"So maybe they didn't go back for the corkscrew," Holly suggested. "What if they had it on them?"

"That doesn't make sense," I said. "Why would they be carrying my corkscrew?"

"Maybe they brought wine on the hike with them and stuck the corkscrew in their pocket."

"No," I said and shook my head. "Laura wouldn't have let them indulge in wine while hiking, and neither would I. It's dangerous, not to mention dehydrating."

"Hmm. I can't think of any other reason for someone to bring a corkscrew other than premeditated murder. And we still haven't established why someone would want to kill Laura. Maybe she was selling information and Dan found out. They fought, but she was an unrepentant criminal and was going to take Dan down with her."

"That sounds a bit out there," I said.

"What if Laura discovered that *Dan* was selling identities? They could've fought. She could've taken the SD card from him and gone to find a good signal to call the police," Holly said.

"I was able to contact everyone on the day of the murder, so I don't think she would've had a problem with a cell signal."

"Too bad." Holly made a face. "It was a good idea."

"Now debunked."

We arrived at the top of the hill to find Millie barking with joy. Her tail was wagging a mile a minute. I glanced around to see why—Aunt Jemma was talking to a shabbily dressed man.

"It's Jack Henry," I said to Holly. "Come on." We hurried over.

"Hello," I said as we arrived next to them.

"Hello, Miss Taylor," he said. "Your aunt tells me that the police are using the jacket against you in court."

"Yes," I said, "unless my lawyer can get the judge to throw it out."

"I'm sorry to hear that."

"Listen, do you remember seeing anything that day? Hearing anything?"

"If you're talking about the murder, no."

"Besides the murder," I pushed. "I thought my group was the only one in the park. Did you see anyone else?"

"Yes, I saw a woman alone. I thought it was a little odd because she parked on the side of the road and walked up. People usually park in the lot."

"A woman? What did she look like?" I asked.

"She was as tall as you, slender, with mousy-brown hair. I remember because she wore all khaki and seemed to blend right into the scenery. The only reason I noticed her was because she parked where she did."

I looked at Aunt Jemma. "It sounds like Dan's sister."

"Why would she come?"

"Maybe Dan called her," I mused. "When did you see this woman?"

"About an hour after your group. You had to be heading down the hill at the time. She took the back trail up. I figured she was going to meet you all."

"Did you see her leave?"

"Naw, I saw the cops come, so I left. I don't like cops."

"Well, thanks," I said. "One more thing . . . Would you be willing to tell the cops about what you saw?"

"Naw. I told ya, I don't like cops. They give me the heebie-jeebies."

"But I could go to prison without your testimony," I said.

"Don't rightly care for cops," he said and started to walk away.

"My lawyer can subpoena you," I pointed out.

"Gotta find me first," he said and melted into the scenery.

"Drat," I said.

"We did get one more piece of information," Holly pointed out cheerfully. "We can add that into our calculations."

"Hmm," I said. "I'm not sure it helps."

"Well, we know that everyone was together here at the prayer tree. You have pictures. Is that the last group picture you got that day?"

"Yes," I said. "I remember after Laura told me she thought she could improve my business—"

"What? That's crazy," Holly said.

"Sounds like she thought she knew more than everyone else no matter what situation she was in," Aunt Jemma said.

"I know, right?" I sighed. "Anyway, I told her no, and she strode off down the trail. She didn't seem happy."

"What about the jacket? Was Rashida wearing it in the prayer-tree photo?" Aunt Jemma asked.

We looked carefully at the picture. "Huh, no jacket," I said and zoomed in on the picture to see if anyone else had it. "No one has it."

"Wait, is that it on the bench?" Holly said.

I zoomed in even closer to see that a corner of the bench was exposed behind the group. There was a scrap of color poking out from the edge of the bench. "It might be," I said and looked at the picture from every angle. "It's hard to tell."

"Well," Aunt Jemma piped up, "let's head down the trail. I'm still Dan. Did he go with Laura?"

I blinked. "Yes, he did."

"When was the next time you saw Dan?" Holly asked.

"He came back to talk to me after we headed down the hill from the prayer tree."

"How much time went by between leaving the prayer tree and him coming back to see you?"

"I'd say a good thirty minutes. I was making sure the ladies didn't get left behind."

"So I'll start and see how far I can go in fifteen minutes or so, then head back to meet you," Aunt Jemma said. "Come on, Millie. Let's see if we can reach the body site and back."

Holly looked at me. "So you think Amy didn't do it?"

"I don't remember exactly, so I can't rule her out. Amy left me when Dan came back," I said. "So there might have been time for Amy to do the deed because the next time I saw her was at the picnic area. She was coming out of the restroom. She could have gone in there to clean up."

We headed down the trail. I wasn't seeing the sculptures or the rare plants—I was thinking about what had been happening to Laura the last time I strolled through these woods.

"I had five minutes at the body site and was able to get back here about the time you arrived," Aunt Jemma said. Millie rooted around in the leaves at the edge of the trail. "Is this where Dan talked to you?"

"I think so," I said. "But I didn't notice Dan having any blood on him. If he had killed Laura, wouldn't he have had blood on him?"

"Unless he found the jacket and used it to cover up his shirt," Holly said.

"Murder is messy," I said.

"What kind of shirt was Dan wearing?" Aunt Jemma asked.

I frowned and pulled out my phone. "A khaki shirt," I said as I pulled up the pictures.

"So his sister could've come up to bring him a new shirt."

"That's pretty premeditated," I said. "It doesn't sound right. Using the corkscrew seems spur of the moment. I mean, there are easier ways to kill someone. I guess the real question is, why would someone have the corkscrew in the first place?"

"Let's think about premeditation. Did anyone bring stuff? A backpack or other gear? Could anyone have had a change of clothes?"

"Again, it would've been pretty premeditated for them to have a change of clothes that were the same so no one would notice."

"Unless Dan called his sister to bring the clothes after he killed Laura."

"They live an hour from here, and Jack Henry saw the woman before the murder happened," I said. "Unless it *was* premeditated, and Dan had set up for his sister to come. That would give her time to get here with a change of clothes. You know, he was the only other person who ended up with Laura's blood on his hands besides me."

"He could've rushed down there to cover his tracks," Holly said.

"The timing would have had to be just right," Aunt Jemma said. "From here Dan walked with you, and Amy went down the trail."

"Yes."

"Okay, Holly, go down the trail. Stop for five minutes at the crime scene and then go to the restroom and pretend to wash. We'll walk the way Taylor remembers and check if we see you at all."

"Got it." Holly strode away with Millie.

"Don't run," I called out. "Amy didn't seem to run."

"Okay."

"Sheesh, we sound so devious," I said as Aunt Jemma and I continued down the hill. We were about ten minutes from the scene of the crime.

"Well, we are trying to save your life. So far, we haven't ruled out Dan or Amy. What about Sally?"

"If I remember correctly, Sally was with Amy at this time. No one has disputed that, so I think we can rule her out. You know, I don't remember Dan being covered in blood," I said. "I think that's something I would've noticed if he had come from the crime scene to me."

"Remember, he could've changed his shirt. Did you look at his hands?"

"No," I said. "I don't remember looking, but I'd think he would've washed them."

"With what?" Aunt Jemma asked. "There's no restroom until you hit the picnic area."

"In the stream?" I wondered out loud.

"Yes, I suppose," Aunt Jemma said. "Did he seem nervous or out of breath?"

"A bit frazzled," I said, "but I thought it was because he wasn't happy with my rejection of their marketing class. I'm getting the feeling that they were running short on cash and desperate to take on new clients of any kind. He said they wanted to expand to marketing and mentoring other small-business start-ups like mine. But I turned him down, and he got quite upset over it."

"What did he do?"

"I don't really know. Mostly I got mad and left to join the ladies," I said.

"Maybe he was still in shock from having murdered his wife," Aunt Jemma suggested. We hit the picnic area, and on cue, Holly came out of the restroom.

"Well," she said. "There was definitely ten minutes when I could've killed someone and gone to wash up."

"So Amy's not in the clear." I sighed. "We need to figure out the motivation. Was Amy mad when she found out that Laura was stealing her identity and selling it?"

"Do we know that Laura was selling it? Perhaps she confronted the identity thief, and they killed her."

"How would she have found out about it if one of her staff members was profiting from stealing identities? Amy said they all got hit by the theft before Laura got them insurance."

"We need to talk to Amy," Holly said.

"We can't," I reminded her. "The lawyer won't let her, remember? She might lose her job."

"Just because you can't doesn't mean that I can't," Holly said. "What if I happen to be going door-to-door, giving out flyers for my next gallery showing? I could talk to her and see what she thinks."

"Better yet, we could pose as surveyors and ask her neighbors about how safe they feel in her neighborhood." Aunt Jemma smiled. "We can talk about the recent rash of identity theft and how it affected them."

"That won't work. I met Amy," Holly said.

"But I didn't. Come on. You can drive me."

"Oh, that sounds good," I said. "Amy doesn't know you. You should hit some of the neighbors as well so it doesn't look like you're targeting her."

"We will do a good job," Holly promised. "All I need is a clipboard and a series of questions."

"Great," I replied. "What's the harm in finding out more information, right?"

Chapter 21

While my friends were out canvassing Amy's neighborhood, I was online digging into Dan's sister's background. According to her LinkedIn page, Ivy Scott was a freelance graphic artist. Her social media page made her look like what my grandmother would have called a barfly. From her pictures, she spent a lot of time at various bars downtown. Most of them in not-so-good areas.

Her favorite spot seemed to be Billy's Bar outside of town. I called Holly.

"How's Operation Survey going?"

"So far, so good. Your aunt has learned that two of Amy's neighbors also had their identity stolen in the last six months."

"That's strange. We should see how many people filed with the police. There has to be someone working on all these complaints."

"Oh, good idea. Or better yet, we can have my friend Chelsea McGartland look into it. She's a freelance reporter for the *North San Francisco Chronicle*."

"Wait—didn't she want to interview me?"

"Yes."

"I told her no. In fact, Patrick said I shouldn't give any statements to the press."

"Chelsea is a good person," Holly said. "We've been friends since college. I bet she would look into all the identity theft even if you don't give her an interview."

"I'll want to meet her," I said.

"Of course. I'll set up lunch."

"Good. In the meantime, want to go out?"

"Honey, I'm always ready to go out. Where are we going?"

"Wear your cowboy boots, your jeans, and a plaid snap-front shirt."

"Sounds like cowboy gear. Are we going to a dive bar?"

"The diviest—Billy's."

"Okay, what got you into the mood for a dive bar?"

"It happens to be one of the places Dan's sister, Ivy, hangs out. Maybe she told someone that she was at Quarryhill that night."

"Won't it look suspicious if we go in asking questions?"

"We'll arrive late, look great, and chat people up. I'll buy drinks, and no one but the bartender will remember we were even there."

"Oh, you are devious," Holly said. "I'll pick you up at ten."

"You'll pick me up?"

"Yes, honey. We can't take your van—that's something people remember."

"Right," I said. "When's your next gallery showing?"

"Day after tomorrow," she said. "I have time for a little fun tonight."

"I'll see you soon."

* * *

I was surprisingly nervous. I had on my oldest cowboy boots from my college days, skintight jeans, and a plaid Western shirt that snapped up the front. I'd done my hair up in hot rollers so it curled in cascades of waves down my back. Some black winged-tipped eyeliner and a pouty red lip, and I looked sufficiently tarty.

"I don't like it," Aunt Jemma said as I waited for Holly to pick me up.

"We'll be safe," I said. "I checked out Ivy's pictures. I'm dressed like all the other girls who go to Billy's. Nothing makes me stand out from the crowd of good-time honeys."

"You're not a good-time honey," she said. "Leading men on is not a good way to investigate. Besides, what if they recognize you from TV? They had cameras showing you walk in and out of the courthouse."

"I was wearing a suit with my hair pulled back and minimal makeup. Besides, the guys at Billy's won't care enough about some random girl to put together who I am."

"Text me every thirty minutes, or I'm calling the police."

"I will," I said. "Can't a girl get out of the house and have fun?"

"Not when she's in a murder investigation," Aunt Jemma said.

"Call your new boyfriend and forget all about Holly and me."

"Milo's not my new boyfriend," she groused.

"Yet," I teased her as Holly pulled up in a convertible. "Bye, Auntie. Don't do anything I wouldn't do." I blew Aunt Jemma a kiss and got into the convertible. Holly stepped on it, her wheels sending gravel flying.

"Wahoo!" she said as we drove out on the highway.

I grinned and raised my hands up to let the air catch them.

It was a fun and carefree moment with the wind whipping through my hair. The night smelled of vineyards and warm earth. Stars twinkled in the dark sky. It had been months since Holly and I were out late. Longer since we were out to party. My nerves turned to excitement as we pulled into Billy's parking lot.

Holly was wearing a cold shoulder shirt, short skirt, and thigh-high boots. She looked like a million bucks. "What's say we go do some investigating," she said as she put her arm through mine and we went to the door. Pounding bass from the speakers filled the air as we opened it. The smell of beer and the sound of peanut shells crunching under our feet gave us that cowboy feel. We went up to the bar.

The bartender had arms that were ripped, and Holly looked from him to me and winked.

"What'll you two ladies have tonight?" he asked.

"Got any craft beer?" Holly asked.

"We've got craft everything," he said and leaned forward.

"Give us your best," I said.

He nodded, sending his thick dark hair into his eyes. He pushed it back absently. The man had the bluest eyes any dark-haired boy could ever have and a California tan to match.

"Wow," Holly mouthed to me. It was useless to talk since the music was so loud. I turned to face the room and saw four pool tables currently in use, some darts that two couples were arguing over, and no empty spots.

"These two are on the gentlemen on the right," the bartender said.

"Well, hello there," Holly said and elbowed me. "He looks like your type, Taylor." The man who'd bought our drinks was tall, dark, and square-jawed. He wore a cowboy hat and tight-fitting jeans. He lifted his beer bottle to salute us. We lifted ours back. It took twenty minutes for him and his blond friend to come over to see us. Another hour until we got a booth where we could sit. I nursed my drink, careful to text Aunt Jemma on time for fear of being embarrassed by the cops.

"So how come we haven't seen you girls here before?" Holly's guy, Matt, asked.

"We're not from around here," Holly said. "Isn't that right, Daisy?" She winked at me.

"That's right, Hanna," I said. "We're tourists."

"Well, welcome to wine country," my guy, Adam, said, toasting us with his beer bottle. "Where are you all from?"

"San Francisco," I said, which was not a lie altogether.

"Hey," Holly said. "Have you ever had your identity stolen?" Okay, so that wasn't subtle.

"I've heard of it. Why?" Matt asked and took a swig of his beer.

"I got mine stolen this week," she said with a dramatic sigh. "Did you know that I have to, like, do all this paper work to stop it?"

"She does," I said and batted my eyelashes. "She had to cancel all her cards too."

"It's like starting over," she went on to say.

"Oh, honey, that's terrible."

"Isn't it?" she said. "Who would do such a thing?"

"What happened?" Adam asked.

"Somehow they got ahold of my name and address and wrote checks all down the five. They hit every big-box store and convenience store for miles."

"I bet they were done with you and onto the next by the time you found out," Matt said.

Holly nodded. "That's exactly what the police told me when I called them and demanded they do something about it."

"Identity theft is big business," Matt said. "You got to be careful with them Central Valley folks."

"Where did it get stolen?" Adam asked.

"Sacramento," Holly said.

"They don't have anything like that here, do they?" I asked and looked around.

"No, no one does that in Sonoma," Adam said and patted my shoulder. "Is that why you keep texting someone every half an hour? Or do you have a guy somewhere?"

I felt the heat of a blush rush up my cheeks. "Goodness me, no. No guy. It's my aunt. She's at the hotel, and she's worried about us out in the middle of nowhere."

"I told her we would be safe enough," Holly said.

"But she insisted that she'd send the police out if we missed a text," I said. Then I excused myself to go to the bathroom. While it was fun to pretend to be good-time girls, it was hard lying, and I felt a little creepy about it. Matt and Adam seemed like nice enough guys. They worked at one of the ranches nearby.

I went into the stall in the ladies' room and overheard two women talking as they came into the restroom.

"I'm sorry to hear about your sister-in-law, Ivy," a woman said. Her voice was hoarse, as if she smoked heavily.

"The witch had it coming," said a surly voice I wasn't sure I could place. Was this Dan's sister? "She was so mean to my brother. I'm glad."

"Seriously?"

"Well, don't tell the cops I said that." Ivy laughed. "I'm glad they caught the woman who did it. Now Dan can move on with his life."

The sound of running water from the sink filled the air.

"When's the trial?"

"Date's not set yet," Ivy said, "but the girl who killed Laura is out on bail. Can you believe that? I don't think she spent more than a day in jail. She should've gotten more jail time, but Patrick Aimes is her lawyer. He's good."

"And good-looking," the hoarse woman said. "I'd like a piece of that, except dating a lawyer would put a serious crimp in my business."

Ivy chuckled. "Good thing Dan never found out about the side business. Too bad I don't have access to his business records anymore."

"It's okay. You need to lay low for a while until this all blows over," the hoarse woman said. "We understand. No sense in throwing the baby out with the bathwater."

"Right?"

I waited while they must have be fixing their makeup.

"You can come back to work for us once the trial is over and the scrutiny is gone."

"Are you and Joe going to be okay?"

"Sure, we have lots of side jobs going on. We can withstand a few months without fresh intel. Better to be safe than sorry."

"I agree." I heard water run as they washed up and the rip of paper towels. I waited until the door closed behind them and I was alone in the bathroom before coming out.

Ivy was here, which meant that if she saw me, she might recognize me. I washed my hands and looked out to ensure she wasn't going to see me right away. I hurried to our booth.

"I'm sorry. I'm not feeling well. We need to go now." I grabbed Holly's arm. "Bye, guys."

"Wait—" Matt said.

"Sorry, we've got to go." I pulled Holly out of the booth.

"But you ladies haven't finished your drinks," Adam protested.

"What's up?" Holly said as we hustled to the door, but it was too late.

"Murderer!" Ivy screeched and rushed toward me.

"Oh," Holly said and put herself between me and Ivy, pushing me toward the door. "I think you have the wrong person."

"Oh, no, I don't." Ivy was headlong into making a scene. Everyone was looking, and I pushed through to the outside, where I ran into a woman with long brown hair and kind intelligent eyes.

"I'm sorry," I said.

"No worries," she replied. "You look like you're in a hurry."

"I'm trying not to cause a fuss," I said. The noise from inside grew as someone else stepped outside.

"Come with me," she said and pulled me around the side of the building. We hid in the dark as the crowd spilled out.

"I'd know that murderer anywhere," Ivy shouted. "Where are you?"

The woman with me put her finger to her lips, motioning for me to be quiet and stay back. She pulled out a pad of paper and a pen and walked around the building into the fray. "Chelsea McGartland, *North San Francisco Chronicle*. What's going on?"

"Nothing," I heard Holly say.

"That woman who murdered my sister-in-law was in here," Ivy said loudly. "Where is she? Did you see her leave?"

"I didn't see anyone leave," Chelsea said. "She murdered your sister-in-law? Tonight? Here? Do I need to call nine-one-one?"

"No need to call anyone," Holly said.

"She ran out of here," Ivy said. "She had to be too afraid to face me."

"She happens to be innocent," Holly said.

"That's not what the cops think," Ivy said.

"I've been trying to get an interview with her," Chelsea said. "I'm sure if I had a chance, I'd be talking to her instead of you."

"Fine," Ivy said. "I swear it was her."

"You ladies all right?" I heard Adam's voice.

"We're fine," Holly said. "It was a case of mistaken identity."

"Funny," Adam said. "She got sick right before this here young lady accused her of murder. She didn't kill anyone, did she?"

"No, she didn't," Holly said. "Now if you'll excuse me, I'm going home."

"That's right. Get out of here," I heard Ivy say.

"Hey, now," Matt said. "Leave the girl alone."

"I'll do what I like," Ivy said defiantly.

"I'd love to interview you," Chelsea said. "Let's go inside. I'll buy you a drink, and you can tell me what it's like to find out your sister-in-law was murdered."

"Why don't you tell her all about how you were there that day?" Holly said.

"What?" I heard the surprise in Chelsea's voice, and I peeked around the corner.

"I was not," Ivy said and put her hands on her hips. She wore skintight jeans and a bustier. Her facial expression was sour.

"Oh, you were," Holly said. "They have a witness who saw you."

"Really?" Chelsea was taking notes. "What's the name of the witness?"

Holly closed her mouth as she realized she might have gone too far, giving away one of our clues.

"I was not there!" Ivy's voice went up two octaves.

"Oh? Where were you, then?" Holly asked.

I bit my lip to keep my mouth quiet. This was a disaster in the making.

"You don't need to know where I was," Ivy said and grabbed a heavy girl beside her. "Come on. Let's go in. I don't want to think about these ridiculous accusations."

"No more ridiculous than the idea that my friend would murder your sister-in-law," Holly called to her back.

"Psst, Holly." I waved at her. I waited until Holly came around the corner, then I peeked back out to see that everyone but Chelsea was back inside Billy's. Chelsea was close behind Holly.

"What were you doing?" I asked Holly.

"Is it true?" asked Chelsea. "Was she at the scene?"

"Let's get out of here," Holly said and put her arm through mine.

"No, don't go," Chelsea said. "I've been trying to get an interview from you forever."

"I can't give an interview," I said. "My lawyer says I can't speak to anyone."

"But that doesn't mean I can't," Holly said. "Meet us at the coffee shop on Main. I'll text you directions." She pulled me toward the car, and I got in as Chelsea walked toward her vehicle.

"Are you nuts?" I asked as Holly pulled out of the gravel parking lot.

"I think some people would say I'm as crazy as a fox," Holly said. "Ivy was trying to incite a riot. She needed to be taken down a peg."

"You let her know that we know about her being there," I said. "Now she can come up with an alibi."

"Only if someone lies," Holly said as we pulled into the coffee shop. "I think it's good for her to know that we have a reporter investigating."

"You know I can't talk to Chelsea," I said.

"But I can. Come on," Holly said. "Let's get a table."

We went inside and got a table by the front windows. Then we ordered lattes and waited for Chelsea.

"I don't know if this was the right thing," I hedged.

"Having coffee?"

"No, talking to the Chelsea. She is the press."

"You have to admit she was good to you back there," Holly said.

"She was," I said. "She stuck me around the corner and stepped out to distract Ivy."

"So let's get her involved. We could use another investigator on our side."

"How do we know for sure she'll be on our side?"

"Because we're the right side," Holly said. We watched Chelsea get out of her car and head in. "Over here." Holly waved her over.

"Hi," she said and stuck out her hand. "Nice to meet you again . . . under better circumstances."

I smiled. "Holly tells me you've been friends for a while?"

"Yes, from college." Chelsea gave Holly a quick hug.

"Thank you for your help back there," I said. "Let me buy you a beverage."

The waitress came over as Chelsea sat down. "I'll take a chai latte," Chelsea ordered. Then turned to me. "Thank you for letting Holly call me about this story."

"You're welcome."

"Of course, since I saved you, I hope to get an exclusive once this is done."

"Now that's something I can promise you," I said. "As soon as my lawyer lets me talk, you'll be the journalist I speak to."

"Wonderful," Chelsea said and sat back. "Now what were you two doing at Billy's?"

"What were you doing at Billy's?" I asked.

"Stalking you," she said with a grin. "A friend tipped me off to the fact that you were there."

"Wow, that makes me nervous," I said and looked at Holly. "I thought we were undercover."

"Your face is the most famous one in the area right now," Chelsea said. "Since I couldn't get you to respond to my requests, I had my friends keep an eye out for you. But don't worry. I'm only able to do that because I'm local. I have friends who grew up in Sonoma."

"Well, that's a relief," I said.

"In fact, Matt was my brother's best friend. He let me know you were there, and I asked him to keep you busy until I got there."

I gasped. "We didn't give Matt our real names."

She grinned. "He knew but figured you were out to try to forget what was going on in your life. So he texted me and then spent time with you."

"Oh, that is so low," Holly said.

"No lower than us pretending to be tourists," I said with a shrug. "So you stalked me."

"It's called desperation," Chelsea said with a sigh. "I'm free-lance for the *Chronicle* right now, and I'm trying to get them to hire me on staff. It's tough these days with so many bloggers writing for free."

"Well, we don't mind helping you get a job," I said, "but not at my expense. So you have to understand that we're trusting you here."

"I have ethics," she said. "Listen, you seem like a nice person. We both love Holly. Seems like we should like each other or at least trust each other. I want to use the angle that you're being railroaded by the local police. I heard that the mayor was pushing for a quick resolution on this murder. I've studied the case. It seems circumstantial."

"Thank you," I said and sat back. I bit my bottom lip to prevent me from speaking more.

Chelsea took out her pad of paper. "Do you mind if I record this?" She put an MP3 recorder on the table.

"Go ahead," I said, "but I'm not speaking. Holly is."

"That's fine," she said. "Now, Holly, tell me about Ivy Scott."

"Well, she's Dan Scott's sister and was Laura Scott's sister-in-law. Laura Scott was found murdered at Quarryhill. We were speaking to one of the caretakers at the gardens, and he described seeing a woman who looked like Ivy Scott park her car along the road—not in the parking lot—and get out to walk the trails."

"That's odd. Why wouldn't she park in the parking lot?" Chelsea asked.

"We think she didn't want anyone to know she was there," Holly said.

"Why?"

"Well," I said, "they found an SD card on Laura with critical identity information from their business. Ivy might've been trying to get that back from Laura."

"Or she might have been trying to sell it, but Laura found out." Holly sent me a look to remind me I wasn't supposed to be talking. Which I wasn't, but it was so hard.

"So maybe Ivy was mad about the data breach or Ivy caused the data breach," Chelsea concluded.

"We don't know which," Holly said, "but you can find out, can't you?"

"I can certainly try," Chelsea said. "This is a good lead."

"I was in the bathroom tonight when Ivy and her friend were there," I said. "They were talking about laying low for a while until things blew over. Do you have any idea what that might mean?"

"It might mean that she was selling data," Chelsea said, "but anyone with a brain would know they can't sell it until you're convicted."

"I won't be because I didn't do anything," I said.

"That's not on the record," Holly said and nudged my latte toward me. "Just spitballing here, but what if Laura's murder was a two-man job? Someone stole the corkscrew out of Taylor's van and used it to hurt Laura."

"Or they could have pushed her down the cliff, then gone down and used the corkscrew to put suspicion on me," I said.

"Interesting," Chelsea said. "Maybe two people *were* involved."

Holly looked from me to Chelsea. "There are really only two ways it could happen: either Ivy did it herself or she had help to do it."

"How did she get the corkscrew?" Chelsea asked.

"The passenger's side door on my van was unlocked," I said. "I suspect it was jimmied. I told the police, and they inspected it and found a partial fingerprint on the door, along with scrape marks that showed it had been jimmied at least once in its life. But there's no proof it happened that day. As far as they can tell, Laura could have simply forgotten to lock it when she left the front passenger seat."

"Except for the partial print," Chelsea pointed out.

"Except for that," I said.

"Now who else didn't have a solid alibi?"

"Dan, the husband; Sally, the HR lady; and Amy, the office manager," Holly said. "Ivy could've been helping any of them."

"Or they could have been helping her," I said.

"There's no telling, at least not yet," Holly said.

Chelsea grabbed her phone and sent out a text.

"What did you do?" I asked.

"I texted Matt and asked him to see if he can't get Ivy to talk."

"About the murder?"

"The identity information," Chelsea said. "If she is selling identities, Matt will find out. He loves this cloak-and-dagger stuff."

"Yeah," I said. "We noticed."

Chapter 22

"Ivy Scott's best friend, Dawn Weller, has been arrested," Chelsea said to me on the phone the next morning.

"What? How do you know? What for?"

"Turns out there was a sting operation in the works for the last two months. They finally got enough evidence to arrest Dawn and charge her as part of an identity-theft ring."

"Wait, was Dawn the woman who was there last night?"

"Yes, she was the woman with Ivy."

"Ivy must be furious."

"I've contacted her to see if she'll make a statement, but she hasn't returned my call."

"She seems pretty press savvy," I said. "I'd be surprised if she talks."

"It doesn't matter. I was able to break the news about Dawn, so I'm hoping this means the *Chronicle* will accept me as staffer. Thank you for the tip to look into Ivy. It's how I learned about Dawn. I have been up all night working on this. I'm stoked."

"I'm glad I could help," I said.

"I owe you. Let's get a drink sometime."

"After I'm free and clear," I said.

"Good. I have a feeling that'll be soon."

*   *   *

Later that afternoon, I drove by Ivy's house. I couldn't help myself. I had to know if she was involved in Laura's murder. Was Ivy the connection between the SD card and Laura's death?

A bit of research online, and I learned that Ivy lived in a tiny two-bedroom house that had been built in the 1930s. The little house was pale blue with white shutters. There was a three-foot picket fence around the front yard. It was the very picture of homey.

I parked in front of the house and noticed that the front door was open. I looked around. There were no other cars in sight. So I got out—maybe if I had a face-to-face talk with Ivy in the daylight, she'd at least acknowledge that I didn't have anything to do with Laura's death. Especially with the evidence that she was at Quarryhill.

I pushed open the little gate and walked up. I was right. The front door was open, leaving only a screen door between the world and the house.

"Hello? Ivy? Hello?" I called through the screen.

There was only silence. I tried again. "It's Taylor O'Brian. I want to talk with you about Quarryhill." Nothing.

I decided to try the back door. Maybe the front was open but she was in the backyard? I walked around the side rock garden. It looked like there had once been a green lawn here, but due to the drought, it had been replaced with curving rocks and gravel.

"Hello?" I called as I rounded the back. I could see that the back door was also open. This door had no screen. No one was in the backyard. "Ivy?" I glanced at the small shed, but it appeared to be locked up tight. She had to be inside.

A nagging feeling hit the back of my neck. Something was wrong. I knocked on the back door, and it opened wider. "Ivy? It's Taylor. I wondered if we could talk about last night?"

I stepped inside the tiny kitchen. I could see Ivy lying face-down on the floor in the hallway that led to the living room. "Ivy?" She didn't answer. I saw the small hole in her back. A pool of blood inched out around her. I went to her and touched her shoulder. "Ivy?" She felt cold to the touch. "Oh, no."

I reached for my cell phone, dialed 9-1-1, and went out onto the front porch to wait. If the killer was still inside, I didn't want them to find me.

The deputy sheriffs got there within five minutes. They drew their guns as soon as they got out of the car.

"She's inside," I said. An ambulance followed shortly after them. One officer went inside, and the other stayed with me.

"What happened?" he asked.

"I came by to ask Ivy a question," I said. "I found the doors open and went inside. That's when I found her dead."

"Did you touch anything?"

"I touched Ivy. I shook her shoulder to start first aid, but she was cold so I called nine-one-one." A mighty shiver went down my back, and I hugged myself as Sheriff Hennessey pulled up.

"The house is clear," the first deputy said as he came out. He held the door open for the ambulance crew. "There's definitely a body inside."

"Taylor, are you all right?" Sheriff Hennessey asked. There was deepening concern in his gaze.

"I know this looks bad. But I came to ask her a question and sort through the confusion," I said and realized how lame my excuse sounded. "Look, I might not have liked the woman, but I didn't want to see her dead."

"Don't say another word," Sheriff Hennessey said. "Blake, stay with her. See that she's comfortable and doesn't move." He went inside to check out things for himself. More police cars showed up, and I dialed Patrick.

"Hey, Taylor, what's up?"

"Well . . ."

"Oh, no, now what happened?"

"I stopped by to talk to Ivy and found her dead in her hallway."

"Taylor!"

"She was shot. I called nine-one-one. The deputies and Sheriff Hennessey are here along with an ambulance crew."

"Don't say another word," Patrick said. "I'll be right there."

Sheriff Hennessey came out onto the porch. "Taylor, do you own a gun?"

"No, sir," I said honestly.

"Good," he said with a bit of relief. "I want you to come down to the station with me until we get this sorted out."

A sedan pulled up, and Dan Scott came running out of the car. "What's going on?" he asked. "What's she doing here?"

"There's been a murder," Sheriff Hennessey said.

"Another? Is Ivy all right?"

"I'm afraid not."

"No!" Dan crumpled to the ground. "No, no, no." Then he looked at me with hatred. "*You.* You did this. You killed my sister and my wife." He stood, looking as if he were going to come after me.

Sheriff Hennessey pushed me behind him and stepped between Dan and me. "Stop. Take a breath. There's no evidence that Taylor did anything but find your sister."

"I think it's pretty convenient that she keeps finding the bodies." Dan bit out the words. His face was bright red with emotion.

"Let's not get ahead of ourselves," the sheriff said. "Come on. I'll have Deputy Blake stay with you." He waved for the uniformed policeman to come down. "I'm taking Taylor into the station."

"Take her," Dan said. "Lock her up, and throw away the key."

I swallowed hard. "I'm so sorry for your loss."

"Right," Dan said, then muttered something dark under his breath. "Why don't I believe you?"

I was glad that Sheriff Hennessey was between me and Dan Scott, who had a murderous look in his eye. "I'll meet you at the station," the sheriff said.

*   *   *

Patrick was at the station when I got there. "I figured they would have you come straight here," he said.

"Dan Scott saw me at Ivy's, and when he learned the news, he accused me of the murder. I know it doesn't look good, but I didn't do it," I said.

"We need to process your clothes and body for trace evidence," Sheriff Hennessey said. "I've got Deputy Linda Moore here to take you back. CSI Ashlyn Cate will take the evidence."

"Do you need to take my clothes? Should I call Aunt Jemma?"

"I'll call Jemma," Patrick said.

"We will take pictures," Deputy Moore said. "If we find anything that needs further investigation, then we'll need to take it."

She took me by the arm and led me back to the area where they had investigation rooms, Patrick following behind.

"Have Aunt Jemma bring me jeans and a T-shirt," I said.

"Don't say anything unless I'm present," Patrick reminded me.

I was taken back to a detention area, and they quickly took pictures of my hands, my clothes, my face, and my hair. Then they took scrapings from under my nails and checked my hands for gunshot residue. I saw that I had blood on my shoes. Not much, but enough that they asked for them. I slipped out of them.

"We'd like inspect your clothes to be thorough," CSI Cate said. She was a small woman with a California tan, blonde hair, and green eyes. I think the camera weighed more than she did. She wore a uniform of khaki pants and a khaki shirt with a name tag over the pocket.

"I've got a change of clothes from your aunt." Deputy Moore came through the door and placed the T-shirt and jeans on the table.

"I don't want to change if there are cameras in here," I said.

"You watch too many cop shows," Deputy Moore said. "We don't tape everything. But come on. I'll show you to the restroom."

We walked down a short hall to a ladies' room, where Deputy Moore waited outside the stall while I changed. I handed her my clothes, and she had me place the shirt and jeans into separate evidence bags, then handed the bags to CSI Cate.

"Can I wash up now?" I asked.

"Yes," CSI Cate said. "Thank you for your cooperation."

I washed my hands with soap and water. I wanted to get rid of the smell of death that seemed to come out of my every pore. I wondered who could shoot a person in the back.

"Sheriff Hennessey will ask you a few questions now," Deputy Moore said as she took me to a small interview room.

"I'd like my lawyer there," I said.

"We'll get on that," Deputy Moore replied and sat me inside the small room. There was a table and two chairs, a camera in the corner, and what was most likely a two-way mirror in the wall. It was all starting to feel wrongly familiar.

I checked my phone. It had taken two hours to collect the evidence. I waited another full hour before Patrick came in. I wondered how I was ever going to pay his fees. "Have you been here the whole time?"

"Yes," he said. "They asked me to stay out."

"I asked for you an hour ago. I guess they're busy."

"It's rather standard," he said with a shrug. "Are you all right?"

"I'm fine," I said. "It's hard to find a dead person. There's a sort of shock that goes through your system. I think I might sleep like the dead tonight once all the adrenaline is gone." I winced at my own grim humor.

"Why did you go to Ivy Scott's house?"

"That's my first question," Sheriff Hennessey said as he came in with a file folder and some papers. "I'll get another chair." He went out, grabbed a plastic chair, and came back in. Then he sat so that Patrick and I faced him. "Now let's try to get you out of here as quickly as possible. Why did you go to see Ivy Scott today? Are you two friends?"

"I ran into Ivy last night at Billy's bar," I said.

Patrick whipped his head around and studied my face. "What were you doing at Billy's?"

"Good question," Sheriff Hennessey said.

"Holly and I went to have a little fun and get out," I lied.

"Please tell me you weren't there to investigate anything," Sheriff Hennessey said.

"I wasn't." I figured it didn't hurt to fib a little. They studied me hard, and I realized I was a very bad liar. I could feel the heat of a blush rush up over my face. "Okay, so we went to see if we could find out any more information on Ivy Scott."

"Why would you want information about Ivy Scott?" the sheriff asked.

"Well, a witness put Ivy at Quarryhill the day Laura died. I wanted to see if I could figure out why she was there."

"You were told to leave the investigating to the authorities," the sheriff said.

"I know," I said, "but no one else who is investigating seems to think I'm innocent. Then I heard her in the ladies' room talking to someone about having to postpone a job or two until after the heat dies down."

"Did you see who she was talking to?"

"No," I said. "I was in a stall, but I left soon after. In fact, Holly and I were in the process of leaving when Ivy came running after me accusing me of murder . . . again."

"So you were embarrassed by her actions and went to see her today about it. Then you had an argument and killed her."

"What? No," I said. "No, no, no."

"No, you weren't embarrassed?"

"No, I got away before she could chase me down," I explained. "I ran into Chelsea McGartland from the *North San Francisco Chronicle*. She helped me get away without Ivy's notice."

"So you ran away."

"Holly and I left."

"And that's all there is to that?"

"Well, I might've given Chelsea a tip about what I heard in the restroom."

"What did you tell her exactly?"

"That I overheard Ivy Scott and her friend talking about how they had to lie low for a while after Laura's death."

"Lie low?"

"That's what they said. I surmised it meant that they had to cease any illegal activity, and I told Chelsea that. This morning, Chelsea called me to tell me that Ivy's friend Dawn Weller was arrested after a sting operation concluded on a ring of identity thieves. It is more than a coincidence, I think."

"So you killed Ivy because she stole identities with Dawn?"

"I think that's enough accusations," Patrick said. "My client has told you that she didn't murder Ivy. She has no gun registered to her or on her person, and you've examined her. I'm sure you know that she has no gunshot residue on her hands."

"Let's talk about why you went to Ivy's house today."

"As I said, I wanted to talk about the fact that Holly told Ivy we have a witness who put her at Quarryhill the day that Laura died. I think it's no coincidence that Laura had an SD card on her with stolen identities."

"You think Ivy was buying them from Laura?"

"Or someone else," I said. "And yes, I thought Ivy knew something about who killed Laura. I even suspected that she might've helped."

"And then you found her dead."

"Then I found her dead."

"Did you see anyone else around when you arrived?"

I closed my eyes and thought back. "No, I think the street was empty. But I noticed the front door was open."

"Yet you went around to the back . . ."

"Well, yes, because she didn't answer the front door. I figured since it was open, she was home and possibly outside in the backyard. So I went around. When I didn't see her, I knocked on the back door and saw it too was open. So I went inside and called her name, but I found her pretty quickly."

"Did you touch anything inside?"

"I touched her to see if I could help her, but she was already cold. So I called nine-one-one and went outside to wait for everyone to arrive."

"The first responders found you on the front porch."

"Yes," I said.

"So you walked through the house."

"It's small."

"I see."

"Do you?"

"You didn't see anyone else?"

"I didn't see or hear anyone, but then I figured I couldn't stick around inside in case the murderer was still there."

"But you said she was cold."

"She was."

"Then most likely the murderer was long gone, as it takes hours for a body to cool."

"Huh, who knew?"

"I'll take that as a rhetorical question."

"It was," I said. "Is there anything else? I've given my statement and my clothes. I'd like to go home now."

"You do that, and we'll be in touch."

"Okay."

A Case of Syrah, Syrah

I got up with Patrick and started to leave.

"Oh, and Miss O'Brian?"

"Yes?"

"I'd suggest you stay at home for the next few weeks. It may be the safest thing for everyone involved."

"I'll do my best to comply, but I'm not making any promises."

Chapter 23

"Now what?" Holly asked.

It was late at night, and we sat outside on the patio, sipping wine and staring at the fire pit. "Now I stay home and wait for them to prosecute me to the fullest," I said.

"That's the saddest thing I've ever heard," Aunt Jemma said.

Millie came and leapt into my lap, turned three times, and snuggled in. I petted her absently. "I don't know what else to do."

"Ivy is dead, Dawn is in jail, and we've narrowed our suspects to Dan, Sally, and Amy," Holly said. "That's not all bad."

"Dan looked like he wanted to kill me," I said. "You didn't see the look in his eyes."

"So maybe he murdered Laura and Ivy."

"Then why would he want to kill me?" I asked. "If he murdered them, wouldn't he be happy that I'm taking the fall?"

"That leaves Amy and Sally," Aunt Jemma said. "It's interesting that Amy quit talking to you as soon as you were arraigned. In fact, we've not heard from her for a while."

"Unless she's dead," I said morosely. "I haven't shown up at her place to verify that she's even still alive."

"My head hurts," Holly said.

"I'll check on Amy in the morning," Aunt Jemma said.

"Even better, send Chelsea," I said. "That way, no one in this house is involved should we find out that Amy is also lost to this serial killer."

"Serial killer?"

"Yes, more than one kill makes you serial, right?"

"I'm not sure what the qualifications are," Aunt Jemma said and sipped her wine, "but it's all quite gruesome."

"With Ivy dead, I'm not sure we'll ever really know what happened that day at Quarryhill."

"We know I didn't do it," I groused.

"True," Aunt Jemma said.

"I think Dan knows more than he's saying. I don't know how to prove it," I said.

"In the meantime, no more wine country tours, and no more visits to suspects' homes," Aunt Jemma warned. "It's simply too easy for you to be framed."

"There's no way they framed me for Ivy. Even I didn't know I was going to go there until the last minute."

"So who would kill Ivy, and why?"

"It could've been Dawn. I know she was arrested, but I saw on the news that she was out on bail. She could have been upset that she was caught in the identity-theft ring but Ivy wasn't," I proposed.

"Or it could be Dan, afraid that his connection to Laura's death and the identity-theft ring would be discovered," Holly suggested.

"Maybe Dan found out that Ivy killed Laura, got mad, and went over there to confront her. They had a fight, and bam! Ivy is dead."

"That would explain why he had murder in his eyes at the scene." Holly tapped her chin. "He might have still been seething."

"Or maybe Ivy found out who the killer was and confronted them," Aunt Jemma suggested. "The killer then killed Ivy out of fear of discovery."

"Ivy might've even tried to blackmail the killer," I said. "It seems like the kind of thing she would've done. She *was* hurting her brother and his wife by selling the information of their staff and clients."

"Dawn might know something," Holly said. "She's out on bond, right?"

"Yes, like me," I said.

"Then I say we go take her out for a coffee," Holly said. "Maybe she'll tell us things."

"We can try that," I said with a shrug, "as long as we meet her in a public place. No more of us going to anyone's houses."

"It's a plan," Holly said. "I'll call Dawn in the morning and set it up." Holly got up and stretched her long limbs. "Now home and bed for me, ladies. Tomorrow things will work out. You'll see."

"Tomorrow is another day," I said in my best Scarlett O'Hara accent.

Holly and Aunt Jemma laughed, and I walked Holly out to her car. I watched as she drove down the driveway between the lines of grapevines. The air was cool and still. I wondered if talking to Dawn would help us at all. It seemed the more I investigated, the more I incriminated myself.

* * *

"Dawn is meeting us at the Leaf and Branch in five minutes," Holly said as I picked her up in my VW van. "It's the coffee shop on the corner of Maple and Main."

"I know it," I said. Holly lived above the art gallery two blocks from Main. It wasn't so far that she couldn't walk, but I'd thought it'd be best to go together. That way, if anything bad happened, I'd have a witness.

I found a parking space a half a block from the coffee shop, and we parked and walked. The streets were quiet. Sonoma was a sleepy little town when there wasn't a holiday or vacation in sight.

"Well, hello, ladies," Chelsea said as we entered the coffee shop. She sat with Dawn at one of the tables nearest the restrooms.

"Chelsea," I said. "Surprised to see you. Dawn, thanks for meeting with us."

"You didn't give me much choice," Dawn said. We sat across from Dawn, and a waitress came over. We ordered chai tea lattes.

"Sorry about that," I said. "Chelsea, how did you know?"

"I was meeting with Dawn to get her side of the story. She simply let me know that you all were coming." Chelsea grinned. "It's good that we all get along."

The waitress brought our teas and left.

"Let's get down to business shall we?" Chelsea put her MP3 recorder down in front of us. "Dawn, how did you get involved in the identity-theft ring?"

"Ivy introduced me to a guy when I told her I needed emergency cash to pay my rent. You know how crazy rents are here. Well, I asked the guy what I had to do for a loan. I wasn't agreeing to no funny business. He says to me, 'Bring me the names, addresses, phone numbers, and e-mails of five people,' and he'd give me one hundred bucks apiece. Well, I went home and dug out my address book."

"Did you know he was selling them to a ring that took the information and used it to write bad checks?"

"No, I didn't know what he wanted. Maybe he wanted them for one of those marketing lists. You know, where they sell the numbers of subscribers to marketers?" She shrugged her wide shoulders. "I didn't ask, and he didn't tell."

"Who was the guy?" Chelsea asked.

"How did Ivy know him? Do you think he killed her?" Holly asked.

"Whoa." Dawn put up her hand. "I don't know the guy. Ivy called him Joe."

"How did you get the addresses to him?" I asked.

"I'd put them on an SD card, put that card in an envelope, and leave it in a post-office box at Mailboxes R Us. After twenty-four hours, I would go back and pick up an envelope with money that corresponded to the number of names."

"What is the post-office box number?" I asked.

"It was number 1352, but he won't touch it anymore."

"How do you know?"

"The cops took away the key," Dawn said. "They caught me, but they didn't catch Joe."

"What about Ivy?"

"Ivy was free and clear," Dawn said and muttered something dark under her breath. "Some friend she was. Left me holding the bag when the cops showed up. She always had an excuse not to leave the names. Funny, but it's almost as if she was working with the cops the entire time."

"Really? Why do you say that?" Chelsea asked.

"She was always going in to town to meet Deputy Ferguson. She said they were dating, but I think it was a setup. She hooked and landed me like a fat fish. Funny how she ended up dead."

"No, it's not funny," I said. "Did you shoot her out of revenge for being arrested?"

"No." Dawn shook her head and scowled. "I don't own a gun. But I wasn't the only one Ivy was working. She had these three chicks her brother knew. Turns out, they each had a list of people and addresses and such. It was like a gold mine for Joe. If it were me, I'd be asking Dan about the three chicks. Any one of them could've found out about my arrest and decided Ivy needed to go before they were next."

"What did the ladies do?"

"They worked with Ivy's sister-in-law. So you see, all I did was gather a few names and addresses. That's all it takes, you know. Some bogus checks, a name and address that match what they find online, and bam. Identity stolen."

"So you knew what they were doing?"

"Ivy did," Dawn said with a shrug. "I recently read how easy it was to use someone's identity. No admission of guilt there." She waved her hand at Chelsea. "Don't put those two things together."

"Do you know the names of the ladies?"

"Me? No," Dawn said. "I didn't want to know. Ivy would get drunk and tell me all kinds of things I didn't want to know. I'm surprised I'm not dead from what she told me."

"Right," Chelsea said.

"Thanks, Dawn," I said. "You were brave to tell us what you know."

She shrugged. "I figure it'll all come out in court anyway. I'm not guilty of anything more than providing a guy with information. Happens all the time."

"Come on, Holly. We have a yoga studio to visit," I said.

Holly and I stopped on our way out to pay the check for all four drinks. Then we got into the van. "Do you really think the ladies killed Laura and then Ivy?" Holly asked as she put on her seat belt.

"I don't know, but we have a motive now," I said. "If they were making money from the list of subscribers to Laura's mastermind class and Laura found out, she would've had a cow."

"It wouldn't take much to imagine a struggle and Laura going down the cliff."

"But why stab her with my corkscrew?"

"To make sure she died," she said.

"Sounds as grisly as it was."

"That's a lot of passion," Holly pointed out. "Are we sure it wasn't Dan?"

"No, I'm not sure," I said. "He may have come to talk to me on the trail to have me be his alibi. I mean, we proved he had time to hurt her and still get back to me. But I didn't see any blood on Dan prior to his touching the body, and we don't know why Dan would do it. The police looked at the family first, and they ruled him out."

"So either we prove the ladies did it or we find out Dan's motive."

"That's the plan," I said.

"What are we going to say to the yoga ladies?"

"I don't know," I said with a shrug. "I'm hoping to figure that out when I get there."

Chapter 24

We sat in the van, parked outside the yoga studio, and watched the ladies file into class. "We can't go in," Holly said. "They've banned us."

"That was pretty convenient, don't you think?"

"Oh, I thought that early on," Holly said. "As convenient as Amy saying Dan's lawyer kept her from talking to us. Speak of the devil." Holly pointed to where Amy was walking into the studio. "Looks like they're all as close as before Laura's death."

"You know the problem with a group of people knowing a secret?"

"What?"

"Someone is going to crack and tell," I said.

"You think we should divide and conquer," Holly surmised.

"Yes," I said. "I don't know who'll be the weakest link."

"We know about Rashida's jacket," Holly said as we watched Rashida walk out of the studio.

"We can try her first," I agreed, and we both got out. We made it to Rashida's car at the same time as she did. "Hello," I said. "Remember us?"

"You two stay away from me." Rashida put her hand up as if to stop us. "I want you to know that Ivy's death hit us hard. I'm getting a body guard."

"Is that because you were working with Ivy stealing identities?"

"What?"

"Dawn told us about your little excursion to the dark side with your lists of names," Holly said.

"We have blood evidence on your jacket that suggests you killed Laura," I pointed out. "With Dawn's testimony, we have motive."

"Oh, I'm not taking the fall for this," Rashida said. "Selling identities was Ivy's idea. She's dead."

"Because you three killed her." I said the words out loud to see Rashida's reaction. Her eyes grew wide as saucers.

"I did not kill Ivy," she said and crossed her arms. "I've done nothing wrong. Ask Juliet and Emma. They were there with me on the trail. I didn't kill anyone."

"But you did sell your lists," I said. "When Laura found out, she was livid with you."

"I've got nothing more to say," Rashida said, opened her car door, and climbed in. "I suggest you leave the premises and never come back."

I nodded toward the studio. "Your friends have been watching you talk to us. What will they say when we go in and ask them about your alibi?"

"Go ahead and ask," she said. "I didn't do anything."

"Except steal your own customers' information." Holly let her disgust come through.

"Please, almost everyone has insurance these days," Rashida said. "No one was harmed."

"Except the insurance company and the businesses that were hit with phony checks," I said. "This is not a victimless crime."

Rashida ignored me, started up her car, and pulled away.

"Well, that was productive," Holly said, her words dripping with sarcasm.

"We can catch the others later," I said. "They have to leave the studio sometime, and when they do, we can ask them why they sold their own clients' names. Someone is bound to tell us something."

"I think Rashida told us a lot."

"Me too," I said and held up my phone. "I'm glad I videotaped the entire thing. Sheriff Hennessey needs to hear for himself what the ladies are up to."

"Do you think they killed Ivy?"

"I don't know," I said with a shrug. "I hope not."

"Me too," Holly said. "Because we might be next."

*   *   *

I went to see the sheriff. It was difficult walking into the building where I was arrested. I tried not to think about the fear and mayhem I'd experienced. Instead, I clung to my recording and hoped it would make a difference in my case.

"Come in," Sheriff Hennessey said when I knocked on his door. "What can I do for you, Miss O'Brian?" He sat back at his desk, looking handsome and self-assured. I blinked.

"I want you to dismiss the case against me."

"I can't do that," he said and leaned forward. "It's up to the courts."

"Fine," I said and put my phone on his desk. "Do you have any suspects in Ivy's death?"

"Off the record? We have a few leads, none of which are you," he advised me.

"Oh, thank goodness." I was more relieved than I knew. "Listen, I learned from Ivy's friend Dawn that Ivy was working with three women who worked for Laura. The women—Laura's yoga instructors—were selling their lists to the theft ringleader, a man known as Joe."

"And?"

"And Laura could've been killed because she found out about them selling her clients out."

"We considered that possibility," he said with a shrug and leaned back in his chair. "There was no evidence."

"Other than the SD card you found. I have a witness who puts Ivy at Quarryhill that day."

"Jack Henry won't testify."

"He will if he's compelled."

"Only if you can find him," Sheriff Hennessey said. "The man's gone underground."

"I say Ivy was there to get the latest list from one of the three yoga teachers. Laura caught them exchanging the SD card for cash and wanted to know what was going on. Then they got into an argument, one of the yoga teachers pushed Laura away, and she fell down the cliff, hitting her head."

"That doesn't explain how she ended up with your corkscrew in her neck."

"The instructor panicked and called the other two. They decided to frame me, and using Rashida's jacket as a shield in case of blood spray, they stabbed Laura in the neck, turning the screw. If she was already dead, it would explain the blood on the jacket not showing signs of arterial spray. Next, they ditched the jacket and headed to the tables, where I saw them on my arrival."

"And their lawyers will tell you it's a wonderful fairy tale," he pointed out.

"Unless you get one of them to crack," I said and turned on my phone, playing Rashida's recording.

"Well, this certainly is interesting," Sheriff said, "but it doesn't prove murder."

"It proves the ladies were working with Ivy," I said. "So they have more motive than I do. Seriously, my motive is weak and where you will lose your case."

"Because you didn't do it."

"Yes, I didn't do it."

"Does your lawyer know you're here?"

"No," I said and looked at him. "Does he need to know I'm here? I handed you a key piece of information."

"In the identity-theft ring," he said. "There is no link yet to Laura's murder."

I rolled my eyes. I couldn't help it. "It's right under your nose."

"I've told you more than once, but because you seem a little bit stubborn, I'm going to tell you one more time. Leave the investigating to the professionals."

I stood. "But the professionals have it all wrong."

"The professionals are doing their job."

"Fine."

"Thank you."

"Are you going to look into the possibility that I'm right?"

"Have a good day, Miss O'Brian."

"It's Taylor," I said, "and my day would be better if I knew you heard me."

"I hear you," he said. "Good-bye."

I walked out of the Sheriff's office, angry that I didn't know what to do next.

*   *   *

"Taylor, Millie's gone." Aunt Jemma met me at the van when I pulled up to the house.

"What? Where? How?"

"I don't know," she said and wrung her hands. "I thought she was in her bed sleeping. I called to her, and she didn't come. Then I noticed the back door was open."

"She's out in the vineyard?" I slammed the van door shut behind me and hurried toward the house.

"Juan and Julio have been looking, but we haven't found her yet." Aunt Jemma sobbed. "I'm afraid. I heard coyotes last night."

"They wouldn't come into the house and get her," I said as I walked inside and called, "Millie, come here, girl." I listened carefully to see if I could hear her whimpering. "Did you check all the rooms and closets? She might have followed you and gotten locked in."

"I checked them all," she said. "When did you leave this morning?"

"I left at nine. Millie was sleeping in her bed."

"Did you lock the back door?"

"Yes," I said and went over it in my mind. Millie stayed in the pool house with me, but I'd known that Aunt Jemma was spending the morning at home. So when I'd left, I'd put Millie in the big house. She had gone straight to her doggie bed in the patch of sunlight by the great room windows.

"Millie," I called as I walked through the house, opening every door. "Come here, girl. Want a puppy treat?" Only silence answered me, and I felt my panic mounting.

What if Jack Henry had come and taken her away? What if she had wandered out in the vineyards and gotten lost again? What if she'd run out in the street and gotten hit by a car? Or had been taken by coyotes, as Aunt Jemma feared?

I couldn't stand the thought of my baby hurting.

My phone chirped with a text from an unknown number. "Is your dog missing?"

"Who is this?" I typed back.

"If you want to see your dog, get ten thousand dollars in small bills and wait for my instructions. No cops!"

"Millie's been kidnapped," I said in horror. I looked at Aunt Jemma. "They must've taken her from the house. I don't think I reset the security when I left. I'm so sorry. It could have been you they took."

Aunt Jemma hugged me. "The good news is, they didn't take me. We have cameras on the parking lots and the entrance. I'll call the sheriff."

"No, they said no cops."

"They always say no cops," she said and frowned. "I'm calling the sheriff. Text them that you want proof of life."

"Oh, right, sheesh," I said. "I watch enough cop shows that I should've thought of that."

"They didn't text until you got home, so they're targeting you, not me," Aunt Jemma said as she dialed Sheriff Hennessey's office. "They have to be nearby to know you're home."

That was a frightening thought. I glanced out the window. They could be on any hillside with a pair of binoculars. I looked around to see if I could see any light reflecting in the distance like in the movies. I had the feeling I was being watched but didn't see anything.

I texted back: "I want proof of life."

They sent a little video of Millie barking in a crate. The video had a time stamp on it. Whoever had her was taking good care of her. That was comforting at least. "I don't have ten thousand dollars."

"Small bills. You have two hours, or the dog gets it."

"Yes, that's right, Sheriff. They're texting her their demands right now. We think they can see the house from wherever they are. It's the only way they could have known that Taylor had arrived home. Yes, yes, so don't come in a marked car. Right, yes, they asked her not to get the police involved."

I showed her my phone.

"They're telling her to have ten thousand in small bills in two hours." Aunt Jemma looked at me. "Yes, I assume they'll expect her to go to the bank. She can meet you at First California. Right. Thank you." Aunt Jemma hung up. "Sheriff Hennessey says to go to the bank. He expects there will be people there watching. Go inside. He will have someone there. They will ask for your phone. Give it to them, and they will do some tracing while you're getting the bills. It takes a lot of time to get that much money in small bills. He says leave now."

"Okay." I grabbed my purse and went to the door. I gave Aunt Jemma a kiss on the cheek. "Lock the doors behind me, and have Juan and Julio nearby, okay? I don't want to come back to an empty house."

"I'll be fine." She pulled a gun out of the credenza in the foyer. "These people messed with the wrong O'Brian."

I felt my eyes widen. "Aunt Jemma, put that away. We're not in Texas."

"I'm licensed."

"What? When?"

"I've had it for a while. I've been practicing out back with Juan ever since that rock came through the window. Why, those kidnappers are darn lucky I didn't see them take Millie."

"No, I think you're lucky they didn't see you. Put that thing away. Someone will get hurt."

"Only if I aim carefully," Aunt Jemma said.

I rolled my eyes and kissed her on the cheek. "Stay inside, and don't hurt yourself with that thing."

"Don't worry. It's not loaded . . . yet."

I got into the van and kept looking around to see if I could spot anyone watching me as I left the winery. I didn't pass anyone on the way to the bank, and I didn't see any other cars on the road. I drove into town and parked in front of the bank. I glanced around but didn't see anything unusual. So I walked into the bank and went up to the counter to write out the check and request for withdrawal.

There was a man beside me, writing one as well. He set his phone on the counter close to me.

"Are you with Sheriff Hennessey?" I whispered.

"Put your phone on the counter," he said as he looked away from me. I did what he said and was not surprised to see him switch phones out of the corner of my eye. It was a sleight of hand that I would've missed had I not been expecting it. I picked up the decoy phone and held it as I got in line for the teller.

When I got to the front of the line, I looked at the girl, whose name tag said, "Arielle." "Hello, Arielle," I said and pulled out my ID card and my checkbook. "I need ten thousand dollars in small bills, please."

"I'm sorry," she said with a shake of her head. "We don't keep that kind of money in the drawer. I can check and see if we have that much available."

"Okay," I said. "Can I see the manager?"

"Certainly," she pressed a button by her station, and I waited until the bank manager came out from around the back.

"Hello, can I help you?" The young manager wore a suit with a name tag that said, "Guy Winnington."

"Yes, Guy." I pushed my ID and bank account card toward him. "I'm Taylor O'Brian, and I need to withdraw ten thousand dollars in small bills, please."

"I see. It sounds as if you are robbing us," he teased.

"What? No, why . . . ? Oh, no, no. I need the withdrawal for a . . . a . . . handyman who is working on my aunt's house."

"That must be some handyman."

I swallowed as tears came to my eyes. "Yes, he's replacing windows." I figured it was best to stay close to the truth. What with the rock throwing, Aunt Jemma did need to replace her windows. "I have five thousand in my account. I need a loan of the next five thousand. I'm good for it. You can check my history and see that I have good credit."

"We don't generally give out loans that quickly," he said.

"I'll sign my van and my shares of Sookie's Vineyard as collateral," I said.

"I don't know. It will take some time to get that kind of cash to this location."

"You don't have ten thousand on the property?"

"Not in small bills, no," he said. "Why are you in such a hurry?"

"He'll be done in two hours and needs his pay," I said, "but that was almost an hour ago."

234

"Come into my office," he said and showed me past the teller area. "I assume there is more going on here than replacing windows."

"No, no," I assured him. "It really is just for windows."

"Then I would recommend you do a cash withdrawal on your credit cards."

"Oh, right, credit cards," I said and fumbled through my purse and pulled out three cards. "Run these."

"It'll take some time to get here and count it out," he said.

"I'll wait."

"Fine. I'll run the cards." He ran all three cards. "Combined I can get you nine thousand in small bills."

"That's fine," I said and looked around. Over my shoulder, I could see people waiting in the bank to do business. The walls were glass. People went about their business as if nothing were happening out of the ordinary today; they had no idea that I was sweating bullets as I dealt with possible dog killers and definite dognappers.

"Let me take a few minutes to collect that amount of cash," he said. "Are you sure a cashier's check won't do?"

"I'm sure." I waited impatiently while he did whatever banks do to transfer cash. I glanced down at my watch—the hour was almost up, and I still needed to get my phone back. What if I missed the call?

"Please, I need the money now."

He got up. "I've contacted the other two banks in town. They are messengering the money over. I'll check and see if it's arrived. I'll be back shortly."

I sat and waited for his return. I was impatient, wishing I had my phone with me. Suddenly, the cop in plain clothes came striding toward the office. I stood as he came inside.

235

"Excuse me, miss, but I think you have my phone," he said as the door closed behind him. He handed me my phone back.

"Oh." I fumbled for the matching phone. "I'm so sorry. Thank you."

"Take care," he said and left.

My phone felt the same, and I wondered what to do next. I looked at the texts. Nothing new. So I texted the dognappers. "I'm getting the money now."

"You have five minutes," came the reply.

I felt a spike of fear run down my spine. "I'm at the bank. They're getting the money. You have to be patient."

There was no answer, and I paced in the bank manager's office. Six minutes later, the manager came in with a full bank bag. "Here you go. Sign here." He handed me the bag. "You should count it."

"I'm sure it's fine." I signed.

"No, count it."

"Fine." I hurriedly glanced at the twenties and fifties. "That's a stack of money."

"It is. That's why you need to count it," he said.

"Sheesh." I counted as quickly as I could and shoved the money back in the bag and hurried to the door. When I got outside, my phone vibrated. I looked down.

"You're late."

"I had to count it," I texted back.

"Go to the corner of Napa and First Street," came the next text.

It wasn't far, so I started walking.

"Faster," came another text. I stepped up my speed. When I arrived at the corner, I got another text: "Cross to the park."

I did as they said and looked around.

"Cross back to the Sebastian Theater."

I jaywalked across, not worried about a ticket at this point. I didn't know why they were taking me back and forth across the same street. I wondered if it was to ensure I wasn't being followed. I waited in front of the theater for what felt like an eternity, but it was only five minutes before I texted.

"Where is my dog?"

"Leave the bag in the dumpster in the alley behind the theater."

I did what they said.

"Your dog is in the park."

I hurried back across the street, calling Millie's name. I heard barking and found Millie tied to a park bench. I fell to my knees and hugged the pup, who licked my face and squirmed in excitement at seeing me. Tears came to my eyes. It didn't matter that I didn't have a job or a business and now all my money was gone. What mattered was that I had my puppy back. It was such a relief.

Chapter 25

"We arrested Joe Smith," Sheriff Hennessey said when I answered the door to the house. I was carrying Millie. It had been five hours since I'd gotten her back, and I hadn't let her out of my sight.

"Come in," Aunt Jemma said over my shoulder.

"Joe Smith?" I asked as he stepped inside. Holly was there with me, along with Aunt Jemma and Chelsea. We had been sipping wine and giving Chelsea an exclusive on what had happened with the dognapping.

"He was part of the identity-theft ring. In fact, we're pretty sure he was the ringleader."

"How did you catch him?"

He held his hat in his hands. "We watched the dumpster until we saw a teen boy climb in, looking for the bank bag. We arrested the boy, and he led us to Joe."

"Why did they dognap Millie? I mean, besides the money."

"Joe blamed you for the sting operation."

"That's ridiculous," I said. "I didn't even know about the sting. I don't even know who Joe Smith is or what he looks like."

"Here's a mug shot of Joe," Sheriff Hennessey said and showed me a picture he brought up on his cell phone.

"Wait—that's the man from the park," I said. "He's not as swarthy as I remember, but I would know those eyes and that nose anywhere."

"What man from the park?"

"When I stayed with Holly after the rock was thrown in the window, there was a man in the park who gave me a scare."

"What kind of scare?"

"He followed me, and I felt threatened, but I lost him in Holly's apartment complex."

"Sounds like he was already surveilling you," Sheriff Hennessey said. There was heat in his gaze from what I thought was anger. "You should have reported that."

"What was there to report?" I asked. "Some guy seemed to follow me, but I lost him?"

"Right."

"Look, I really don't know the guy. Why would he hurt my dog?"

"He said that Ivy told him the sting was your fault."

"And now Ivy's dead," I pointed out. "Wait. That doesn't mean I had motive to kill her."

"No, there's no evidence you were involved, other than finding her body."

"It's the same thing for Laura, you know that, right?"

"I can't talk about that case," he said.

"So Joe Smith masterminded a dognapping to get back at me for the bust of his identity-theft ring. That's crazy. Why did he ask for ten thousand dollars?"

"With the new bank rules, anything ten thousand or less doesn't necessarily have to be reported to the federal government.

We've seen a lot of small money thefts lately as the crooks have gotten smarter about things."

"Wow. That's horrible. I'm thankful it wasn't a larger amount because there's no way I could've come up with the money. This whole murder thing has put a real crimp in my finances. Any idea when I'll get my money back?"

"We're working on that," he said. "Listen, we have Joe in jail, and I don't think he'll be bothering you any time soon." Sheriff Hennessey hunkered down and petted Millie. "You're safe now, little girl."

She jumped up, putting her front paws on his shoulder, and gave him a lick on the cheek.

"You're welcome," he said and stood. "Good thing I speak fluent dog."

We all laughed.

"Keep your doors locked and your security cameras on," he said with a nod. "I think it's best until we get things to settle down a bit."

"Thank you," I said and walked him to the door. "We will."

"Listen," he said to me in a low voice, "I know that you didn't know about the identity-theft ring, but I suggest you stay away from Dawn for the time being. At least until I get Ivy's murder under wraps."

"Do you think Dawn killed Ivy?"

"I'm not sure," he said and put on his hat as he went outside. "Better to be safe than sorry. Good night."

"Good night, Sheriff. Thank you for stopping by."

*　*　*

The next day, I stayed at home and did chores. Millie stayed near me and slept in the sunshine. The dognapping had taken a lot out of us both. The sheriff said I'd get my money back that week, which was a good thing so I could pay back the credit cards and my bills. The sad thing was that, until I was no longer a suspect in Laura's murder, I couldn't do any new tour work.

I pulled out the file folder with the notes from that fateful day when Laura had died. I went over all the information I had. It had been Amy who had contacted me initially about the tour. Laura had then vetted me, and we'd gone over the hike and picnic plans with a fine-tooth comb. Laura put the "micro" into "micromanager." I remembered that, at one point, she'd told Amy to get out of the way so that she could go over a list that Amy had written word for word on what had been said. It was embarrassing, and I'd sensed Amy's humiliation.

I remembered asking Amy what kept her on the job. She'd told me that I needed to see Laura with the yoga ladies and that she was truly inspirational. I guessed we all had our good sides. I simply hadn't seen it with Laura.

It all came down to the idea that Laura could have been killed by anyone there that day—anyone but me.

The doorbell rang, and I got up. Millie went barking and slid into the door. The cat slunk away with a hiss at the excited dog. I opened the door to find the sheriff.

"What brings you back here today?" I asked.

"I know you needed your cash, so I sped things up," he said and handed me the bank bag filled with cash.

"Oh, thank you so much. This is needed. I was looking at my bills and don't know how I'm going to generate any cash with no work."

He removed his hat when I waved him into the pool house apartment. "Justice always wins out. I wouldn't be a sheriff if I didn't believe that."

I looked him in his gorgeous blue eyes. "I thought being a sheriff was more political than law enforcement."

"I like being a part of the community," he said. "If I can make a suggestion, I'd recommend that you do something that has nothing to do with your case."

"Like what? I can't work. You don't want me talking to anyone."

"Anyone involved in the case," he clarified, "but that doesn't mean you can't get out and do some volunteering. Anything for the community will help with your reputation."

"That's a great idea. How do I start?"

"There are a few organizations—besides the church ones, of course."

"Of course," I said and tapped my chin thoughtfully. "Can I offer you some coffee?"

"That'd be nice."

We walked into the living area, which opened to a breakfast bar and a tiny kitchen. I had a pot of coffee on already, so I pulled down two mugs. "Cream and sugar?"

"Yes, ma'am," he said and sat down at the breakfast bar.

"Won't you get in trouble for mixing with a murder suspect?" I asked as I poured the coffee and placed it in front of him. I pushed the creamer and sugar dishes toward him and handed him a spoon.

"Well, I might," he said. He slowly added cream and two teaspoons of sugar and stirred the coffee. Then he looked me in the eye. "But I wanted you to know that my office hasn't stopped looking into your case. The prosecution went forward way too fast. They were getting some political pressure and rushed to judgment, but I'm not convinced of your guilt."

"Wow, thank you," I said.

"That said, I'll do my duty should you be convicted."

"I understand," I said, my heart warming for the first time in weeks. I hadn't realized how much the suspicion had weighed on me. "Thank you. It means something to know I'm not alone in looking for Laura's killer."

"See, now that's the main reason I bring this up. I've been thinking about you talking to the yoga ladies and doing some investigation on your own. I want to stress my point that you don't need to do that. People are looking out for you. I know you've been through a lot lately—"

"You think?"

"—but for your safety and that of your family, I think it's best you let me do my job."

"You see, I can't," I said seriously. "Not if it means I end up in prison for a crime I didn't commit."

He put down his coffee. "I'm afraid if you don't let this investigation of yours go, you might end up a lot worse than in prison." He stood. "I don't want to see you get hurt."

"I'll be careful."

He frowned at me. "Seriously, Taylor, you're vulnerable doing this on your own. Let me do the looking. You have to trust someone. I'm hoping that it's me."

"But I did trust you and ended up with a million dollars in bail that my aunt leveraged her vineyard for. I can't have her lose the vineyard."

He reached down and tilted my face up to his. His eyes held the heat of attraction, and I was shocked into stillness. My brain froze. Was he going to kiss me? Did I want him to?

"Trust me," he said after what seemed like forever. "I care." He put on his hat and walked out. Millie barked and ran around my legs. I stood there for a long time, trying to figure out what it all meant. It was crazy—I was attracted to the strong, handsome sheriff, but I also liked Patrick, my lawyer. My feelings were as tangled as my life. If I had had the chance, would I have kissed the sheriff? I didn't know. Maybe. What a mess.

I knew one thing for sure—I wouldn't let anything deter me from my mission to prove my innocence.

Chapter 26

Later that afternoon, I went to settle my account with the bank and get the money out of the house. I found a parking spot a block and a half away and parked Aunt Jemma's car. I'd tried to listen to the sheriff's warning and decided that I'd leave the van parked at the winery. It was easy to identify as my car and perhaps seeing someone was here would deter any other would-be puppynappers or kittynappers.

The cat was not as happy with Millie's return as the rest of us were. At least, she acted put out, but I suspected she was secretly happy to have the little ball of energy back in the house.

As I exited the bank, money safely deposited, I glanced down the opposite side of the road and noticed Amy walking down the street. Lawyer's orders or not, I had so many questions that I simply had to have answered. I crossed the street and followed her. She went a block down the street and through an alley to a small 1920s bungalow. There was a car parked outside, and I was surprised to see Dan get out.

He kissed her quick as she unlocked the door, and they both went inside. This was a new development. I ducked behind a building, hoping they wouldn't see me. I noticed that Dan closed the curtains on the front windows.

I phoned Holly.

"Hello?"

"Holly," I whispered, "it's Taylor."

"Taylor, why are you whispering?"

"I followed Amy," I whispered.

"Oh! What's going on?"

"I saw her kiss Dan and go into a house with him."

"*What?*"

I flinched at her volume and glanced around. The streets were quiet, but I wasn't sure if our voices would carry to the house. No one seemed to have overheard. My heart was beating fast.

"Are they having an affair?"

"Well, it sure looked like it," I said. I took a picture of the house with the address. "I'm sending you a picture of the house. Can you run a Google check to see who owns it?"

"This would be a strong motive to get rid of Laura," Holly said, her tone excited as I sent her the picture.

"I know. One or both could've been involved."

"I'll see what I can find out. You go get Sheriff Hennessey."

"Do you think he'll come?"

"Hopefully."

"Maybe I should confront them first and see what they have to say."

"Not alone," Holly said. "Hold on. I see where you are. I can be there in a few minutes."

"Hurry," I said. "I don't want them to see me when they come out."

"If they do, then it's too quick for them to be having an affair."

I felt my excitement flow away. They could simply be looking at new houses for Dan or places of business for him. I checked Zillow and saw that the property was up for sale or rent. It was zoned residential and commercial, so they could technically be there to see about renting the property. Except they hadn't come outside yet.

"Holly, over here," I said in a stage whisper as my friend came walking down the alleyway.

"You saw them go into the house?" Holly asked as we both peered around the corner of the building to study the two cars parked outside.

"Yes, and they kissed before they went inside."

"Was it a passionate kiss or a hello kiss?" Holly asked.

I struggled to remember. "I think it was a hello kiss."

"Hmmm," Holly said. We continued peering around the corner, but there was no movement.

"Amy's not in real estate," I pointed out. "If they were looking to buy, wouldn't they have a realtor with them? They had a key."

"Maybe they already own it," Holly said. "I think we should go ring the doorbell."

"What? No."

"I'm doing it."

"Holly, wait!" But she was already striding up the sidewalk toward the house. I hid on the other side of the building, mortified. I peered around to see Holly go up on the porch and ring the doorbell. What would she say? How would she explain? Didn't she remember that Amy knew who she was?

I hid and waited for what seemed like forever but was merely five minutes. I looked again. Holly said good-bye to someone with a wave and moved down the porch steps.

Dying of curiosity, I hopped from one foot to the other. Finally, Holly came around the corner. "What happened?" I asked. "Did Amy remember you? What did you say to them? Is there motive there?"

Holly put her arm through mine and walked me toward Main Street. "Amy answered. I pretended to be surprised to see her. I told her I was interested in the property and wanted to know if I could tour it."

"And?"

"And Mr. and Mrs. Scott told me they were waiting for the inspector to do the final inspection before they signed for the property today."

"Amy recognized you and wasn't upset by it?" I said. "Wait—*Mr. and Mrs. Scott?*"

"It seems that Dan and Amy got married two nights ago in Las Vegas. She was quite happy to show me the ring."

"That's, what, a week or two after Laura's death? She's barely in the ground. I find that highly suspicious."

"I agree," Holly said and walked with me to the police station. "But I don't think it proves anything."

"Except they were most likely having an affair, and Laura may have found out the day she was murdered. We have to tell the sheriff."

"Good thing we're close to the station," Holly said, and we walked inside.

"Sheriff Hennessey, please," I said to the receptionist.

We waited a half an hour for the sheriff to come out and see us. "Ladies, what brings you down here?"

"Can we talk in your office?" I asked.

"Certainly," he said and opened the door to the back room. "Do you want your lawyer present?"

"It's not about me," I said as we walked to his office and stepped inside. He bustled passed us and sat down behind his big desk.

"Taylor, what's up?" He crossed his arms on the top of his desk, which was covered with paper work in various stages of completion.

"Did you know that Dan Scott married Amy Hampton?"

"No, but what does that bit of gossip have to do with anything?"

"Don't you find it suspicious that they married so quickly after Laura's death?" Holly asked.

"Look"—he wiped his hand across his face—"I know you're desperate to find a guilty party, and this does seem a little shady. That said, lots of guys get married soon after a spouse dies. It can be part of the grieving process. Especially if they're close to the woman they marry. Amy worked for Dan for three years."

"And that's not suspicious?" Holly said. "I thought whenever a person died the spouse was the first on the list of suspects."

"Without further proof, there's little I can do."

"How do we get proof?"

"Someone has to confess," he said, "and no one does that willingly."

"But—"

"Good day, ladies."

"Still," Holly said as we stood. "Isn't it more likely he and Amy were having an affair and killed Laura than Taylor getting mad and killing her? I mean, both Taylor and Dan were covered in Laura's blood."

"Listen, it's not that I don't want to help. It's that the system works the way it does for a reason. I need you to trust me and the system."

That was hard to do when the system saw you as a criminal.

Chapter 27

"Dan and Amy marrying seems so crass," Aunt Jemma said. "Why wouldn't they wait?"

It was the morning Ivy's funeral, and Aunt Jemma, Holly, and I sat outside on the patio drinking coffee and discussing everything we had learned.

"Sheriff Hennessey says it could be part of the grieving process," I said and lifted my face to the warmth of the morning sun. "He also said the only way to drop the charges at this point is to get the real killer to confess. I don't understand how I'm supposed to do that. It seems to me that Dan and Amy are happy, the yoga ladies are busy with their new business obligations, and no one cares that I'm going down for a crime I didn't commit."

"All secrets come out in the end," Aunt Jemma tried to reassure me.

"That's no help," I said.

"I know it sounds like a platitude," Aunt Jemma said and daintily picked a donut up from the tray of pastries on the patio picnic table. "But it is usually a true statement."

"It's hard to keep a secret," Holly agreed from her seat on the other side of the table. "There are three of them. If we can get one to crack, then it'll bring down the entire plot."

"What if it wasn't them?" I fretted. "What if it was Dan?"

"I know, but we can point the finger at Amy, and if Dan did it, he might crack," Holly said.

"And if Amy did it?" I asked.

"Then point the finger at Dan," Aunt Jemma suggested.

"Sounds like we'd need a crazy amount of luck," I said with a sigh. "Maybe Sheriff Hennessey is right. Maybe we should let the system prove my innocence and go from there."

"That's nuts," Aunt Jemma said. "It will all but squash your business. And it might be helping the winery right now, but it could hurt us in the long run."

"What do you mean 'helping the winery'?"

"We've seen a twenty percent increase in people tasting and buying. They're all coming out to see the woman accused of murder."

"People are morbid," I said and sipped my coffee.

"Once this is over, you could do murder tours," Aunt Jemma said. "There's plenty of dark history in Sonoma County."

I rolled my eyes. "No."

"It's still a good idea." Aunt Jemma and Holly nodded at each other. "But back on the subject of murder, who do you think did it?"

I frowned. "It could be anyone. The thing is, I think Dan is the least suspicious since Ivy was murdered. His actions seemed to say that he truly loved his sister. You should have seen his anger and grief when he learned she was dead."

"Hmm, the yoga teachers might be easiest to crack since there are three of them," Holly said.

"We need a plan," I said.

"We'll work on that," Aunt Jemma said. "In the meantime, are you sure you want to attend Ivy's funeral?"

"I feel like it's the right thing to do," I said and stood.

Holly and I were dressed in simple black dresses. Ivy's funeral was in an hour, and we were heading out.

"I'm curious to hear who shows up," Aunt Jemma said as she gathered up the tray and walked with us back into the house. "Maybe the killer . . ."

"I'll take notes," I said and put my coffee cup in the sink. Holly followed suit.

"You girls try not to make a scene."

"I realize it will be a bit awkward," I said, "but if we show up and are respectful, it should be fine."

"You can't simply 'show up' places anymore," Aunt Jemma said. "You are a bit of a celebrity, you know. People are coming up from San Francisco to see you."

"Listen, I can't control what others do," I said. "I'm innocent, and I'm going to pay my respects."

"Yes, we know you are innocent," Aunt Jemma said. "But if an innocent person can be on trial for murder, that means that anyone can find themselves in that situation at any time. It's like waiting for a train wreck or seeing an accident at the side of the road. Everyone wants to know what really happened."

"Maybe I should start telling them," I said, half in jest. "I should give Chelsea an exclusive and see if that'll draw the real killer out."

"You can't cast accusations without proof," Aunt Jemma said.

"I know, I know," I said. "It's a recurring theme in my life, but that said, I *can* tell everyone what happened from my point of view. Let them think what they want. If I get my story out there, then perhaps the jury will be a little more willing to hear me during the trial. If it goes that far. I'm calling Chelsea after the funeral."

"Call Patrick as well," Aunt Jemma advised. "You don't want to make things worse by trying to make them better."

"I don't see how anything could get worse."

*   *   *

Ivy's funeral was small. We entered the funeral home, and there weren't a lot of people there. Amy was there with Dan. The preacher had already started the service by the time Dan spotted me. His gaze shot daggers at me, and I wiggled uncomfortably.

"Oh, he's upset you're here," Holly whispered.

"I figured he might be, but I needed to pay my respects," I said. "Let's be as quiet and respectful as possible."

"Okay," Holly said, "but I'm taking notes on who else shows up."

It was hard to sneak out of a funeral. Dan and Amy were the first to follow the casket out. There were maybe ten other people there. Rashida, Juliet, and Emma were present, along with Sally. They all looked at me with various amounts of horror or interest.

Holly got up to leave, and I held her down. "Let's wait until they all go to the cemetery."

"Oh, good idea," Holly said. "Did you notice the grief and anger on Dan's face?"

"I did," I said. "Amy's attention was all for Dan."

"I didn't expect the yoga teachers to come."

"Well, we know they knew Ivy pretty well. If what Dawn said was right, they were working with Ivy."

"All three looked pretty torn up," Holly observed.

"Sally was the only one not crying," I pointed out. "Do you think that's suspicious?"

"No, she's in human resources. She's probably seen everything," Holly said.

"Excuse me, ladies, but everyone is leaving for the burial," the funeral home attendant informed us.

"That's our cue to leave," I said, and we got up. Upsetting anyone further was the last thing I intended.

We stepped out into the sunshine and watched as the cars pulled away.

"Well, that was interesting," Holly said. "I'm bummed we didn't learn anything new."

"We learned that everyone was closer to Ivy than we thought," I pointed out. "I wonder why she wasn't in business with her brother. Or at the very least, invited to the retreat."

"You told me that she and Laura didn't get along. Remember?"

"Right," I said, "that's when we thought Ivy might have killed Laura."

"And now Ivy's dead."

"Pretty convenient, don't you think?"

"Only if the killer was trying to cover their tracks," Holly said.

"So there's still a chance that we can find out who really killed Laura," I concluded. "I'm calling Patrick to let him know I'm going to talk to Chelsea. I'm hoping that by sharing my story with the press, someone else who knows something will come forward."

"Good luck with that," Holly said and hugged me. "I'm leaving to prep for a gallery showing tonight."

"Take care," I said. "I've got a tasting for Aunt Jemma. It seems she was right. People are coming down to catch a glimpse of the murder suspect."

Holly rolled her eyes. "Don't let them get you down."

"I'll do my best." Watching the procession leave, I realized it bugged me to not see the whole picture. Maybe, if I was careful, I could watch the rest of the funeral from a distance . . . I smiled and got in my car.

*   *   *

Patrick did not get back to me so I went ahead and called Chelsea.

"I have a better idea," Chelsea said on the phone after I explained everything. "Let's do a stakeout and follow the new Mrs. Scott for a while."

"I don't want to get into more trouble," I said.

"There won't be trouble. You will be with me. I'll be your alibi."

"I don't know . . ."

"What can it hurt? I'll pick you up, and you can sit in the car with me and tell me your story. If we happen to run into Amy Scott, then we run into her."

"But we'll be sitting outside her new home."

"Actually, her place of business," Chelsea said. "They bought the house to start the brain wave–training business out of."

"Fine." I didn't really care about their business. "We'll talk about Amy outside her new place of business. What if she sees us?"

"Then we ask her how things are and leave," Chelsea said. "Trust me. She won't be looking for us."

"Fine," I said.

"Good," she replied. "Wear black in case we need to follow someone on foot."

*   *   *

"So you went to the bank, came out, and saw Amy walking this way," Chelsea said as we sat in her car.

"Yes," I said. "I wanted to ask her some questions, so I followed her, but then I saw her meet Dan. She kissed him, and they went inside the building."

"Then what happened?" Chelsea faced me and took notes. I faced the house and tried to keep an eye out for Amy or Dan.

"I called Holly. I mean, what if they were having an affair this whole time? Wouldn't that be motive for murder?"

"Sounds like motive to me," Chelsea said. "Suspicious, anyway. What did Holly say?"

"She came right down and knocked on the door on the pretense of wanting to rent the building. She spoke to Amy and learned that she and Dan were newlyweds and that they had first dibs on the property."

"Wow, and now we're sitting outside the house on a stakeout."

"Yes," I said. "Despite my better judgment."

"It'll be fine," Chelsea said. "I brought donuts."

"Right."

We sat and chatted about nothing as time passed. The sun went down, and I felt as if we were wasting time.

"What if they don't come out?" I said.

"We'll spend the night in the car," Chelsea said, unfazed by the prospect. "We'll follow Amy around during the day and see what she's up to."

"What if it's nothing?"

"Then we'll give her a few days," Chelsea said. "She has to slip up sometime."

"I don't think she will," I said. "My case is going to trial. She's married Dan. All is well as far as she's concerned."

"Wait. Is that her?" Chelsea said.

I watched as a woman came out of the back of the new house. It was dark, so I couldn't be sure if it was Amy or not.

"Duck," Chelsea said, and we both scooted down to avoid being seen. My heart beat fast as I listened to footsteps on the sidewalk. They came closer and closer, then passed by without pausing. We both sat up and looked to see the woman turn down the street.

"Do we follow in the car or walk?"

"Car," Chelsea said and started the engine. She wheeled us in a fast U-turn, then drove down the street to see the woman cross the next street. We stopped at the stop sign and watched as she continued down the street and turned right. Strange, but it looked like she was carrying a shovel and something else . . . a tote bag with something in it? It was hard to tell at this distance.

"I'll go up the next block and then turn onto that street," Chelsea said. We got to the street to find that the woman was walking into the cemetery where Ivy and Laura were buried. "That's interesting," Chelsea said, found the closest parking space, and parked. "Come on."

We got out of the car and crossed the street, following the figure ahead of us.

"She's going to Ivy's grave," I said.

"How do you know?"

"I went to the funeral," I said. "I stayed back out of respect for Dan, but I wanted to see who all showed up."

"Who showed up?"

"Dan and Amy, of course."

"Of course."

"Emma, Rashida, Juliet, and Sally from the yoga company. Then a few men I didn't know—I assumed they were Dan's family."

"Did Ivy have a boyfriend?"

"I don't have any idea. For all I know, she didn't have any friends except for her best friend, Dawn, who was charged with identity theft. There was some talk that she was the one who killed Ivy, so she wasn't there."

"Sad not to go to your best friend's funeral."

"I agree," I said softly. "Anyway, Dan was really upset I went to the funeral, so Holly and I left after everyone. I intended to go home, but decided to see if Dawn showed up at the burial."

"Did she?"

"No," I said. "So I left. But it's how I know we're heading for Ivy's funeral plot."

We walked through the dark toward the spot where Ivy was buried. The ground was still freshly disturbed. They had rolled sod on top to help it blend in, but there was still a bit of a mound from where the casket was lowered.

We stopped, and I grabbed Chelsea's arm. The woman was digging in Ivy's grave.

"Get out your cell phone and record this," Chelsea said. She took out her phone, turned on the camera, and motioned for me to go to the opposite side and get some video. I walked as silently as possible. I didn't need to. The woman was busy digging. She had moved a swatch of sod from the top of Ivy's grave and dug a small hole about two feet deep. I videoed her placing something wrapped in a pillowcase inside the hole and covering it with dirt. She replaced the sod and stomped on it.

Chelsea sneezed, and I caught the woman's face as she looked around. It was Amy.

"Who's there?" Amy called.

I kept quiet and hid my phone light but kept the video recording.

"Hello?"

"Hello," I heard Chelsea say as she walked out into the light outside the grave site. "I'm sorry. I didn't mean to startle you. I'm Chelsea McGartland."

"You're that reporter."

"Yes," she said. "I was visiting Laura's grave, and I noticed she had fresh flowers. Then I came over to see Ivy and saw you standing there by the grave. I see you have a shovel. Are you planting flowers?"

Nice save, I thought.

"No," Amy said. "I . . . I found the shovel. One of the workers must have left it. I was missing Ivy and came to talk to her," Amy said.

"Oh, so you knew Ivy well?"

"She was my husband's sister," Amy said. "I worked with her for three years before she moved onto other business ventures."

"Your husband is Ivy's brother? Dan?"

"Yes," she said. "We're newlyweds."

"Didn't his first wife die recently?"

"Laura was found murdered," she said. "I know it seems fast, but Dan and I have been in love for years. We didn't do anything about it because he was married."

"Why didn't he get a divorce?"

"Laura had terminal cancer," she said. "He couldn't abandon her in her time of need."

"But I thought she was building a yoga empire."

"Teaching others how to improve their business was Laura's passion. She wanted to do as much as she could as long as she could. Dan and I supported her. We knew our love would last, so we waited patiently."

"Did Laura know about you?"

"I don't think so," Amy said. "I'd like to think she felt loved up until the end."

"Don't you think that your love for Dan might be a motive to murder Laura?"

"Why? She was already dying. All we had to do was wait. He was caring for her. She knew she was terminal. They tried several doctors, but the prognosis was the same. So she set about eating well, meditating, and doing her yoga."

"I'm sorry for your loss."

"Ivy was as big a loss for Dan as Laura," Amy said. "Bigger because it was unexpected."

"I heard they had a fight the day Ivy was killed."

"Who?" Amy asked, suddenly looking guilty.

"Dan and Ivy," Chelsea said. This surprised me. I hadn't heard anything about Dan and Ivy fighting. "I've got an eye-witness who tells me that they were overheard fighting before Dan stormed out. Do you know what the fight was about?"

"I don't know anything about a fight," Amy said, her face darkening with fear.

"Neither did I," I said as I approached.

"What are you doing here?" Amy screeched. "Are you two together? Did you bring this woman here?"

"I'm sorry for your loss," I said. "What were you burying with Ivy?"

"I wasn't burying anything. Why are you here? Don't you know that Dan doesn't want you near his family?"

"I didn't kill Laura, and you know I didn't kill Ivy," I said. "Let's see what you buried."

"Get the police out here," Chelsea advised.

"No!" Amy said and threw herself on the ground as if to cover what she'd buried with her body.

I nodded at Chelsea, who dialed 9-1-1. "I recorded you with my phone. Chelsea is calling the police. What did you bury, Amy?"

"It's nothing," Amy said. "Go away."

"I'm not going anywhere, and neither is Chelsea. You might as well tell us what's going on."

"There's nothing going on," Amy said. "I wanted Ivy to have something. The ground wasn't settled yet. I don't know why you have to dig it up."

"I'm not digging it up—you are."

"I refuse." She crossed her arms.

We waited uncomfortably in the cemetery, Amy refusing to speak, until the authorities arrived.

"What's going on?" Sheriff Hennessey asked as he walked up the drive. "We got a phone call about suspicious activity."

"We found Amy burying something in Ivy's grave," Chelsea said.

"Taylor, what are you doing here?" he asked.

"Chelsea and I were talking. We saw Amy coming this way so we followed her."

"That's stalking!" Amy pointed a finger at me.

"It's not stalking," Chelsea said. "It's a public cemetery."

"We caught her burying something," I said and showed him my phone. He took it and watched the video.

"It's not a crime to bury something, is it?" Amy said. "It's a memento for Ivy."

"Let's see what you buried," the sheriff said. "Then we'll talk to the cemetery keeper and see if it's okay to bury it or not."

"I'd rather not," Amy said and held her expression firm.

The sheriff pushed his hat back so that his full face was showing. "What you'd prefer is not my concern here," he said. "Let's take a moment and see what you buried."

"No."

"I'll get a crew of forensic specialists to come out. Do you really want to make me do that?"

"If you can justify the expense, then go for it." Amy was quite stubborn.

"Fine." He made a quick call to his dispatcher.

"I'm not sticking around for this ridiculousness." Amy started to walk away.

"Oh, no," the sheriff said. "You aren't going anywhere until we get this figured out."

"I'm calling my husband and my lawyer," Amy said.

"You're free to do that," he said as another police vehicle appeared. Two deputies got out and came over. Chelsea took pictures with her phone.

"This is great for my story."

"What if she was burying a memento like she said?" I whispered to Chelsea. "Then you don't have a story, and we both look stupid."

"We'll cross that bridge when we come to it."

Dan showed up next and rushed to Amy's side and hugged her. They locked hands and he scowled at me. "Why is it you're always messing up my life?"

"I didn't do anything," I said.

"You followed my wife. You called the sheriff. What is wrong with you?"

"She wouldn't tell us what she buried," I pointed out. "So this mess is her fault."

He turned toward Amy. "What did you bury?"

"Don't answer," an older man in his midfifties said. He was portly and walked up wearing jeans and a dress shirt. His gray hair stood up on one side as if he'd been in bed and hastily dressed.

"Who are you?"

"I'm Eric Jones, attorney at law. Amy and Dan hired me."

"I didn't do anything," Amy said. "I want to go home."

"I have her on tape burying something in Ivy's grave," I said.

"Where is this video?"

"The sheriff took my phone," I said and put my hands in my pockets.

"Burying something is not a crime," Eric said. He turned on his heel and went to where the police were gathered. The crime investigator showed up in his van and brought out a shovel. Before he started, he took Amy's shovel and bagged it. Then he bagged my phone.

They brought in two big lights and illuminated the grave site. After studying my video, the CSI guy rolled up the sod and stuck in the shovel. Two shovels of dirt later, we all heard a clink.

"I'm sorry," Amy said and turned to Dan.

"Don't say another word," Eric advised as the crime scene guy dug with his hands and pulled up a pillowcase with something metal inside.

"We have a gun," he said.

"I'm going to have to take you to the station," Sheriff Hennessey told Amy. He turned her around and cuffed her hands.

"Don't say anything," the attorney advised.

"Amy?" Dan looked surprised.

"It's a 9mm," the investigator guy said. "The same type of gun that killed Ivy."

"I tried to get rid of it," Amy said. "I tried to save you."

"What?" Dan looked confused.

"I think you should both come down to the station with me," Sheriff Hennessey said.

"I don't understand." Dan looked confused.

"Don't say another word," the attorney said.

"I'm sorry, Dan," Amy said. "I found the gun, and I thought I could save us both and bury it with Ivy. It needed to go away."

"What gun? I don't own a gun," Dan said.

"You didn't kill Laura and your sister?" Amy asked.

"How could you think that?" Dan asked her, astonished.

"Let's take everybody down to the station," the sheriff said.

"Wait. Everyone?" I asked.

"Yes, everyone," Sheriff Hennessey said, "including you and Chelsea."

"Man," I said as he escorted me to the back seat of his car. Two deputies took Amy and Dan. Chelsea was able to take her car. "Why can't I drive with Chelsea?" I asked as the sheriff got into the front seat.

"Because you're under investigation for Laura's murder," he said. "You were present when a key piece of evidence was found. Under an abundance of caution, I'm taking you to the station." He started the car and backed away. "It's for the best. We're going to check your fingers for dirt and prove you didn't have anything to do with the gun."

"I didn't," I said.

"It's standard—"

"I know, I know, standard procedure." I was not liking the fact that I was getting used to being suspect number one.

Chapter 28

Three hours later, Sheriff Hennessey finally walked into the little interrogation room where he had put me. "How are you doing? Do you need any coffee or water?"

"I'd like to go home," I said. It was strange being alone with him again after the last time. Neither of us mentioned the strange heat that had passed between us.

"I understand," he said and handed me my phone. "Our experts in digital forensics downloaded the video, so you can have this back."

"Thanks."

He took a seat across from me. "Let's talk about the day you found Ivy's body."

"Okay," I said cautiously. "Do I need my lawyer?"

"I'm sure he'll advise you not to say anything." Sheriff Hennessey sighed. "It sounds like a chorus to me right now."

"They're doing their jobs," I said.

"And I'm trying to do mine. What you did today, staking out Amy and following her to the cemetery, was ill advised."

I shrugged. "I was indulging Chelsea. I didn't really think anything would happen."

"Well, because of you and Chelsea, we caught a break in Ivy Scott's murder. So thank you."

I drew my eyebrows together in confusion. "You're welcome?"

"Tell me about the day you went to see Ivy. Why did you go to her house?"

"I thought maybe she knew something about who had killed Laura."

"Why did you think that?"

"She was part of the identity-theft gang. She was seen at Quarryhill the day Laura was killed, and Laura had that SD chip on her with everyone's identity information. I thought maybe someone in the group was working with Ivy, and Laura had caught them in the act of handing over secure information . . . Did you know that Laura had cancer and was terminal?"

"Her autopsy report showed that," he admitted.

"I suppose that'll come out at the trial."

"Only if it's relevant," he said. "Now tell me about the day you went to see Ivy. Did you see anyone on the street?"

"No." I shook my head. "We've been over this. I didn't see anyone. The front door was open, but the screen door was closed. No one answered when I knocked, so I went around the back to see if Ivy was working in her garden."

"And entered the house through the back door."

"Yes," I said. "The back door was also open, and this one didn't have a screen. When I saw that Ivy wasn't in the back, I became worried that something was wrong and went inside. I saw her almost immediately and called nine-one-one."

"And then you exited the house through the front."

"Yes," I said.

"Did you see a gun?"

"No." I shook my head. "I didn't see any weapon. I only saw Ivy lying in blood. I touched her shoulder. When I realized she felt cold, I called."

"Why did you leave the house?"

"I thought that the killer might still be inside, so I went outside where the neighbors could see me."

"Except you didn't see any neighbors."

"No, I didn't," I said and sighed. "I didn't see anyone, but it still felt safer on the porch."

"How long were you there before the first responders showed up?"

"I don't know," I replied. "I didn't think to time them. I'm sure you have record of my call and when the first responders got there."

"It was ten minutes," he said casually. "You saw Dan shortly thereafter."

"Yes," I said. "The first responders weren't there long before Dan showed up. He got out of his car and threatened me."

"Did you call him?"

"Me? No, why would I call him?"

"You'd found his sister dead."

"I thought it was your job to call him. No one called him? He just showed up?"

"Yes, it appears that way," Sheriff Hennessey said.

"Do you think Dan killed Ivy?" I hugged myself. "That would mean that Dan and Ivy probably killed Laura." I drew my eyebrows together. "But why would they when they both knew she was dying anyway?"

"We have no evidence that the two murders were linked," he said.

"But the SD card and the identity-theft ring link them."

"Circumstantially."

"Which is what your entire case against me is—circumstantial."

"Let's talk about Ivy's death," he said. "Did you see Amy there?"

"No, I didn't."

"But you saw Dan."

"Yes, I saw him show up a few minutes later. Tell me about the gun," I said. "Is it the gun that killed Ivy?"

"Yes," he said. "A simple ballistics test proved it. They found two sets of prints on it—one is Dan's and one is Ivy's. Dan has confessed to killing his sister."

"What? How terrible."

"I think he's covering for someone."

"Why?"

"Because Amy also confessed to killing Ivy," he said. "Their stories don't jive, so I think they're covering for each other."

"You mean Amy thinks Dan did it and is covering for him, but Dan thinks Amy did it and is covering for her?"

"Yes," he said. "I have two people who have confessed to the same crime. I'm pretty certain that Amy is lying because she can't tell me where Ivy was shot. Dan knows where Ivy was shot—"

"In the back," I said.

"Yes," he said, "but Dan can't tell me why he shot his sister."

"So you're going to let them both go?"

"I'm going to hold them both while we go over the evidence with a fine-tooth comb," he said. "I was hoping you could shed some light on that day, but it sounds like you didn't see anything."

"I didn't," I said.

"It's amazing how we can miss things when we're shocked by an accident or death," he said. "Don't worry. I'm going to let you and Chelsea go. I suggest that you go home and leave the rest to me and my team."

"You keep saying that."

"You keep ignoring that," he pointed out, stood, and opened the door for me.

Chelsea was waiting for me in the lobby along with Aunt Jemma.

"Well, that was an adventure," Chelsea said as we walked out.

"What were you girls thinking?" Aunt Jemma asked. "Amy could've used that gun on you."

"She didn't," I said and walked Chelsea to her car.

"She confessed," Chelsea said.

"So did Dan," I pointed out. "I think they're trying to save each other."

"A credible source told me that Dan and Ivy had an argument the day she was killed," Chelsea said.

"I heard you tell Amy that. What were they arguing about? Do you know?" I asked. "Was it about the identity-theft ring?"

"Or Amy," Chelsea said. "I bet it was quite the surprise when those two got married so quickly."

"Was Ivy protective of her brother?" Aunt Jemma asked.

"Yes!" Chelsea and I said at the same time and laughed.

"She threatened me to an inch of my life when she thought I killed Laura," I said.

"I bet she was not happy when she discovered that Amy married Dan," Chelsea said. "My source told me there were witnesses to the argument. I'm going to call on them tomorrow morning and see what they can tell me."

"I want to come," I said.

"No," Aunt Jemma said. "Enough is enough. You must stay out of the investigation and let Chelsea see what she can drum up."

"I understand they found both Amy's and Dan's fingerprints on the gun," Chelsea said, "so that didn't help them determine who was lying."

"What about DNA?" I asked.

"I'm sure the police are already on any kind of lead like that," Aunt Jemma said. "For now, let's go home. It's nearly three AM. Chelsea, follow me. You can spend the night in the guest room. I'm not sending you back to North San Francisco at this time of night."

"Thank you," Chelsea said. "That'll help me get an early start on finding and interviewing witnesses tomorrow. I'm going to get to the bottom of this."

We arrived at the winery to find Clemmie waiting for us at the door. She wound between my legs and rushed into the house as Aunt Jemma opened the door.

"What a night," I said.

"A real adventure," Chelsea said as she followed me inside. Aunt Jemma turned on the lights as I let Millie out of her kennel.

"Do you really suppose that Dan thinks Amy did it, Amy thinks Dan did it, and they are covering for each other? That would be real love," I said as I picked up Millie and gave her a hug. "Imagine going to prison in the place of the person you love."

"What I think is that Ivy knew who killed Laura and was killed for her knowledge," Chelsea said.

"Seriously?" I asked. "If she knew, then why would she accuse me? I mean, she practically attacked me."

"Maybe she only recently discovered who did it," Aunt Jemma said. "That would explain getting shot in the back. She might've been trying to get to the phone to call the police."

"That would mean she knew the killer," I said. "So it might have been Dan or Amy."

"I'd bet on Amy," Aunt Jemma said. "After all, Dan was with you at the end of the hike."

"But he also set out alone to help you find her and in the end had Laura's blood on his hands. He might have found her, killed her, then hurried up the trail so that when you found her, he could hurry down and ensure you saw him touch her."

"But," I pointed out, "he knew she was dying of cancer. Why murder her?"

"I thought Amy would be his motive," Chelsea agreed, "but it seems like he would simply wait out her disease."

"Well," Aunt Jemma said, "that's enough speculation for one night. Let's get some sleep. Things might be clearer in the morning. Good night, girls."

"Good night, Aunt Jemma," I said. "Thanks for coming down to the police station to check on me."

"Your aunt is great," Chelsea said. "My family is a little nuts."

"So are we. We just hide it better." I showed her the guest room and gave her fresh towels, a new toothbrush, and spare toiletries.

"I hope you don't mind the cat," I said as Clemmie scooted into the room and sauntered toward the bed. "She likes to sleep in here whenever possible."

"I love cats," Chelsea said and ran her hand over the kitty. "We'll keep each other company, won't we?"

"Her name is Clemmie—short for Clementine."

"It's a pleasure to meet you," Chelsea said to the cat, and then she looked up at me. "Good night."

I closed the door to the room behind me and called Millie to follow me to the pool house. Millie helped me feel safer in the small apartment. It was mere yards from the main house, but ever since the picture window had been shattered, I hadn't been comfortable sleeping alone.

* * *

I was up by ten AM the next morning. Millie licked my face and nudged me out of bed to feed her and ensure she went outside to do her business—after all, we were still potty training. By the time I got dressed and had a cup of coffee, I saw that Chelsea's car was gone. I sat outside on the patio and listened to the men start to work on the vines.

Holly had texted me, "Did you catch Ivy's killer?"

I texted her back, "Both Dan and Amy confessed. The sheriff thinks they are both lying."

"Then who?"

"I don't know," I texted, "but I've been banned from trying to find out."

"What will you do today?"

"I'm going to meet with Emma to see if she'll volunteer to come out to the winery for Wine Down Wednesdays."

"I thought none of those ladies were talking to you."

"I e-mailed her yesterday and got her to agree to meet me outside the studio," I wrote. "She needs the money. Her son started soccer."

"Expensive sport."

I laughed and texted, "Only if you want to give them private lessons. Emma is competitive. If her son is going to do soccer, then he's going to be the best of all the soccer players."

"How old is he?"

"Four," I texted. "Got to start early if you're training for the pros."

"Poor kid."

"I know."

"Why don't you stop by for lunch?"

"Okay." We finished up the details, and I got dressed and went into town. Emma had agreed to meet me at the coffee shop closest to the yoga studio.

"Hi," I said as I walked in. I gave her a quick hug and ordered a chai latte. "Thanks for meeting me. I'm sorry it's been a while since we last spoke."

"I was surprised to see you at Ivy's funeral," Emma said. "Are you still investigating things?"

"No, I was paying my respects. I found her and wanted closure."

"I get that," Emma said.

"How are you?" I asked.

"Going crazy," Emma said. "With Laura gone, I've inherited a third of her client list. It keeps me busy. I had no idea how much she and Dan did for us."

"Is coaching difficult?"

"Not difficult, but time consuming." Emma sipped her tea.

"Oh, does that mean you can't commit to doing a Wednesday evening yoga class? My aunt and I were thinking about having a six PM class outside on the winery grounds and then finishing with light refreshments. We think it could be a way to get people out to the winery and to enjoy the fresh air."

"What is the time commitment?" she asked.

"An hour a week from, say, May through September?" I said. "If you can't make a day, you could send a substitute. We'd pay a hundred dollars for that hour, plus snacks and wine if you want them."

"Let's see, a hundred a week for twenty-six weeks . . ." She did the math in her head. "Yes." She nodded. "That sounds fair."

"Fabulous," I said. "I'll have a contract written up."

"Sounds good to me." She sipped her beverage. "I want you to know that I don't believe you killed Laura."

"Thank you," I said. "That means a lot."

"The case seems weak to me. I mean, you barely knew her, unlike the rest of us, who'd worked with her for the last four years."

"Did you know that Laura had cancer?"

"What? No! Was it bad? How could she keep something like that from us?" Emma nearly dropped her drink. Eyes wide, she looked stunned by the news.

"She thought she was in remission," I said. "She didn't want anyone to worry. Amy told me that Laura had just learned it was terminal. Also, I guess Dan and Amy got married."

"Yes, I heard at Ivy's funeral." She shook her head. "I would've never guessed those two would do such an impulsive thing. I suppose I've been busy with my boy, running him to and from school and lessons and playdates, and then trying to pick up the slack on my third of the client list. It was no wonder Laura could be a bit of a bear. She must've been exhausted. I know I am, and I'm healthy." She paused. "As for Dan and Amy? I suppose I can see it now that I think about it. Dan is a nice guy, and Amy was always there to help."

"So you don't find it odd that Laura let them continue their affair while she was dying?"

"Oh, no, I highly doubt Laura knew about Dan and Amy. She would have exploded if she found out."

"Huh," I sipped my drink. "How do you have an affair under someone's nose and keep it secret? Especially if she is a micromanager like Laura."

"My guess is they didn't do anything about their feelings until Laura died," Emma said. "Dan is a man of honor, and Amy liked Laura no matter how mean she was. Wow, the secret must have been tearing Amy apart. I'll have to call her and see how she is."

"I'm afraid that might be impossible," I said. "Amy confessed to killing Dan's sister."

"Why would she do that?" Emma's eyes grew wide.

"She was caught burying the gun that killed Ivy," I said.

"What? No, no I can't believe it."

"I don't think she did it. I suspect she thinks Dan did it and is covering for him."

"Dan killed his sister?"

"He confessed as well," I said, "but I don't think he did it either. He probably thinks Amy did it. They're in love, and each is willing to fall on the sword for the other."

"That's terrible," Emma said, "but if they didn't do it, how'd Amy get the gun?"

"I'm not sure," I said and sipped my drink. "Good question."

"Ah . . . so you don't know," Emma said. "Do you think Laura's killer killed Ivy? I mean, it'd be a strange coincidence that they were both murdered within weeks of each other."

"I don't know that either. I can't figure out who killed Laura or why. I thought perhaps it had something to do with the identity-theft ring."

"You think Laura found out and confronted the killer."

"It sounds like something Laura would do," I said.

"Yes, it does," Emma said and chewed on her bottom lip.

"What I want to know is why the killer used my corkscrew," I said. "I think if I could figure that out, then I might be able to figure out who killed Laura and most likely Ivy. But you see, the police have told me I have to have concrete proof before I float any of my ideas past them again."

"I see."

"Do you?"

"Yes," she said. "You think I know who killed Laura, and I can help you out. But I don't."

"Are you worried that you are on the suspect list?" I asked. "Because I wouldn't be meeting you for coffee if I thought you murdered anyone."

"Well, that's a relief," she said.

"I have one more question."

"Go ahead," she said.

"Who do you think was helping Ivy steal the client list? Is there anyone else who needed extra money?"

"We all needed money, so I highly doubt it was the only factor in Laura's death," Emma said.

"Yes," I said and frowned. "It had to be something more."

"Well, good luck with it. It sounds to me like the only ones with motive were Amy and Dan, but they knew of Laura's illness and didn't need to kill her."

It seemed my investigation was once again stymied.

* * *

"There you are." Chelsea spotted Holly and me at the Taco Heads on the corner of Maple and Pine. We sat outside and were talking about my adventure the night before.

"You look excited," I said as Chelsea pulled up an extra chair and joined us.

"Well, I have news."

"Good or bad?" I asked and eyed my lunch of two fish tacos.

"Interesting," Chelsea said and flagged our waitress down. "Iced tea, please," she ordered before turning back to us. "I filed my report and can now tell you that my source was Ivy's neighbor, Mrs. Hernandez, who heard Dan and Ivy arguing the day Ivy was killed. She saw Ivy slap Dan in front of Ivy's house. Mrs. Hernandez was not close enough to hear what the argument was about." Chelsea read her notes then looked up. "My guess is that Ivy wasn't happy with the wedding."

"Wow, Ivy slapped Dan? Was Amy there?" I asked.

"She was in the car. Mrs. Hernandez told me that she'd stepped outside to get her newspaper when she saw the slap. But she has no idea what led up to it." She checked her notes. "After the slap, Amy got out of the car, pulled Dan away, and begged him to leave. So they did."

"Did any of the neighbors hear the gunshot?" I asked.

"No," Chelsea said. "Mrs. Hernandez left for work. No one else saw or heard anything until the police were there."

"Sounds like Amy thinks Dan shot his sister, and Dan thinks Amy did. But if neither of them did it, how did they get the gun?"

"Neither one of them is saying," Chelsea said.

"But they can't both be guilty," I pointed out. "One or both of them is lying."

"My guess is that Ivy encountered Laura's killer," Holly said. "If we can find out who killed Laura, we will most likely know who killed Ivy."

"What if Ivy killed Laura, and Dan discovered it and killed Ivy?" I said. "Amy could have decided that's what happened and tried to cover for Dan."

"But Dan isn't confessing why he killed Ivy, so we're no closer to solving Laura's murder."

I frowned. "If I didn't do it, and Dan and Amy didn't do it, that leaves Ivy, Emma, Sally, Rashida, and Juliet. I really haven't talked to Sally since that day. Maybe we should go see her."

"They kicked us out of the yoga studio."

"I can follow them like we did Amy and see if I can't find a time to talk to them."

"I don't think that's such a good idea," Holly said. "You can get into big trouble."

"Not if I go with her," Chelsea said.

Holly rolled her eyes. "You two got into trouble last night."

"Then come with us," I said. "You'll see it's mostly waiting in cars for people to go places."

"Fine. When do we start?"

"What are you doing this afternoon?" I asked.

"Getting into trouble, I guess," Holly answered. Chelsea laughed.

"Who are we going to follow first?"

Chapter 29

We decided on Sally. She was working at the yoga studio, so we hung out in two cars—one at the front of the studio and one at the back. Chelsea was in front since fewer people would recognize her. We made a pact to text each other should anything interesting happen.

"You were right," Holly said as she leaned back in her seat. "Stakeouts are dull. We need donuts and coffee."

"There's a coffee shop at the end of the strip. Why don't you go get us some?"

"Me? Why don't you go get the coffee?"

"Fine," I said. "What do you want?" I wrote down her order of a large triple expresso macchiato with a shot of raspberry and cream.

"Oh, and bring a box of those little donuts. You know, the powdered sugar ones?"

"Okay," I said as I got out of the car. "Promise you'll text me the minute you see Sally."

"Will do," Holly said and leaned back into her seat. She had on her sunglasses, and I wasn't sure if she was watching or sleeping. I texted Chelsea to see if wanted anything. She sent me a request for a latte.

The coffee shop was crowded, and it took me longer than I thought to get the food. I walked to where Chelsea sat first and got into her car. "Did you see anything?"

"Class got out," she said and took her latte from the paper holder. "I counted ten people leaving. Does Sally have another class?"

"No, I think Juliet's the next instructor—I saw her go in a few minutes ago on my way to get coffee. But Sally usually stays and cleans up and does paper work.

"Do you really think Sally or Juliet killed Laura and Ivy?"

"I don't see it," I said.

"Sally or Juliet could've picked up Rashida's jacket and used it to shield them from the blood when they killed Laura."

"Do you think they did it together? One could have knocked her down and the other stabbed her."

"That's an interesting theory."

"I'm going to text Holly and let her know I'm coming around the back. Keep me posted if you see Sally leave."

"Will do."

I cut through the cycle shop next to the yoga studio and headed toward Holly's car. I noticed it was empty. "Holly?" I called, looking around. The driver's side door was open. My heart went into my throat, as there appeared to have been a struggle. I looked around. The parking lot was void of people. A few cars remained parked. "Holly!" Nothing. I called Chelsea.

"Hey, what's up?"

"Chelsea, did you see Sally leave the studio?"

"No, why?"

"Holly is missing. It looks like she was forcibly taken from the car."

"*What?* I'll be right there."

"Stay on the phone with me," I said.

"Will do. I'm backing out of my spot now. I need to drive around to the back of the strip mall."

"Hurry."

"I'm hurrying."

"Holly!" I called again and took steps from the car to the bushes that lined the front and side of the parking lot. I saw Chelsea come around the corner in her car. She parked next to me and stepped out.

"Are you okay?"

"Holly's gone," I said with fear in my voice. "It looks like there was a struggle." I pointed to the open door and the spilled bag of chips on the driver's seat.

"That's not good. Call nine-one-one." Chelsea took pictures with her phone as I dialed.

"What's your emergency?"

"I'm in the parking lot behind Divine Yoga, and it looks like my friend has been abducted."

"What is your name, please?"

"Taylor," I said as I looked around in vain. "Taylor O'Brian."

"I'm sending a squad car now. Wait. Are you the suspect in the Laura Scott murder?"

"What does that have to do with my friend's disappearance?"

"You also discovered Ivy Scott's dead body."

I grew impatient. "What does that have to do with now?"

"Is anyone with you?"

"Yes," I said. "Chelsea McGartland is with me. Are you sending help?"

"Help is on its way," she said. "Please stay on the line. Who do you think was abducted?"

"Her name is Holly Petree, and she works at Le Art Galleria."

"And she was taken from the parking lot?"

"I left her in the car when I went to go get coffee, and now she's gone. The door was open, and there were signs of a struggle when I got back." My voice rose in panic.

"Please stay calm. Help is on the way."

I watched as Chelsea took more pictures and video. "What good is a video?" I asked, covering my phone with my hand.

"We might see something later that we can't see now in our panic," she said.

The sound of sirens filled the air.

"I hear the squad car," I said. "They're here."

"Best of luck, Miss O'Brian."

I hung up as Deputy Ferguson stepped out of the car. A junior deputy was with him. I told them both the whole story.

"I see," said Deputy Ferguson. "Did you call her cell phone? Are you sure she didn't step away?"

"She didn't," I said and dialed Holly's cell. "We were on a stakeout."

"A what?"

Lucky for me, the sound of Holly's cell ringing distracted everyone.

"The phone's in the car," the junior deputy verified after sticking his head into the vehicle.

"See? There's no way she would walk away willingly and leave her phone when the car door was open," I pointed out.

"Is Holly a minor?"

"No. She's my age."

"We're in broad daylight in the middle of a parking lot with lots of people coming and going. It seems highly unlikely she was abducted. Are you sure she didn't just run into the yoga place to use the bathroom?" Deputy Ferguson asked.

"Oh, this is ridiculous," I said and dialed the sheriff directly.

"Hennessey," he said as he answered his phone.

I explained what was going on.

"Give Deputy Ferguson your phone," he said.

I narrowed my eyes, trying to convey that he was going to be in big trouble, and handed him my phone. "The sheriff wants to talk to you."

"This is Deputy Ferguson," he said as he took my phone. "Yes, sir. Yes, sir. Right. Will do." He handed me back my phone and walked over to the junior deputy to discuss something in private.

"Hello?" I said into the phone.

"Don't go anywhere. I'm on my way down," Sheriff Hennessey said.

"Okay," I replied and hung up. I looked at Chelsea. "I think I got his attention."

"Let's hope so," she said. "Holly's been missing nearly an hour."

"He said not to leave, but I'm going to walk the perimeter of the parking lot," I said. "Will you come with me?"

"I will," Chelsea said.

We walked in silence. I kept my gaze down on the ground, looking for clues. Chelsea looked at the bushes and shrubs to see if they might produce some kind of evidence.

"I'll go inside the yoga studio and see if anyone saw anything." She left to go into the back door. I noticed that the flashing police lights were drawing a bit of a crowd, both inside the building and outside.

"What's going on?" someone in yoga pants and a T-shirt called out.

"Were you inside?"

"Yes," she replied. "We got out of class and saw the lights."

"Did you happen to see Holly Petree?" I asked.

"Who?"

"She runs the art gallery. She's tall, brunette, and slender with big brown eyes."

"No, I haven't seen her."

"She's missing," I said. "I'm afraid someone took her from the car."

"That's terrible," the woman said and turned to the person beside her. "It's an abduction." The news spread like wildfire through the crowd.

If Holly were around, she would surely have heard and stepped forward.

The sheriff pulled up in his squad car. I went over to him as he stepped out. "Sheriff Hennessey, please tell them we have to find Holly."

"Listen, I told you to stay home. What were you doing out here anyway?"

"We were . . . well . . . following Sally."

"Why were you doing that?"

"We wondered if she or Juliet had anything to do with Laura's death."

"I asked you to leave that to me," he said with a stern face.

"I'm sorry. My entire life is on hold while I wait for you."

"Now your friend's life may be in danger," he said.

"What do you mean? Do you know who might have taken Holly?"

"There's been a break in your case, and following Sally was the last thing you should have been doing."

"Why? What happened? What did you find out?"

"They found a thumbprint on the bullets. We ran it through the DMV since everyone with a California driver's license is required to have a thumbprint taken."

"Bullets—what bullets?"

"The ones in the gun that shot and killed Ivy."

I put my hand to my mouth in shock. "Whose thumbprint was it?"

"Sally's," he said grimly. "I'd hoped you girls would stay away."

"She was the one Laura caught with the SD chip."

"That is a safe assumption," he said. "I've got squad cars going to her house right now."

"We just saw her inside the studio."

"I'll send an officer in to check if she's still there."

"Do you think she took Holly?"

"I don't know, but I don't like it."

There was a squawk on his radio, and he stepped aside to listen. He turned to the other deputies. "We have a hostage situation. Wait for the crime scene folks to come, and preserve the evidence. I'm going to help with negotiation."

"I'm going with you," I said.

"Me too," Chelsea said.

"No!" The sheriff was stern. "I need you safe and as far from the scene as possible."

Then he turned on his heel and left. I looked at Chelsea, and she looked at me.

"Are you willing to leave your car with the deputies?" she asked.

I looked at my car and the two men and held up my keys. "Yes, let's go."

Chapter 30

We got into Chelsea's car, and she did a quick Google search to see where Sally lived. It was only two blocks away. We were able to get a block closer, but the police had her street closed off. I jumped out of the car and ran to the barricade.

"That's my best friend inside," I said to the policeman patrolling the barricade. "Please let me in."

"I'm sorry. I have strict orders."

Chelsea came up behind me and flashed her press badge. "I'm with the press. Let me in."

"Not for an active scene," he said stubbornly. "You ladies are going to have to wait here like the rest of the lookie-loos. It's not safe."

The wait was excruciating. My phone rang, and I saw it was Aunt Jemma.

"Are you all right? I heard there was a hostage situation not too far from the yoga studio."

"I'm fine," I said. "It's Holly. The police think Sally took her from our car while we were on our stakeout."

"Where were you when that happened?"

"I was getting coffee," I said. "I feel horrible. She might not have taken Holly if I'd been in the car with her."

"No, she might have taken you both, and then no one would know you were missing."

Aunt Jemma's argument helped me feel a tad bit better.

There was a sudden bang, and shots rang out. I couldn't stop myself. I raced passed the police barricades toward the house. Someone grabbed me by the arm before I could bolt up the sidewalk and run inside. "Holly!" I shouted.

"Stand back!" It was Sheriff Hennessey who had ahold of me. His handsome face was stern. "Do not go inside. The SWAT team is handling it."

"But Holly—"

"They're professionals," he said.

I turned toward the house to see two men in SWAT gear walking out. "Holly!" I shouted again. The next person out was Holly. She stepped out and looked a bit dazed. There was a bruise on her forehead. I jerked myself free of the sheriff's grip, ran to her, and hugged her. "I'm so sorry," I said. "I never would have left if I'd thought for a moment she would attack you."

"She needs to be checked by the paramedics," the sheriff said and gently pushed me away from Holly. He took her arm and escorted her to the paramedics. Chelsea was beside me, snapping photos and taking video.

"Looks like the police got Holly out safe," Chelsea said. "This is a great news story." She was quickly typing in her words and sending the video to her editor. "Where's Sally?"

"There was no one else in the house," the SWAT leader told Sheriff Hennessey.

"She got away?" I asked.

"We'll get her," he said, his tone flat and professional.

"It looks like Sally killed Ivy," Chelsea said.

"My guess is that she killed Laura too," I said. "I don't know why."

"That's something for the police to determine," the sheriff said as he motioned for us to move on. "You two need to leave now for your own safety."

"What about Holly?"

"They're taking her to the clinic to check her over. You can pick her up there."

"Come on, Chelsea," I said. "Let's go."

"I want a few more pictures," Chelsea said.

Sheriff Hennessey put his hand on her phone. "No more. Leave the scene, or I'll confiscate your phone."

"Fine," Chelsea said and hitched her purse up on her shoulder. She put her arm through mine. "Come on. Let's go see Holly."

We walked to her car, ignoring the questions of the crowd and the glares of the barricade cops. It was a short trip to the clinic, where the staff kept us waiting for two hours before they released Holly.

She came out looking pale and shaken but was none the worse for wear.

"Holly," I said and stood. "I'm so sorry."

"You cracked the case," Chelsea said. "Maybe even two cases if Sally killed Laura."

"She did," Holly said. "That's why took so long for them to release me—I had to debrief the sheriff and deputies about what happened."

"Come on," I said. "Let's go to the winery. You can tell us all about it over dinner. Aunt Jemma is so worried."

"Yes," Holly said. "Let's go. I hope to never have to see the inside of this place again." She shivered. I wrapped my arm around her to keep her warm and walked her to Chelsea's car. Holly's car was still being processed at the yoga studio parking lot, so Chelsea drove us back to the winery.

"Oh, Holly!" Aunt Jemma came running out and hugged her hard. Millie also raced out and jumped up on Holly. The cat prowled in the doorway. "Come in, come in. I have a fire going in the fireplace and fresh beef stew in the Crock-Pot."

"Sounds wonderful," Holly said.

It took a few moments to get everyone settled. Holly was bundled in a blanket and sat on the couch in front of the fireplace. She had a glass of wine on the end table nearest her and a bowl of hot stew in her hands. I noticed that she didn't touch it, and my heart squeezed.

"What happened?"

"Well, you left to get coffee."

"Yes, I know," I said with great sadness. "I didn't know any harm would come to you."

"Neither did I," she said and patted my hand. "You couldn't have prevented what happened next. You see, I saw her come out of the yoga studio and got out of the car to speak to her."

"No! That's not part of the stakeout."

"I know, but I didn't think anything of it."

"What did you say?"

"I told her that we knew about her connection to Laura's murder, and it'd only be a matter of time before we proved it."

"Why would you say that? We didn't know anything of the sort."

"I know," Holly said. "I was being dramatic. I thought I could get a rise out of her—a swift denial, and then we could concentrate on watching Juliet."

"But she didn't deny it," Aunt Jemma said.

"No," Holly said and took a sip of her drink. "She looked relieved. She told me that she hated selling out everyone she worked with to Ivy."

"Then why had she?"

"She was in love with Ivy."

"What?"

"Yes," Holly said. "She pulled out a gun after she told me that."

"What did you do?"

"I ran, of course, to the car."

"That's why the door was open."

"I went to get my phone to call the police, but she grabbed me by the arm. I struggled, but she held the gun to my side and told me she would shoot."

"So you went with her."

"I had no other choice." Holly's voice cracked, and she teared up. "I was scared to death."

"Did she walk with you to her house?"

"Yes. Once inside, she tied me to a chair and put a gag in my mouth. All the while, she told me what happened that day."

"What happened? Can you tell us?"

"She went to meet Ivy, but Laura discovered them exchanging the chip for cash. Laura freaked out and went ballistic on Ivy. Laura said she'd suspected it was Ivy who was part of the theft ring. Laura was going to call the police. She got out her cell phone, but Ivy attacked her. She and Laura struggled. Sally tried to break it up, but Laura pushed her aside. Sally panicked and stabbed Laura with the corkscrew. Ivy pushed her body down the side of the cliff."

"So the corkscrew was a weapon of opportunity."

"Yes."

"How did she get it?"

"She said that something bumped against her foot in the van while you were driving to the quarry. She reached down, found the corkscrew, and put it in her pocket, thinking you'd need it when you brought out the wine."

"Instead, she used it on Laura."

"Afterward, Ivy demanded to know where the SD card was. Sally said that Laura had taken it. They both looked down at the body, but there was no going down after it. So Ivy helped Sally wash up in the stream, and Sally went to join the others."

"What about Rashida's jacket?" I asked.

"Sally picked it up from a bench where Rashida had left it and used the jacket to help wipe away the blood. Ivy took it and buried it."

"So why kill Ivy?"

"They got into a big fight," Holly said. "Sally felt guilty. She wanted to tell the police what happened—that she had done it to protect Ivy. But Ivy argued that they should let you go to jail for it. Sally said she wanted to put all her cards on the table. She declared her love for Ivy, but Ivy rejected her, and Sally shot Ivy for the rejection. After all, she'd killed for Ivy. To have Ivy reject her was awful."

"Sally told you all this?"

"Yes," Holly said. "You should've seen her expression. She looked quite mad and yet happy to be free of the secret. She said she'd have to kill me as well since I knew. Her goal in kidnapping me was to flush you out, Taylor. She hoped to pin my death on you as well."

"That's crazy!"

"She is crazy," Holly said.

"Did you tell the police?"

"Yes, but right now all they can prove is that she kidnapped me and held me at gunpoint."

"They have other proof. She put the bullets in the 9mm that killed Ivy," I said. "The sheriff said they found her thumbprint on the bullets."

"How did he know it was Sally's thumbprint?"

"We all had our thumbprints taken when we got our driver's licenses. He ran the print through the DMV, and her name popped up."

"So we can get her for kidnapping and for Ivy's murder, but that still doesn't free you from suspicion in Laura's murder."

"But Holly can testify that Sally admitted to killing Laura."

"They'll throw it out as hearsay," Aunt Jemma said.

"But I didn't do it!"

"We have to get Sally to admit to doing it where we can record it or have the police involved."

"How are we going to do that?"

"Let's get Juliet to help us out. She's close to Sally. Maybe she can get her to confess."

"Why would Juliet help us?" I asked.

"Because she also benefitted from Laura's murder. Her alibi was Sally—if Sally killed Ivy and is suspected of killing Laura, that leaves Juliet without an alibi."

"We need to talk to Juliet first thing in the morning."

"Do you think that's safe, considering all that's happened today?" Aunt Jemma looked concerned.

"As long as no one goes alone," I said, "we should be fine. It sounds like we know the killer. It's a matter of proving it."

"We don't know for sure that Juliet knew anything," Chelsea pointed out. "I say we meet at ten AM and go see Juliet. She has a class at nine and should be at the studio."

"Sounds like a plan," I said.

"If you don't mind, I think I'll skip this one," Holly said with a shiver. "I've had enough adventure for a while."

I hugged her. "We don't mind. Don't worry. It'll all be okay. What could possibly go wrong?"

Chapter 31

It was sort of anticlimactic when we arrived at the yoga studio the next morning to discover that Juliet had called in sick.

"Well, shoot," Chelsea said. "I was looking forward to really filling out the story. Do you think we should go to her home?"

"I'm not so sure that's a good idea considering what happened to Holly yesterday."

"But I'm a reporter, it's what we do," Chelsea reminded me. "So are you coming or not?"

"Fine," I said. "I'll go."

"Good."

We decided to leave my van at the yoga studio and take Chelsea's vehicle to Juliet's house. She lived in a small home on the edge of town flanked by a vineyard. It was a bit run-down looking, but her car was in the driveway. So we got out and walked up. The curtains were all closed.

Chelsea knocked. There was no answer, so she knocked again and rang the doorbell. "Ms. Juliet Emmerson," she said. "My name is Chelsea McGartland, and I'm here with Taylor

O'Brian. We want to talk to you about what happened last night. We want to get your take on the Sally Miles story."

There was no answer.

"Do you think she's okay?" I asked. "The last time there was no answer, I found a dead body."

"Maybe we should go around back," Chelsea said. We turned to leave when the front door cracked open.

"I'm fine," Juliet said. "Please go away. I don't want to talk to anyone."

"Are you alone?" I asked when a sudden chill went over me.

"I don't want to talk to anyone," she said, her eyes wide. "Please go away."

"Okay, okay," Chelsea said. "We'll respect your privacy."

We left, and she closed the door. I didn't like it. It didn't feel right to leave her. We got into Chelsea's car, drove two blocks away, and parked.

"I think we should call the sheriff," I said.

"I agree," Chelsea said. "Something's wrong."

I called Sheriff Hennessey's direct line.

"Hennessey."

"Hello, Sheriff, it's Taylor O'Brian."

"What can I do for you, Taylor?"

"Chelsea and I went to visit Juliet, and something isn't right."

"What do you mean?"

"We knocked on the door, but all the curtains were closed. She told us she didn't want to talk to anyone."

"I can understand that. You and Chelsea aren't exactly the best people to talk to these days."

I frowned at his insinuation that the bad things that happened were somehow my fault. "I asked her if she was alone, and she didn't answer. I think she's in trouble."

"I'll send a car over there," he said. "In the meantime, you two stay away."

"Sure."

"I mean it, Taylor."

"Okay. I'll be watching for the squad car." I hung up and looked at Chelsea. "It could be another five minutes before they get here. What do you want to do?"

"I say we get out, walk back there, and go around back and see if we can see anything in the windows."

"But her curtains were all closed."

"In front, but she didn't want us around back. It's the only reason she popped her head out."

"Then let's go," I said, more bravely than I felt. We got out of the car and took the alley behind the house. There was a carport behind the house but no fence. "If someone's watching, they'll see us," I pointed out.

"Let's hope their attention is on the front," Chelsea answered.

"Wait," I whispered, but it was too late. Chelsea hurried to the corner of the house. There was a tiny back patio and patio doors. The long vertical blinds were partially open. Chelsea was peering in, and I couldn't take the suspense. I dashed across the lawn on the opposite side from Chelsea and looked inside.

Sally was inside with a gun. Juliet sat in a chair in the living room looking terrified, while Sally ranted and waved her arms around.

"We have to do something," I whispered. "Can we distract her? Maybe get her to come out so that Juliet can get away?"

"The police are on their way," Chelsea said.

"But that might make things worse," I said. "How about you tip the trash can over, and I'll stay beside the door when she looks out?"

"What good will that do?"

"It'll distract her for a few minutes while the police are on their way."

"Even better—look around the corner. See if there are any open windows," Chelsea said.

"What are you suggesting?"

"That one of us distracts her while the other climbs in and saves Juliet."

"But Sally has a gun."

"All the more reason we need to hurry."

"Fine." I looked around my side of the little house and saw that there was a window open. "I think I can go through the bathroom window. It has to be a bathroom, right?" It was a little higher off the ground than the front windows.

"Fine," Chelsea said. "You distract her, and I'll go in."

"No, it's on my side of the house. I'll go in. You distract her."

"Be careful."

"Right," I said and slid around the edge of the house. The window was at eye level, and I peered in. It was the bathroom. I pushed the window up higher and held my breath as I listened. I could hear Sally yelling at Juliet that it was all her fault. That she should've never introduced her to Ivy.

I heard the trash can being knocked over and grabbed the windowsill. My heart thumped loudly in my chest as I slid into the bathroom. I landed awkwardly in the bathtub and held my breath as the house went silent.

"What is it?" I heard Juliet ask.

"Something's gotten in your trash can," Sally said, and I listened as she walked back to the living area. She paused by the bathroom door, and I held my breath. What was I thinking? What could I do against a woman with a gun?

"Please, Sally, put the gun down. I'm certain that Taylor and Chelsea knew there was something wrong. They may have called the cops."

"The only way they could've known something was wrong is if you let on. I swear, you've messed things up so badly, I don't know why I trusted you in the first place."

I realized I didn't have a weapon, but I did have my cell phone. I hit the record button—if nothing else, I could catch the encounter on video.

"I'm sorry. I should have never involved you with Ivy. I didn't know that Ivy would double-cross you," Juliet said. "You asked for a way out from under Laura's strict management. I was only trying to give you that."

"Now I'm wanted for kidnapping and murder," Sally said. "They can't find out about Laura too."

"I won't tell anyone what happened that day," Juliet said.

"I can't trust you to do that," Sally said. "I need to get rid of you."

"What about Taylor, Holly, and Chelsea? Are you going to murder them too? It's gone too far. Give it up. Don't let the police find you with my gun. Things will only get worse for you."

"Stop trying to talk me out of things," Sally said. "If Ivy hadn't been there that day, she and Laura would never had fought, and I wouldn't have had to stab Laura. You started this whole thing with your push to become part of Ivy's ring."

"It wasn't me. It was Laura. She threatened us all," Juliet said. "If you hadn't killed Ivy, our plan would've worked. They indicted Taylor. No one would have thought otherwise."

"You know as well as I do that three people can't keep a secret," Sally said. "I'm the one who wanted to tell the truth. I wanted to go to the police. Then Ivy told me she never loved me. She used me to get rid of her sister-in-law so that her brother would be free from Laura's tyranny."

"You mean Ivy set it up so that Laura found out about the SD card?"

"That's what Ivy told me. I got so angry, I picked up her gun and shot her."

"I don't understand. How did Dan get the gun?"

"I don't know. I left it at the house. I was in shock and dropped it. Dan must've picked it up."

"So he's covering for you by confessing to having killed Ivy?"

"No, the idiot thinks Amy did it." Sally waved the gun around. "As far as I'm concerned, they can both go to prison for it."

"Sally, please," Juliet said. "Why don't you put the gun down? I'm with you all the way. I mean, I even threw a rock with the word 'murderer' on it into that window. I did that for you."

"It didn't stop that woman from investigating, now, did it?"

"Look, I'm almost certain those two meddlers called the police. Let's let them find two old friends having tea."

"It's too late for that," Sally said and leveled the gun at Juliet.

My heart raced, and I rushed out of the bathroom and into Sally, knocking her and the gun to the floor.

"What the . . . ?"

"Juliet, get the gun," I said when I saw the Juliet was not tied to the chair.

"How did you get in here?" Juliet screamed. When she didn't move, I scrambled for the gun, but Sally grabbed me by the leg.

"You meddling girl. You need to be taught a lesson. It wasn't bad enough you nearly got your friend killed, but now you need to put yourself in danger?" Sally said. There was a pounding at the door.

"Police."

"Help!" I shouted.

The door was busted open, and Sheriff Hennessey and two deputies came in with guns pointed. "Freeze!"

"She has a gun," I said and pointed at Sally, who was inching her way toward the gun.

"I said freeze," the sheriff said and kicked the gun out of the way.

I put my head down and my hands over my head.

"She invaded my home," Juliet said, and I glanced over to see her pointing at me. Me! "We were having tea, and she burst in. She grabbed my gun. I think she was going to kill us both."

"Oh, no," I said and reached for my phone.

"Don't move!" Sheriff said.

"I have it all on video," I said.

"Lies!" Sally said.

The deputies put cuffs on all three of us and got us sitting up. "I'm not lying," I said. "Sally was trying to kill Juliet. I caught it all on video. She killed Laura and Ivy. They were in it together to cover up Laura's death."

"Don't listen to her jabbering. She wants free from the charges," Juliet said. "We were having tea, and she came bursting in. I think through the bathroom window. Although I have no idea how she got through such a tiny space."

I winced at the insult. "Chelsea's outside. We called the police. Please check my video."

Sheriff Hennessey shook his head. "I thought I told you girls to stay home."

"But I've got your proof," I said as triumphantly as I could despite being handcuffed. "Sally killed Laura; Juliet and Ivy helped cover it up. Sally killed Ivy, and Juliet was next. Check my phone."

"We'll check your phone," the sheriff said. "But first, let's get you all down to the station and processed, shall we? After all, we have procedures for a reason."

"I suppose," I said and looked at Chelsea. "Let Aunt Jemma and Holly know I'm okay."

"I will," Chelsea said. "Then I'm posting my story."

The deputy helped me to my feet and walked me to one of three squad cars outside. I was glad not to be riding with Sally or Juliet but sad to be riding anywhere at all. I saw flashes of light as people took pictures with their cell phones. *Great.* I was going to be on the evening news yet again.

The ride to the station was short, and I was put in a small interrogation room where I waited for three hours. Finally, Patrick walked in. "What happened?"

"We wanted to talk to Juliet about the case. When we arrived, all her curtains were closed, and she seemed in distress."

"So you broke into her home?"

"We called the sheriff's office. Then we saw Sally inside waving a gun, and Juliet looked like she was tied to a chair. What would you have done?"

"Waited for the police."

"Well, good for you," I said flatly. "I thought it'd be better if I tried to save Juliet."

"She wants to charge you with breaking and entering."

"That's ridiculous. I didn't break anything. I went through her open window, and I saved her life. I've got it all on video."

The door opened, and Sheriff Hennessey entered. "That was the stupidest thing you could have ever done."

"Wait. What? I saved Juliet, and I proved my innocence and got a confession on tape. It wasn't coerced. There's no reason to not believe it."

"You could've been killed."

"But I wasn't," I said.

He went around behind me and unlocked the handcuffs. "You're darn lucky."

I rubbed my wrists. "I solved your case."

"I told you I had it covered."

"Except I was still preparing for trial."

"The charges have been dismissed," Patrick told me.

"Yes!" I jumped up and hugged him. He stood very still. I turned to Ron Hennessey and hugged him too. "I told you I was innocent."

"Next time, leave the sleuthing to me, okay?" Ron said.

"There better never be a next time," I said and rubbed my wrists. "I'm not good at going to jail."

"So I can tell," the sheriff said.

"What happens now?" I asked.

"We'll process you out, and your aunt will get back her collateral for the bail minus the bond fees."

An hour later, I walked out a free woman. The winery was back in Aunt Jemma's hands, and all was well.

Later that night, Chelsea, Holly, and Aunt Jemma sat around the fireplace and sipped wine with me. "What a story," Chelsea said. "I've cemented myself as a staffer for the *Chronicle*—thanks to you all."

"Thanks to you, I was able to prove my innocence."

"Thanks to you both for rescuing me last night," Holly said.

"Thanks to this caper, the winery is more popular than ever," Aunt Jemma said. "I guess it's true that any publicity is good publicity."

"The major news channels all called," Holly said. "They want to interview us both and feature the story on one of the network crime shows. We're going to be famous."

"Good famous, I hope."

"Enough that people have been calling all day trying to line up one of your wine country tours. There's one catch."

"What's that?"

"That you feature crime scenes. It seems that crime is as popular as ghost tours."

"So instead of Taylor O'Brian Presents 'Off the Beaten Path' Wine Country Tours, I should call it . . ."

"Wine and Crime Tours. Remember that investor who was chased through the vines by the proprietor when he demanded his money back?"

"You keep bringing that up. Didn't he end up shooting him?"

"And it was all recorded because the proprietor was on the line with the police at the time."

"Yes, I remember," I said.

"That'd be a great place to tour first," Holly said.

"Isn't that a bit grim?" Aunt Jemma asked.

"Hey, my college mentor said the best thing you can do is ride the horse you came in on."

"What does that mean exactly?" I asked.

"If life hands you crimes to solve . . ."

"Solve them," I finished.

"Yes," Holly said and sat back. "Of course, it's better if you only do sites where murders have already been solved, if you get my meaning."

"Oh, I get it. No more dead bodies for me."

"I don't know," Chelsea said. "We make a heck of a team."

"Yes, well, it wasn't you in handcuffs and facing jail time."

"Not this time," Chelsea said and wiggled her eyebrows, "but that doesn't mean we can't try again."

I rolled my eyes as she lifted her glass. "Here's to Wine and Crime Tours," she said. "Long may it last."

"Hear, hear," the others agreed.

I lifted my glass reluctantly. I wasn't too sure that Sheriff Hennessey would be as excited about the prospect.

"Here's to the best friends a girl can have," I said and raised my glass. Now that was something we all could agree on, including the cat sauntering in to taunt Millie, who growled playfully. Friends were the best things in life.

A Case of Syrah, Syrah Wine and Food Pairings

Sonoma's cooler climate usually leads to a lighter Syrah. The lighter Syrah uses less oak aging and can taste a little more tart. It's best to pair lighter Syrahs with delicate flavors. The lamb recipe below is great choice. Or if you prefer vegetarian recipes, you'll find a grilled eggplant that goes wonderfully with the mouth-watering fruit flavor.

Grilled Lamb Chops

¼ cup apple cider vinegar
2 tsp. salt
½ tsp. black pepper
½ tsp. allspice
¼ tsp. clove
2 tbsp. grape-seed oil or olive oil
1 yellow onion, thinly sliced
2 pounds lamb chops

Place vinegar, salt, pepper, allspice, clove, grape-seed oil, and onion in a resealable bag and mix until salt dissolves. Place lamb in the bag and toss until coated. Marinate in the refrigerator for two to four hours. Preheat outdoor grill to medium-high heat (400° F) or set oven to broil. Remove chops from marinade and discard marinade. Grill or broil lamb until desired doneness. Three minutes per side will achieve medium doneness on the grill (five minutes per side under the broiler).

Serve with grilled veggies and Sonoma Syrah.

Grilled Eggplant

1 eggplant, ends trimmed and cut into ½-inch slices
1 red pepper, seeds removed and cut into rings
1 cup spinach leaves, chopped into 1-inch (fork sized) pieces
½ ounce feta cheese, crumbled
1 tsp. sundried tomato paste
1 tbsp. grape-seed oil
1 tbsp. balsamic vinegar
Freshly ground salt to taste

Preheat broiler or grill to medium-high heat (400° F). Arrange slices of eggplant and bell pepper on baking sheet and broil/grill until soft (approximately seven minutes).

Arrange spinach on a serving plate and drizzle with grape-seed oil and vinegar. Sprinkle with salt. Arrange grilled red pepper on top. Spread a small amount of tomato paste on eggplant slices and arrange in a spiral on spinach and red peppers. Sprinkle with feta.

Serve immediately with your favorite Sonoma Syrah.

Spicy Chocolate Chili Cookies

Spicy, smoky dark chocolate pairs well with Syrah. Try these cookies for a dessert that goes with your favorite dessert Syrah.

⅓ cup unsweetened cocoa powder (61 percent cacao)
½ tsp. ancho chili powder
¼ tsp. salt
1¼ cup flour
¾ cup sugar
½ cup unsalted butter, room temperature
1 large egg
Confectioner's sugar to dust

Preheat oven to 350° F and grease or line a baking sheet.

In a medium bowl, sift together cocoa, chili powder, salt, and flour.

In a large bowl, cream the sugar and butter until light. Add egg and mix. Slowly add flour mixture and mix until it becomes smooth. Roll the dough into a 1½-inch-wide log. Wrap in wax paper or plastic and let dough chill in freezer for one hour.

Cut dough into ½-inch thick circles. Bake about sixteen minutes until even in color but still chewy. Let cool and dust with confectioner's sugar if desired.

Looking for a Cheese to Pair With Your Syrah?

Pair Syrah with the following Cheese and Herbs:

Softer, stinkier cheese with fat texture and earthy flavors will absorb the high tannin in Syrah.

TRY:

Abbaye de Belloc
Applewood Ilchester
Asiago
Beecher's Flagship
Bleu d'Auvergne
Blue Shropshire
Cahill's Irish Porter
Cheddar
Comte
Dubliner
Gorgonzola
Gouda
Gruyère
Mahon
Manchego
Mimolette
Parrano
Tomme de Savoie

HERBS:

Lavender
Fennel
Thyme

Acknowledgments

Every book takes a village to produce. Thank you to Matt Martz and the staff at Crooked Lane Books for their hard work and dedication to this book. Thanks to Paige Wheeler for helping me find a good home for the series. Thank you to my friends and family who supported me through the process and most importantly to the readers who make every work come to life in their imaginations.